FAY WELDON is a novelist, screenwriter and cultural journalist. Her novels include *The Life and Loves of a She-Devil*, *Puffball*, *The Cloning of Joanna May*, *Big Women* and *Rhode Island Blues*. She has also published her autobiography, *Auto da Fay*. Her most recent book was *Mantrapped*. Fay Weldon lives in Dorset.

Visit www.AuthorTracker.co.uk for exclusive information on your favourite HarperCollins authors.

From the reviews of *She May Not Leave*:

'I relish Fay Weldon's books and read them as slowly as I possibly can, but still couldn't put this one down'
TRACEY COX, *Independent*

'A spine-chilling black comedy . . . it held me absolutely gripped in between rushing around with a Hoover, a laundry basket and a frying pan for the children's tea before working until midnight. It has already been placed on the shelves of my next au pair's room'
AMANDA CRAIG, *Daily Telegraph*

'This hilarious and disturbing cautionary tale gives a modern twist to an old scenario'   *Mail on Sunday*

'Very entertaining'   *Time Out*

'*She May Not Leave* is a modern morality tale, an Aga saga for the post-feminist age, and an inter-generational story of love, marriage, family and the importance of good lunches and good genes. It's also a ripping great read'   *Sunday Business Post*

By the same author

FICTION

The Fat Woman's Joke
Down Among the Women
Female Friends
Remember Me
Little Sisters
Praxis
Puffball
The President's Child
The Life and Loves of a
   She-Devil
The Shrapnel Academy
The Heart of the Country
The Hearts and Lives of Men
The Rules of Life
Leader of the Band
The Cloning of Joanna May
Darcy's Utopia
Life Force
Affliction
Splitting
Worst Fears
Big Women
Rhode Island Blues
The Bulgari Connection

CHILDREN'S BOOKS

Wolf the Mechanical Dog
Nobody Likes Me

SHORT STORY COLLECTIONS

Watching Me, Watching You
Polaris
Moon Over Minneapolis
Wicked Women
A Hard Time to be a Father
Nothing to Wear and Nowhere
   to Hide

NON-FICTION

Letters to Alice
Rebecca West
Sacred Cows
Godless in Eden
Auto da Fay
Mantrapped

FAY WELDON

She May Not Leave

HARPER PERENNIAL
London, New York, Toronto and Sydney

Harper Perennial
An imprint of HarperCollins*Publishers*
77–85 Fulham Palace Road
Hammersmith
London W6 8JB

www.harperperennial.co.uk

This special edition published by Harper Perennial 2007

1

First published in Great Britain by Fourth Estate in 2005

PS™ is a trademark of HarperCollins*Publishers* Ltd

Fay Weldon asserts the moral right to
be identified as the author of this work

A catalogue record for this book is available from the British Library

ISBN 978-0-00-779116-3

Set in Sabon by Palimpsest Book Production Limited,
Grangemouth, Stirlingshire

Printed and bound in Great Britain by Clays Ltd, St Ives plc

Martyn And Hattie Have Employed An Au Pair

'Agnieszka?' asks Martyn. 'Isn't that far too long a name? If she wants to get on in this country she'll have to shorten it. People are just not familiar with *sshzk*.'

'But she won't want to shorten it,' says Hattie. 'People have their pride, and a loyalty to the parents who named them.'

'If we pay her,' says Martyn, 'she may have to do more or less as we ask.'

Martyn is in conversation with Hattie in their economical, comfortable first-time-buyers' house in London's Kentish Town. Both are in their early thirties, handsome, healthy and educated, and for reasons of principle not lack of affection are not married but partnered. Baby Kitty, twenty-four weeks old, sleeps in her cot in the bedroom: Martyn and Hattie fear that she may not sleep for long. Martyn is just back from work. Hattie is ironing: she is unused to the task, and making a rotten job of it but she is, as ever, doing her best.

Hattie is my grandchild. I spent many years bringing her up and I am fond of her.

1

They have been talking about the possibility of employing an au pair, Agnieszka, recommended by Babs, a colleague of Hattie's at Dinton & Seltz, Literary Agents. Hattie took maternity leave: now she wants to return to work, but Martyn is resistant. Not that he says so, but Hattie can tell because of his feeling that the girl's name is too long. About Agnieszka they know very little, except that she has worked for Babs's sister, the one with triplets, and left with good references.

In the circles in which Martyn and Hattie move as many babies are implanted as conceived, and so do often arrive in twos or threes. Kitty was an accident which served, after initial confusion and dismay, to make her the more precious to her parents. Fate had intervened, they felt, for the good. Man proposes, God disposes, and for once the result was satisfactory.

'I don't think it would be right to ask her to change her name on our account,' says Hattie. 'She might be offended.' 'I am not sure,' says Martyn, 'that we should define right as what does not offend.'
'I don't see why not,' says Hattie. Her brow darkens as she comes to grips with what Martyn has just said. Surely not offending other people has a large part to play in what is defined as 'right'? But since Kitty's birth she is less sure than before about what is right and what is wrong. Her moral confidence is being eroded.

She can see it is 'wrong' to jam a comforter in baby Kitty's mouth to stop the crying, as poorly educated mothers from the housing estates do. 'Right' would be searching for the cause of the crying and attending to that. If this is the case she chooses wrong over right at least five times a day. She can see she is also guilty of élitism, in not wanting to be numbered as one of the estate mothers. The family income may be currently below the national average, but even so the notion of her own superiority increasingly flits across her mind. Does she not read books about child-care, instead of waiting two weeks for the health visitor to turn up? Surely she is someone who controls her own destiny? But she has been so a-mush lately, so driven by hormonally based emotions, so much a prey to unaccustomed resentments and gratifications that she swings from conviction to doubt within minutes. She did wake this morning, leaning over to the crib beside the marital bed to put the comforter in Kitty's mouth, with the comforting understanding that people are as moral as they can afford to be, no more nor less. She should not blame herself too much.

'Then you *should* see why not,' says Martyn. 'Social justice can't be achieved by simply letting everyone do what they want. A fox-hunter might well be offended if you pointed out that he was a cruel sadistic brute, but that doesn't mean you shouldn't say it. We should all be working towards the greatest good of the greatest number and sometimes hard words and tough choices must be made.'
'How would telling someone to shorten their name further social justice?' asks Hattie.

She feels mean and petulant; she knows she's being obstructive, but if Martyn can be so can she. Hattie has already asked Agnieszka to come round for an interview but hasn't told Martyn. She has not yet quite brought him round to the idea, though the arrival of the electricity bill and the community charge, both in the morning's post, has had its effects. Hattie must go back to work. Really there is no choice.

'For one thing,' he says, 'think of the delays while the name was spellchecked. Agnieszka Wyszynska! Computer operators all over the country will be at their wits' end. It would be a simple kindness to others to simplify it.'

'What to?' asks Hattie. 'What do you suggest?'

'Agnes Wilson? Kay Sky? Short and simple and co-operative. She can always change it back when she goes home to Poland.'

'I have no problem spelling Agnieszka Wyszynska. You just have to get used to certain combinations of consonants and realise "y" is a vowel. But then I studied modern languages and I'm not bad at spelling.'

Hattie is indeed good at spelling, but when she talks about Agnieszka's pride she may well be talking about her own. People tend to invest others with their own qualities be they desirable or otherwise. The generous believe others will be similarly generous: the liar accuses the other of lying: the selfish see selfishness in everyone else. If Hattie declines to use Microsoft's Spell-check, preferring to use her own judgement, or call her great-aunt the writer if in doubt, it is because she too has her pride. She has a highly developed superego. This may well be why she and Martyn, a man from the working-class North with high social principles and well-developed class-consciousness, are joined together in committed partnership, if not holy matrimony.

Hattie comes from the bohemian South, from a family for whom morality tends to concern itself with the integrity of a particular art form and the authenticity of emotion. It is a family in which Hattie's particular temperament is seen as something of an anomaly. There is something rigorous and nonconformist about her which echoes the same tendencies in Martyn. In this she is unlike her mother Lallie the flute player, or her grandmother Frances who is married to an artist currently in prison, let alone like her great-aunt Serena, the well-known writer. Heaven knows through which genetic route 'the responsible tendency', as Frances refers to it, has come. It may well be from Hattie's father Bengt, a schoolboy at the time of Hattie's conception. But who is to say? Bengt was so quickly whisked off to Sweden by his parents for a new and better start in life, that the details of his character were never fully apparent to Lallie's family. We could only watch and observe Hattie as she grew to find out what she would be like.

Bengt was to become a pharmacist in Uppsala and live quietly and decorously with a wife and three children, so with time it was assumed that he had left responsible, competent, if possibly rather priggish genes behind. The single brief act which resulted in Hattie occurred in what was known as the Tranquility Hut at the progressive and very expensive school the two young people attended.

Once a year, if Lallie can find a window in her busy international schedule, Bengt will bring his family over from Uppsala to visit her and Hattie, his ill-begotten daughter. Everyone is most courteous on these occasions but can't wait to get back to normality, which is to forget any of it ever happened.

Hattie is polite to her father but cannot be very interested in him. She found out and filled in details of his medical history to the researchers at the hospital where she went for antenatal care, but could find nothing but good health and non-event to report. If Hattie didn't resemble Bengt other than in a certain heaviness of jaw and brusqueness of temperament, she would have thought her mother had made a mistake and somebody quite other was responsible for her, Hattie's, existence. Like the rest of her family Hattie does like things to *happen*. Bengt is, frankly, dull.

But since she had Kitty it's the wrong kind of things which seem to happen. The district nurse, who calls regularly because Hattie has declined to join the weekly mothers' and babies' club, and this goes down on her notes, complains that the baby's motions are too loose and accuses Hattie of eating garlic. Hattie has not eaten garlic since Kitty was born. The district nurse does not even ask but just assumes Hattie is the kind of mother who would. Is this how she seems to others? Irresponsible, biddable, and dumb?

'Anyway,' says Martyn now, 'it's all hypothetical. We don't need, want, let alone can afford an au pair. Forget it. It's just an idea of Babs's. I know she's your friend but she has an odd idea of how the world works.'

Martyn is not too keen on Babs as a friend for Hattie and not without reason. Babs is married to a Conservative MP and although Babs declares herself scornful of her husband Alastair's political opinions, Martyn has a feeling that something political must surely rub off in the marital bed, and that perhaps some essence of the amended Babs could in turn be transferred to Hattie. He feels that he has already personally osmosed a lot of Hattie's being by virtue of sharing a bed with her, and is happy enough about this. Why should he not? He loves her. They have the same outlook on life. The arrival of Kitty, half him and half her, has bonded their beings more closely still.

Hattie has no choice now but to tell Martyn the truth. Not only has she already spoken to Agnieszka of the too long name, but she has told Neil Renfrew, executive director of Dinton & Seltz, that she would like to come back to work within the month, having sorted out her child-care arrangements. Martyn and Hattie had decided to opt for a year's leave of absence: now Hattie, unilaterally, has halved that. Neil has found a space for her in Contracts, working opposite Hilary in the Foreign Rights Department. Hattie has lost some seniority as a result of taking maternity leave but it's not too bad. She should be back on career course within the year. Hattie reads and speaks French, German and Italian; she is suited to the job, and the job to her.

She would perhaps rather be working at the more literary end of the agenting business – it's more fun: you go out to lunches and talk to writers – but at least in foreign rights you go to the Frankfurt Book Fair and deal with overseas publishers. Eastern Europe is an important and expanding market in which Hattie will need to be active. The job is going free since Colleen Kelly, who has become pregnant after five years of IVF, is stopping work early to write a novel. It has occurred to Hattie that Agnieszka will help her to learn Polish.

'But you haven't even met her,' says Martyn now as Hattie reveals truth after irritating truth. 'You have no idea what's she's like. She could be part of some international baby-theft ring.'

'She sounded very nice on the phone,' says Hattie. 'Well-spoken, quiet and calm and not at all from the criminal fringes. Agnieszka looked after Alice's triplets until they moved to France last month. And Alice told Babs that she was a gift from heaven.'

'A gift to you, perhaps,' says Martyn. 'But what about Kitty? Do you really mean to compromise our baby's future in this way? Research shows that babies with full-time mothers in their first year are at an advantage intellectually and emotionally.'

'It depends which research report you read,' says Hattie, 'and sorry about this, but I do tend to believe the ones that suit me. She'll be fine. We're living on nothing, I have to ask you for money as if I were a child, we are unable to pay the community charge so I have no choice but to use child-care for Kitty. You've already told me I'm mad. What use is it to Kitty to have a mad mother?'

'You're being childish,' says Martyn, with some truth. 'And "mad" is not a very helpful word to use. Let's say you have been a little disturbed lately. But what's the point of my saying anything; you've jumped ahead and taken my approval for granted.'

He slams the fridge door a little harder than is necessary or desirable. Indeed, so hard does he slam the door, that the floor shakes and in the next room baby Kitty stirs and lets out a cry, before fortunately falling asleep again.

One of the unspoken rules of engagement in the battle for the moral high ground waged so assiduously by Hattie and

Martyn is that the weapons of bad temper – bangings, crashings and shoutings – should not be used.

'Sorry,' he says now. 'I haven't had all that brilliant a day. I know I've more or less turned over Kitty's care to you, and I'd so much hoped we could do fifty-fifty parenting, but that's because I have to, not because I want to. All the same, you could at least have called me at the office and warned me.'
'I didn't want Agnieszka to get away,' says Hattie. 'Someone like her can pick and choose. As a fully qualified nanny in Kensington she could get £500 a week and her own maid.'
'That is revolting,' says Martyn.
'But she wouldn't be happy doing that. She's a real homebody, Babs says. She prefers to live as family, work in a real home, halfway between au pair and nanny.'
'She'd better make up her mind,' says Martyn. 'Au pairs are covered by strict guidelines: nannies are not.'
'We'll sort that out when the time comes,' says Hattie. 'I took to her on the phone. You can tell so much from people's voices. Babs says she's exactly right for us. She got such a good reference from Alice that Alastair said it sounded as if Alice was trying to get rid of the girl.'
'Ah, the Tory MP. And was she?' asks Martyn.
'Trying to get rid of her? Of course not,' says Hattie. 'Alastair was joking.'
'Funny sort of joke,' says Martyn.

Martyn is still cross. His blood sugar is low after a day in the office. Obviously he is right; it is not ethical to exploit another in this way, especially if they have little power in the labour market, but it would be kinder to everyone if he left the matter alone.

He can find precious little in the fridge. Since Hattie took maternity leave they have not been able to afford dinners out, take-aways or luxuries from the delicatessen. Supper tends to be chops if he's lucky, with potatoes and vegetables and that's it, and served in Hattie's own good time, not his. He finds some cheese in the salad drawer and nibbles at it, but it is very hard. Hattie says she is saving it for grating.

Martyn feels Hattie rather overdoes what he refers to as her 'frugal number'. Anything will do at the moment to make life bleaker for both of them. She hates spending money on food. Food is full of pollutants which if she eats might end up in Kitty via the breast milk. Since the birth, it seems to Martyn, Hattie has gone into rejection mode. Sex also has become a rare event – rather than the four or five lively times a week it used to be. He can see it might be a good idea if she did go back to work, but he does not like her organising their joint life behind his back. He is Kitty's parent too.

Frances Presents Some
Authorial Background

Let me make clear who is speaking here, who it is who tells the tale of Hattie, Martyn and Agnieszka, reading their thoughts and judging their actions, offering them up for inspection. It is I, Frances Watt, aged seventy-two, *née* Hallsey-Coe, previously I think, but for a short time, Hammer: previously Lady Spargrove: previously – we would have got married but he died – O'Brien. I am Lallie's bad mother, Hattie's good grandmother – determined to get my money's worth from my new laptop, bought for me by my sister Serena. Write, write, write I go, just like my sister. '*Scribble, scribble!*' As the Duke of Gloucester said to Edward Gibbon, on receiving *The Decline and Fall of the Roman Empire*, a million and a half words long: '*Always scribble, scribble, scribble! Eh! Mr Gibbon?*'

Serena is the one with the reputation for writing: she has been writing steadily since she was thirty-odd, scarcely giving herself a minute's time for reflection: she pays everyone – the household helps, the secretaries, taxi drivers, accountants, lawyers, the Inland Revenue, friends, grocers – just to make them go away so she can get on and write. But this doesn't mean she has a monopoly on writing skill. I myself have finally found the time and courage to do it, while my husband Sebastian is in prison. The presence of a man in the house can be inhibiting to any endeavour which does not include him, such as writing a book. I run a little art gallery in Bath, but I choose not to open every day, so I have time and to spare.

Hattie, beloved only child of my only daughter Lallie, called me this evening to say she was going back to work, and had found an au pair for her baby, and Martyn was being a bit iffy about it. Is her return to work a good thing or not? What can I say? Speaking as the great-grandmother she has made me, she should sacrifice her life to the baby. Speaking as her grandmother, I want her to get back into the world and live a little and have affairs with men – life is for living, not just handing on. I am actually very fond of Martyn, but so far as I know he is only the second man she has been to bed with, and that does seem to me to be rather limiting.

Hattie will not settle easily to domesticity, that I do know. The Victorians used to pity girls like her, born too clever for their own good, never content as appendages to the Male – daughter, mother, sister, wife – forever striving for an identity which was theirs and theirs alone, whilst living in a society which forbade them to find it. Such girls made bad mothers and worse wives. That was the old world wisdom.

Martyn, I know, has romantic ideas about having a full-time wife and mother for his child, but I know he is being unrealistic. Couples today need two incomes to get by. And Hattie is bound to pay the new girl too much: she has her great-aunt Serena's generosity but not the means to fund it. The guiltier the mother, the higher the au pair's wages – or else it goes the other way and the mother, identifying, is furious that the girl expects any salary at all, let alone any free time, let alone boyfriends in the house. But Hattie will be the concerned kind, and that can come expensive.

My grand-daughter Hattie is thirty-three. She has a sharp nose, a square jaw, and a mass of striking red-gold Pre-Raphaelite hair, curly on some days, frizzy on others, which she keeps in a cloud around her face. I have the same hair, but mine has gone rather satisfactorily all-over white. It too is striking, and suits me. Hattie has very long legs: this she must get from her father, since her mother Lallie's are rather short and plump of calf. Not that anyone has seen Bengt's legs, other than Lallie (presumably) briefly, once, long ago and far away when Hattie was conceived. Lallie is a pouting, fleshy, sensuous beauty with a high colour, very different from her daughter's lean, high-cheekboned, abstemious, long-fingered paleness. You would think from the look of them that the daughter, not the mother, would achieve world fame playing the flute but it is the other way round.

Hattie has what her great-aunt Serena calls 'good bones' and men can be guaranteed to turn and stare at her when she walks into a room: amazing what confidence this can give to a girl. But she is currently thin to the point of gaunt-ness. The strain of looking after a new baby has told on her. Or perhaps it just is that some women do get pale and thin after having babies, just as some stay with the rounded pinkness of a good pregnancy. The body is wilful and usually goes the way a person very much hopes it won't.

13

The trick with bodies, as with so much in life, is not to let the Fates know just how desperate you are about anything. You must look casual and act casually, play Grandmother's Footsteps with life. Hattie and the cousins used to play it at Caldicott Square. One child stands in front of the group with her back turned. The others move forward stealthily. The one in front turns swiftly. Anyone who's caught moving or giggling is out, and has to leave the game. So don't move; don't giggle; don't show the Fates you care, and the less likely you are to develop a cold sore before the wedding, tonsillitis before the holiday, thrush before the dance, and your period won't come on as you're putting on your tennis skirt.

Hattie is really happy to be thinner than she was, but placates the Fates by saying aloud she doesn't mind what size she is so long as she and Kitty are happy and healthy. Martyn – she likes to add – is certainly not one of those men who would be put off by a few extra pounds.

Likewise, Hattie does not show how she looks forward to going back to work, but murmurs to others that she might have to start earning again, since it's such a problem managing on one salary. These sops thrown to destiny are working for the moment: she has got thin by sheer force of secret yearning, a job is waiting for her and now a kindly destiny has put Agnieszka her way. Hattie loves little Kitty, of course she does. Indeed, she is sometimes quite over-whelmed by love, and presses her face against the baby's firm, soft, milky flesh, and thinks that is all she needs in life; but of course it is not. It's just so dull at home. You listen to the radio, and struggle to stem a sea of disorder –

the trouble with babies is that it's all emergency: you keep having to stop whatever you're doing. She craves gossip, infighting, the amphetamine effect of deadlines, and the swirling soap opera of office life. She misses conversation as much as her salary. Kitty lies around gurgling and disgorging the food that's put into her and is not a valid source of entertainment, only of love, received and given. Songs and scriptures tell her that love is all she needs, but it is not true. Love is all she needs just for some of the time. So Martyn is being 'a bit iffy'. I can imagine.

A Bit Iffy

'But Hattie,' says Martyn, 'we have a problem here.'

'What's that?' Hattie asks.

'Just how ethical is it to ask another woman to look after one's child? Perhaps using child-care is in itself exploitative. I know it's convenient but is it right?'

'It's always been done,' says Hattie, allowing a hint of irritation to enter her voice. 'Those with the best education get the most money. I use my skills to earn: she uses her human instincts to earn. There are more women like her than there are women like me, so we get them to look after our babies.'

'But in an equitable society,' says Martyn, 'the scale would be reversed and we would be paid to make up for the pain of our work, not rewarded for the pleasure we take in it.'

'It isn't an equitable society,' says Hattie. 'That's it.'

'You are so argumentative,' he complains. But he is pleased at the return of her spirit.

Soon she may be back to normal, and their diet will improve. But he's not finished yet.

'We both agree that raising a child is the most important thing anyone can do, and it should be paid concomitantly.

And a nursery is probably the best option if you don't want to look after your own child.'

But Hattie has won, and his voice fades away and she gives him a half kiss, half nibble on his ear to show there are no hard feelings. If there is to be better food in the fridge Hattie must go out to work, and when it comes to it Martyn would rather that his child was looked after in the home than be sent to a nursery. He has not liked to ask what age Agnieszka is, nor whether she will be a pleasure to look at or otherwise. He is above such enquiry. He has a stereotyped Polish girl in his head: she is pale, thin, high-cheekboned, small-breasted, attractive but out of bounds.

Hattie has it all arranged. Agnieszka is to live in. This unknown and untested person is to have the spare room, look after the baby as a priority and do such domestic work, cooking and laundry that she can find time to do: she is to have Saturday and Sunday off and three evenings a week to go to evening class. She will be paid a generous £200 a week, with of course full board and lodging. Babs, who is accustomed to employing staff, has been consulted on these matters and this is what she recommends.

Martyn points out that Hattie will have to earn at least £300 a week to break even on the deal – perhaps more if the girl is a big eater. Hattie says she will be paid £36,000 a year and Martyn complains that that is ridiculously low: Hattie explains that instead of taking statutory maternity leave she actually handed in her notice, so certain was she that she would never want to return to work, and though she expects rapid promotion, she will formally have to start work fairly low down the end of the pay scale.

'With any luck,' says Martyn, 'this Agnieszka will be anorexic. That will save money on food. But hey, if she's what you want, go ahead. Let's share our evenings and our lives with a stranger. So be it. Only do be sure to ask for written references.'

Martyn loves Hattie. Dissension is just part of their life. He loves brushing up against her in the kitchen; he loves the warm roundness of her body, so different from his own angularity. He loves the ease of her conversation, her ready laugh, her lack of doubt, the way she didn't hesitate when she found she was pregnant and just sighed and said it was fate, why fight it?

Martyn comes from an awkward, belligerent family who look for slights and insults and find them, and would root out an unwanted baby without a second thought. He had no idea, when he met Hattie at a peace demo, that people could be like this, that sheer affluence of good feeling, not a superfluity of rage, could drive them on the streets in protest. It was a destined encounter. Surging crowds pushed them into each other's arms in an alley behind Centre Point. He had an erection, and deeply embarrassed, blushed and apologised when it would have been more fitting to over-look the matter, pretend it had never happened. She said, 'Not at all, I take it as a compliment.'

In three weeks he had moved in with her, and now they have a house and a baby. He would like to marry her but

18

she won't do it. She says she has no respect for the institution, as indeed neither does he, at least in principle. Both look at marriages within their immediate families and decide it is not for them. The complexity of divorce, and also its likelihood, alarms them both. But he has less objection to being owned by her, than she does by him. That worries him. He loves her more than she loves him.

'What's for supper?' asks Martyn, having abandoned any hope of finding something edible in the fridge, kissing the back of her neck, melting her wrath at once.

'I must finish the ironing first,' says Hattie. Her mother Lallie has hardly used an iron all her life long. It can hardly be in the genes. But then Lallie's a creative artist and Hattie is avowedly not, and so the daughter must take the normal route to a satisfactory environment, not by filling the air with music, but by providing an easy background for others.

All the same Hattie stops ironing. She needs little incentive. She bought pure cotton, wool and linen fabrics, natural fibres dyed with organic dyes, to cover the baby's back. Now she regrets it. Unnatural fibres dry faster than natural, don't matt, shrink or discolour with washing. They were developed for very good reason. The cot is always damp because ecologically-sound terry nappies are less effective than disposable ones. It doesn't make much difference to the baby what fabrics it regurgitates over. But Hattie is stuck with what she committed to, if only by virtue of the cost of replacement, and she does like things to look nice. There are still some few items left to iron but when were there ever not? Martyn may feel less stressed if he eats. She is not hungry herself. She opens a can of tuna and a jar of mayonnaise and heats up some frozen peas. Martyn once, rashly, said how much he liked frozen peas.

'Babs and I will be in adjacent offices,' she says, as the peas come to the boil and bob about at the top of the pan. 'And we'll be able to share a taxi home.'
'A taxi!' says Martyn. 'If we're to afford an au pair there won't be much taking of taxis anywhere.'

He knows tuna is nutritious and with bread and peas makes a balanced meal, but that doesn't mean the tinned fish doesn't clog up the mouth. The peas are not even bright green *petits pois* (too expensive) but large, tough and pale green. The bread is sliced brown Hovis. In his mother's household, meals were frequent, generous and on time, no matter how paranoiac and backbiting those who sat around the table were. The bread was fresh, crusty and white. But now in his own home the very concept of 'meals' has been abandoned. Since Kitty's birth he and Hattie eat to assuage hunger, and the desire seldom strikes them simultaneously. Yes, it is time she went back to work.

Demotic Credentials

'Hattie,' I say, 'what I think about you going back to work or not going back to work is irrelevant. You will do what you will do, as ever.'
'But I do like to have your permission, Great-Nan,' she says. I know she does. It touches me but I have asked her not to call me Great-Nan. 'Grandmother' is best, 'Gran' will do, 'Nan' is vulgar and 'Great-Nan' ludicrous, but Hattie will do what she will do.

Since Kitty came along, she claims her right to set me yet more firmly in the past and advance me a generation in public disesteem. She called me Grandmother in a perfectly proper way until she met Martyn, after which she took to calling me Nan, presumably out of loyalty to her partner's demotic origins. To possess a father who died in an electricians' strike is a rare qualification in the political media circles in which Martyn works. Anyone who does may feel the urge to make the most of it. Grandmother or even Granny smacks of the middle class, and the young these days are desperate to be seen to belong to the workers.

But I daresay next time she sees me she will hold Kitty out to me and say, 'Smile at Great-Nan,' and the infant will bare its toothless gums at me, and I will smile back and be delighted. I am totally dedicated to my family, and to Hattie, and to Kitty, and even to Martyn though he is not always a bundle of laughs, but then neither is Hattie, certainly not since they had the baby.

Martyn is tall, over six foot, solidly built, sandy-haired, and hollow-cheeked but otherwise attractive enough. Girls like him. He has a First in politics and economics from Keele University, and is a member of Mensa. He tried to get Hattie to join but she declined, finding something distasteful about setting herself above others, intellectually. This may be because her mother also once belonged to Mensa, having joined in the days when you could send the qualifying questionnaire by post, so you could get your friends to supply the answers. Martyn has worn glasses since he was five. His shoulders are slightly rounded, from bending over so many computers, so many textbooks, so many reports and evaluations.

His mother Gloria, forty-three years old when Martyn was born, the youngest of five, had the same big-boned build, making twice of Martyn's father Jack. The latter was slightly built, although like his son sandy-haired and hollow-cheeked. But Martyn looks healthy. Jack never did, certainly not by contemporary standards. Chip butties, fried fish, mushy peas and sixty cigarettes a day made sure that his arteries were clogged and his lungs black-lined. It was surprising he lasted as long as did. Gloria is still alive and in a nursing home in Tyneside. Martyn and Hattie visit her twice a year, but neither looks forward to the visits. She finds Hattie too fancy and strange-looking. The other siblings live closer to their mother, and visit more often.

Martyn is the only one who went to university. The others could have, but chose not to. They were like that: so sharp they cut themselves. Their father, Jack, joined the Communist Party as a boy in 1946, leaving when Russia invaded Hungary in 1968 to become a less extreme labour activist, but fighting as ever for the rights of the working class. He died of a heart attack when on the picket line during a strike. Waste of a good death, his friends said, better had it been from police brutality. Jack's hair thinned and went in his thirties.

Martyn fears that the same thing will happen to him: he hates to see hairs in his comb when he gets to the mirror in the morning. The bathroom is small, and usually hung with wet, environmentally-friendly, slow-drying garments.

My own demotic credentials are rather good, these days. My husband Sebastian is in a Dutch prison serving a three-year sentence for drug running. His name works against him. It is too posh. It attracts attention. I have suggested he calls himself Frank or Bill, but people are oddly loyal to the names that their parents gave them, as Hattie has observed to Martyn in relation to Agnieszka. Sebastian was, I believe but do not know, trying to supply the Glastonbury Festival with Ecstasy in yet another doomed attempt to solve our financial problems. These of course have become much worse as a result, but there are consolations. I have my new computer and a novel I can write in peace. I can sleep in all the bed, not a third of it; I can listen to the radio all I want, and now the panic fear, the anxiety as to how Sebastian is faring, and my own sense of social disgrace have faded, I can almost call myself happy. In other words, one can get used to anything.

And it's surprising, even at my age, how suitors cluster round as soon as the man of the house is away. The newly divorced woman, the grass widow and the prison widow are as honey to the wasps of the passing male, in particular the best friends' husbands. If there is no man to begin with, the attraction is not so great. Men want what other men have, not what they can have for the asking. So the lonely stay lonely, and the popular stay popular; the leap from one to the other is hard but not impossible. True widows do all right if they have come in to a great deal of life insurance. But otherwise their lot is hard: a grave too new for a headstone is disconcerting, and once it's up it's worse. Lose one husband, lose another. But the grass widow is in a good position, the promise of a short-term exercise in love and desire with a finite end is tempting. Age has little to do with it, in these days when a man of sixty seems old and a woman of sixty seems young. So I have suitors who do not interest me – they include a retired Professor of Philology from Nottingham, an art student who mistakenly thinks I have money and 'likes older women', and a television dramatist of the old school, largely unemployed, who thinks a connection with Serena would be a good idea. But like Penelope I encourage the suitors so far, and no further. I have no real intention of betraying Sebastian. I love him, in the old-fashioned, critical, but steadfast manner of my generation, we who loved first and thought afterwards. '*Men have died from time to time, and worms have eaten them, but not for love*,' said Shakespeare, and that is true for women too today, if not for the women of my generation. We lot died for love, all right.

'How am I *really*?' I respond to Hattie's question. 'How I am *really* is angry with Sebastian.'
'Oh, don't be,' she says, 'I am sure he is suffering enough.'
'I am suffering too,' I say, 'I have suitors. But I must say I am faltering in my Penelope role. Three years is a long time.'
'Oh, don't!' she implores. 'Just give up and behave like a grandmother and wait.'
'He should have looked behind him,' I say. 'A police car followed them for forty miles and they didn't even bother to look behind. In a car packed with illegal drugs!'
'Perhaps he didn't know they were in there. And he wasn't driving.'
'Oh, come off it,' I say. 'Don't you start excusing him too. Last time I saw him he said, "I did it for you." That made me really cross. He committed the crime, not me.'

Hattie laughs and says it's true, men have a knack of making their womenfolk responsible for everything that goes wrong. Martyn will open the front door and turn to her and say 'but it's raining' as if it were her fault.

Sebastian is my third husband, fourth if I include Curran, so I like to think I have some knowledge of the ways of men, in the house and out of it. I regale her with tales of husbands who pat their pot bellies and smile and tell you it's your fault because your cooking is so good, blame you for their adulteries (your fault I slept with her: you were too cold, snored too loudly, not there enough – anything). Your fault I lost my job, you did not iron my shirts. Your fault I am in prison, I did it for you. Serena's previous husband George gave up painting pictures and in future years was of course to blame Serena for failing to dissuade him from doing so. You should never try to make a man do anything, Serena says, that he doesn't want to. It always bounces back to you.

I love you, I love you, is the mating cry of the arriving male. *All your fault*, as he departs.

I met and married Sebastian when I was thirty-eight: he was forty. We had no children together: he had two by an earlier marriage: I had accumulated two along the way. I can only hope that imprisonment will not have the same effect on Sebastian as the heart attack had on George: that he will not, like George, encounter some therapist who will encourage him in the belief that it's all the wife's fault and the only way to survive is to leave her. To break the ties that bind. It is a fairly absurd worry. Fortunately counsellors are in short supply in Dutch prisons.

'Codswallop,' I say to my grand-daughter, 'Sebastian just wanted some excitement.' But I tell her I am only joking about the suitors, I will wait patiently for my husband's return, and I will.

Miraculously, we have managed to keep Sebastian's conviction from the press. He is Serena's brother-in-law, and as such could attract attention. And though I tell her publicity is good for sales, she says she is never sure of that; the more people know about your feet of clay, the less they want to buy your books and she certainly does not want to be pitied on account of a feckless brother-in-law. At seventy-three she is still working – novels, plays, occasional journalism – if you are self-employed there is always last year's tax to be paid.

When Sebastian went inside, Serena paid off our mortgage, so I can just about manage the bills. A small amount comes in from the gallery; in these days of conceptual art normal people still buy paintings in frames. Serena flies Club Class on a scheduled flight to Amsterdam every six weeks or so to visit Sebastian: Cranmer, her much younger husband – though at fifty-five he's scarcely a toyboy – or some other family member goes with her. As a family we give each other what support we can. I mostly go on my own, on easyJet from Bristol airport at a quarter the cost.

I can feel Martyn in the background, thinking Hattie has been on the phone too long, chattering, and wanting her to pay more attention to him. His family don't chatter, as Hattie's does. I hear him putting on the radio in the background, clomping about. Well, why should he not? When the man works and earns and the woman does not, it is only meet and fitting that his interests should take precedence over hers. 'I'd better go,' I say. 'Bless you for calling. I'm just fine and I think you should go back to work.'

'Thanks for your permission, Gran,' she says, but stays on the line. 'Don't worry about Sebastian; he'll be all right. He has his art to keep him warm. I remember Great-Gran saying in the middle of the trial, just before she died, that at least prisons were comparatively draught-free. He should think himself lucky.'

Hattie's great-grandmother Wanda had three daughters: Susan, Serena and Frances the youngest, that is to say myself. And Frances gave birth to Lallie, and Lallie gave birth to Hattie, and Hattie gave birth to Kitty. Wanda died the day Sebastian was sentenced to his three years – leaving her descendants, though distraught at her loss, at least now with time and energy to go prison visiting. I do not say she timed her death for Sebastian's benefit, but it would not have been out of character if she had. She brought us up to be dutiful and attentive to family responsibilities at whatever cost to ourselves. Susan, our eldest sister, died of cancer in her late thirties. My mother was a stoical person, but ever since then, she complained, she felt the cold. Draughts loomed large in her later life.

Hattie has not been to visit Sebastian in prison, though she always asks after him, and writes. Well, she has been pregnant and now she has a small baby, and though of course he has not said so, Martyn would feel easier if she did not go. He has his position at the magazine to think about, and his political ambitions. He hopes to stand for Parliament at the next election, and does not want his position compromised by a step-grandfather in prison.

'All right, darling,' she says to Martyn. 'I'm just coming. I think I left the car key under the nappies.' And she says goodbye to me and is gone.

Sebastian In Prison

Sebastian is allowed two visitors once a week, if all goes smoothly at the Bijlmer prison, and so far it has. The authorities encourage him to paint. They changed his cell so that he could stand an easel up in it. They like their prisoners to be creative. They can hang his paintings on the walls of that bleak place. He is, after all, a Royal Academician. He cooks excellent curries for other prisoners in his block. No one has raped him or even sworn at him. The wardens address him as Mr Watt. Even so, the Bijlmer is a horrible, frightening, noisy, clanging, terrible place, but villains are villains only some of the time and if you are careful to be out of their way when they are in violent criminal mode, you can get by. So Sebastian tells us.

But I want him home where he's safe, and can hear birdsong. I try not to think of him too much. He paints in oils: the house still smells of them, though the turps is drying up in the jam jars and the brushes stiffening: sometimes I catch a movement out of the corner of my eye and see what can only be his shadow through the open door of the attic. I never knew before now that the living could haunt a place. But Sebastian manages. It's a kind of company but I would rather have the real thing.

Sebastian became an RA twenty-five years ago; he had his name in the gossip columns and an exhibition at the Marlborough Gallery. He was once a member of the Arts Council, but no longer. He went on painting landscapes in frames long after everyone else had stopped. He is an idealist and a romantic. This is why he is in trouble.

Sebastian believes in the right of the artist to live in whatever state of mind they choose, natural or one that is chemically induced, drugs also being God-given. In the same way, he tells me, that women with pale lips choose to use lipstick to make them brighter. He denies the right of Government to deny choice to the individual. He is perfectly intelligent in other ways, and indeed charming, but he does not hear me when I say, in my mother Wanda's voice, that a principle so convenient can hardly be counted as a principle, it is too laced with self-interest.

Sebastian, after the manner of men, tends to be deaf to uncomfortable truths. He believes himself to be a favourite of the God who gave him his artistic gift. His defence lawyer described him as paraphrenic – a person sane in all respects except one. His capacity for trust is pathological. He would meet up with his criminal associates in the Royal Academy restaurant, thinking that was perfect cover, though the ladies up from the provinces would look askance over their quiche and the white wine at the expensive, flashy suits and talk knowingly about 'bling'. When he was in Holland and fingered by these friends of his, Sebastian was the only one surprised. That is my reading of the situation. He never told me the detail. He was ashamed.

A Further Ethical Discussion
After Supper

'With your Swedish background,' says Martyn to Hattie, 'I am surprised you take the view you do.' He will not let up. He is no longer hungry but he is unsatisfied, and deprived of sensual pleasures. Baby Kitty still sleeps in a cot next to their bed. Martyn can see the sense of it, but wishes the baby slept in a separate room. Sometimes he wakes in the night and reaches out for his wife, which seems his natural right, and finds Hattie sitting up and feeding Kitty. (He knows she is not his wife but his partner, and thus 'natural right' is the more questionable: it is one of the subliminal reasons why he would marry her if he could.)

Hattie will look at the child with what Martyn hopes is adoration, but suspects it is something more like amazement. She feels uneasy about making love while dripping milk from her breasts. For someone who rather dislikes the thought of breast-feeding – so cowlike – she produces a remarkable amount of this sweetish, delicately scented liquid from her nipples. Martyn, too, is amazed. It puts him in mind of a film he saw as a child about the exploitation of workers in the Malaysian rubber plantations. Cuts were made in bark and a strange yellowish goo would seep out.

He was revolted. He knows breast-feeding is natural and right but he wishes Kitty fed from a bottle. He preferred it when Hattie's breasts were erotic signifiers rather than dedicated to feeding another, even though that other has sprung from his seed. Indeed, Martyn finds the processes of parturition so bizarre as to be almost beyond belief.

Since the birth, he, who was once so scientifically reluctant and talked about Nature in the same way as people once talked about God – as the source of all goodness – finds himself all for cloning, test tubes, stem cell research, artificial wombs, GM crops and the like. The further from Nature and the more subject to intelligence and contrivance, the better. It has crossed his mind that an au pair would take up the spare room, and that this postpones the baby having a room of its own, and makes the likelihood of any decent, noisy, bounce-around-the-house sex even more remote than before.

'What has my Swedish father got to do with anything?' asks Hattie. Martyn points out that a Swedish Prime Minister's wife, a full-time working lawyer, was lately in trouble for employing a maid to clean their house. That she should do so was seen as demeaning to her, her husband and the maid. In Sweden, people are expected to clean up after themselves.

'Now we, who are meant to be working for the New Jerusalem, are to have a servant?' Martyn asks, 'Where are our principles?'

Hattie almost giggles. Sometimes she thinks he is addressing a public meeting, not her, but he has a future as a politician so she forgives him: he has to get into practice.

'She's not a servant,' says Hattie, firmly. 'She is an au pair.

Or a nanny. I don't know which she will prefer to be called.'
'Whatever – she will be doing our dirty work because we
can afford to have her do it, and she can't afford not to do
it,' says Martyn. 'What's that if not a servant? Get real,
Hattie. By all means do what's convenient, but understand
what you're doing.'
'*We* are embarking on a fair and sensible division of labour,'
says Hattie haughtily, seeing that mirth will not distract him.
'Have you thought about the consequences of being an
employer?' Martyn asks. 'Are we doing it officially, paying
for insurance stamps, taking tax at source and so on? I
certainly hope so.'
'If she's working part-time and lives in, she doesn't need
stamps,' says Hattie. 'She counts as one of the family. I asked
Babs.'
'I assume you've seen her visa, and she's entitled to be in
this country?'
'Agnieszka doesn't need a visa. She's from Poland,' says
Hattie. 'We're all Europeans now. We must be hospitable
and do everything we can to make her welcome. It's all
rather exciting.'

She has a vague idea of Agnieszka as a simple farm girl,
from a backward country, with a poor education, but well-
trained by her mother in the traditional domestic arts. Hattie
will be able to teach her, and enlighten her, and show her
how forward-thinking people live.

'I wouldn't be too sure,' says Martyn. 'She'll probably hate
it here and leave within the week anyway.'
Both come from long lines of arguers and defenders of
principle in the face of all opposition.

To The Left!

In 1897 Kitty's great-great-great-great-grandfather, a musician, joined forces with Havelock Ellis the sexologist and wrote to the Archbishop of Canterbury urging him to acknowledge the entitlement of young women to free sex. He forthwith lost his job as Director of the Royal Academy of Music, and had to flee to San Francisco, but it was a sacrifice gladly made in the interest of early feminism and the onward march of humanity.

Kitty's great-great-great-grandfather, a popular writer, went to the Soviet Union in the mid-thirties and came back to report a socialist and artistic paradise. Thereafter there was no stopping the left-footed march of the family, certainly on the female side.

When the Campaign for Nuclear Disarmament began, Kitty's great-great-grandmother Wanda walked from Aldermaston to London, her daughters Susan, Serena and Frances at her side. In 1968, Serena's second husband George was arrested for his part in the Grosvenor Square demonstration against the Vietnam War. In the seventies Serena's boys Oliver and Christopher put on balaclavas and threw aniseed balls over walls to distract guard dogs – though I can't remember what that was about. Serena and George housed an anti-apartheid activist in their house in Caldicott Square. Susan's children and grandchildren still turn up to march against the war in Iraq. It's in the blood. Even Lallie signs petitions to save veal calves from export. Hattie has demonstrated against GM crops – that was probably the time she and Martyn met crammed up against one another in an alley. One way and another it is amazing that the world is not yet perfect. The forces of reaction must be strong indeed not to fall in the face of so much good feeling and hope for the future, over so many generations.

From Kitty's father comes a different strain, a more orderly, stubborn, self-righteous kind of gene: oppressed and poor, the family rise up to demand their rights. Martyn, educated and sustained by the kindly State they have brought about, works as a commissioning editor for *Devolution*, a philosophical and cultural monthly. It runs articles about plenary targets, enablement, and the statistics of State control. These days Martyn feels he has the opportunity to change the world from the inside out, and no longer needs to go on demos, which are only for those who don't know the inner story, as he does. He too is certain that he is helping the world towards a better future.

I wonder what Kitty will do with her life? If she takes after her father's side, she will end up working for some NGO, I daresay, looking after the asbestos miners of Limpopo. If she favours her mother's side, and all the mess and mayhem attendant on their particular talents, she will be a musician, a writer, a painter, or even a protesting playwright. You may think I'm obsessive about the gene thing, but I have watched it work out over generations. We are the sum of our ancestors and there is no escape. Baby Kitty looks at me with pre-conditioned eyes, even as she holds out her little arms and smiles.

Acceptance

Martyn cheers up, for no apparent reason, rolls the name around his tongue, and likes it. 'Agnyeshh-kah,' he says, savouring the syllables. 'I suppose it is less gloomy than Agnes. And you're quite right. It's antisocial to have a room going spare at a time when there's such a pressure upon housing. Tell you what, Hattie, I'm still hungry. Supposing I get some fish-and-chips?'

Hattie looks at him in no little alarm. Hasn't he just eaten? Can he still be hungry? Is this why he wants the car keys? To buy fish and chips? A dozen thoughts flow through her mind, oddly disorganised. Fish fried in batter is unhealthy on many counts, not just for the individual but for the planet. Re-used oil has carcinogenic properties. The batter itself is fattening. The wheat used, unless organic, will have been sprayed many times with toxic chemicals. Batter can be removed before eating, true, but the seas are being denuded of fish and good citizens are cutting down on their consumption. And isn't there something about dolphins? Don't they get caught in the trawler nets and die horribly? Hattie seems to remember that though dolphins occasionally save swimmers from sharks, they also get a bad press these days: apparently the young males chase and gang-rape the females. On the other hand Martyn has often said that fish and chips remind him of his childhood in Newcastle and doesn't she love him and want him to be happy?

'You could get an Indian, I suppose,' she concedes. 'Though the District Nurse is against curry. It gets through into Kitty's milk.'
From time to time Martyn goes into what Hattie calls 'shaggy mode': his sandy hair sticks up, the skin on his face seems too loose for its bones, his eyes are too large for their sockets. It happens when he is in despair but doesn't know it. At such times Hattie feels both great affection and pity for him. She capitulates.

'Oh all right,' she says, 'go out and get us some fish and chips.'

Agnieszka Comes Into Hattie's Home

A week later and Agnieszka rings the doorbell of the little terrace house at 26 Pentridge Road. Hers are strong, practical hands, the skin rather blotchy and loose and much lined upon the palm. They are not her best feature. She is in her late twenties and wears a brown suede jacket, a knee-length black skirt and a white blouse. Her face is pleasant, broad, high-cheekboned, her demeanour quiet and restrained, her hair cut in a neat, thick, brown-to-mouse bob. Apart from the slightly sensuous air imparted by the short, full upper lip she seems to present no danger to marital harmony. She is far too serious for sexual hanky-panky.

The doorbell needs attention. There is a loose connection somewhere and the buzzer seems in danger of giving up completely. Agnieszka does not ring a second time but waits patiently for the door to open. She hears the sound of infant wailing growing nearer and Hattie opens the door. Hattie's hair is uncombed and she is still in a blue velvet dressing-gown, with dribbles of porridge down the front and what looks like infant vomit on the shoulder. It needs to go in the washing machine.

Agnieszka holds out her arms for the baby, and Hattie hands the child over. Kitty is taken aback and stops crying, other than for a few more gulping sobs while she gets her breath back. She looks at Agnieszka and smiles divinely, revealing a tiny little pink tooth which Hattie sees for the first time. A tooth! A tooth! Agnieszka wraps the child more securely in its blanket and hands Hattie her bag to hold. Hattie takes it. It is a capacious black leather bag, old but well polished. Hattie thinks perhaps Kitty won't like having her limbs constrained but Kitty doesn't seem to mind. Indeed, Kitty exhales a deep breath of relief as if she had at last found her proper home, closes her eyes and goes to sleep.

Agnieszka follows Hattie through into the living room, and lays the baby on its side in the crib. She folds crumpled baby blankets neatly, holding them against her cheek to test for dampness, putting those that pass the test over the edge of the crib and gathering up the damp ones.
'Where do we keep the laundry basket?' she asks. Hattie stands gaping, and then points towards the bathroom. The 'we' is almost unendurably reassuring.

Hattie, dressing in the first-floor bedroom, catches a glimpse of Agnieszka in the landing bathroom, sorting the overflowing washing basket. Whites and coloureds, baby and non-baby. All get filed into plastic bags before being put back in the basket. Nothing overflows. Soiled nappies go into a covered pail.

Hattie remembers Martyn's strictures about the necessity of checking references, but to do so would be insulting. She feels she is the one who should be giving references.

40

Agnieszka asks if she can see her room. Martyn has piled his suits onto the spare bed before setting out for work that morning, and Hattie has not yet found space for them elsewhere – she has had a bad morning with the baby. Agnieszka says she is satisfied with the accommodation, but perhaps she could have a small table to use as desk? Would Hattie like Kitty to sleep in her cot in the spare room with Agnieszka, or stay in the bedroom with her parents? She is sleeping through the night by now? Good. Then the former will be preferable, because then she, Agnieszka, can get Kitty up and dressed and having breakfast before Mr Martyn, as she already calls him, needs the bathroom. Early-morning routines are important, she says, if a household is to run smoothly. While Kitty sleeps she, Agnieszka, will get on with her studies.

Agnieszka now picks up and carries a chair to the front door, climbs on it, and does something to the wires that feed the bell. Hattie had never noticed those wires existed. It certainly has not occurred to her that the bell can be mended. Agnieszka tries the bell and lo! it rings firmly and clearly, no longer hesitant and hard to hear.

'Don't wake the baby,' says Hattie. 'Hush.'
'It's a good idea to get baby used to ordinary household sounds,' says Agnieszka. 'If Kitty knows what the sounds are about she won't wake. Only unaccustomed noise wakes babies. I was told this in Lodz, where I studied child development for two years with the Ashoka Foundation, and it checks out.'

She gets down from the chair and replaces it in its original position, and takes the end of a damp cloth and removes a little wedge of encrusted baby food where it's been stuck for some time.

Agnieszka tells Hattie that she is married to a screenwriter in Krakow, and plans to be a midwife, but must first perfect her English. Yes, it is difficult being away from her husband, whom she loves very much. She would like ten days off over the Christmas period to visit him, and her mother and her younger sister, who is not well. She is very close to her family. She produces photographs of all of them. The husband has a lean, dark, romantic face: the mother is dumpy and a little grim: the sister, who looks about sixteen, is fragile and sweet.
'Ten days seems rather a short time,' says Hattie. 'Make it two weeks and we'll manage somehow.'

Thus, without further argument or discussion, Agnieszka is engaged. But first she says she must put the damp washing into the machine. Plastic bags are invaluable for sorting laundry in an emergency, she says, but she will bring her own cotton ones for household use in future. Sorting prior to the wash makes sure mistakes are not made: white nappies do not pick up colour from black underpants, or cotton jerseys stretch in the boiling wash. Hattie might like to look into the local nappy laundry: this collection/delivery service can work out cheaper in electricity and soap powder than a home wash, and is less strain on the environment.

Still the baby sleeps, smiling gently. Hattie's life slips into another, happier gear. While Agnieszka keeps an eye on the white wash – Agnieszka has put the machine on its ninety-degree cycle, she notices, something she, Hattie, never does in case the whole thing boils over and explodes, but Agnieszka is brave – she goes round the corner to the delicatessen, ignoring the common sense of the supermarket, and buys two large pots of their fake but convincing caviar, sour cream, blinis and champagne. She must stop being mean, rejecting and punishing. She can see this is what she has been doing. Not his fault the condom broke. She and Martyn will live happily ever after.

Frances Worries About Her Grand-daughter

I hope Hattie understands the complexities of having an au pair in the house. For one thing Hattie is not married, only partnered, which in itself is rash. 'Partnerships' between men and women, as everyone knows, are more fragile even than certificated marriages, and the children of such unions likely to be left without two resident parents. Any disturbance to the delicate balance is unwise. If introducing a dog or a cat into a marriage can be difficult, how much more so a young woman? Some kind of female rivalry is bound to ensue. And if it all goes wrong the decisions are the more painful. Who takes the dog, who takes the cat, who takes the au pair when couples split? Forget the children.

Martyn is a good enough boy in his terrier fashion, never willing to let go, and as a couple they are affectionate – I have seen them go hand in hand – and he is a responsible father, having read any number of guide books to parenthood, but I am left with the feeling that he has not yet arrived at his final emotional destination, and neither has Hattie, and that makes me uneasy.

They have their shared political principles to fall back upon, of course, and I hope it helps them. I am an upright enough person myself and a socially conscious one, and in my youth, once the wild years were over, kept the company of kaftan-clad hippie girlfriends and bearded boyfriends with flares and sang along with Joni Mitchell. There was a time when all the men one knew in the creative classes had Zapata moustaches: it is difficult to know what a person with such a moustache is thinking or feeling, which may be why they were so popular.

That was in the sixties when women and men hopped in and out of each other's beds with alacrity, trusting to luck and the contraceptive pill to save them from the consequences of broken hearts and broken lives, and before venereal diseases (now called STDs to remove the sting and shame) put a blight on the whole enterprise – herpes, Aids, chlamydia and so on – but I never urgently sought after righteousness or thought the world could be much improved by the application of Marxist theory.

In any case I had too little time or energy left over from successive emotional, artistic and domestic crises to concern myself with political theory. The creative gene is strong in the Hallsey-Coe family, and we tend to marry others like us, so lives of quiet respectability amongst them are rare. We end up writers, painters, musicians, dancers – not metal-lurgists, marine biologists or solicitors. In other words we end up poor, not rich.

Hattie, a linguist and a girl of high principle and political awareness, is fortunate enough to be born without a creative spark in her, though this can sometimes flare up quite late, and there may yet be trouble ahead. Serena did not start writing until she was in her mid-thirties: Lallie on the other hand was an infant prodigy, performing a Mozart flute concerto for her school when she was ten.

The Effects Of Bricks
And Mortar On Lives

Let me tell you more about Hattie's and Martyn's house. Houses are not neutral places. They are the sum of their past inhabitants. It is typical of the English of the aspiring classes that they prefer to live in old places rather than new. They crawl into someone else's recently abandoned shell and then proceed to ignore whoever it was who went before. Tell them they're behaving like hermit crabs, and they raise their eyebrows.

Pentridge Road was built towards the end of the nineteenth century, rooming houses for the working classes, few of whom ever grew to optimum size or lived beyond fifty-five. The young couple see themselves as somehow set apart from the heritage of bricks and mortar in which they live. They feel they have sprung into existence ready-formed and into a brand new world, blessed with more wisdom and sophistication than their predecessors. Tell them they inherit not only the genes of their forebears but the walls and ceilings of those socially and historically related, and they look at you blankly.

Some things do happen which are an improvement – facts are certainly easier to come by in the twenty-first century than in the age of the printed page. News of the outside world flows like chlorinated water from radio and television: houses are better warmed and food cupboards more easily filled, but those who live in them are as much as ever at the mercy of employers and whatever rules of current cultural etiquette apply, whether it's the obligation to fear God or to own an iPod.

Tear off the old wallpaper – as Hattie and Martyn did when they bought the house – and find yellowed scraps of newspaper beneath – accounts of the Match Girls' Strike, the force ten gale which brought down the Tay Bridge, the costumes worn at Edward VII's coronation. Hattie and Martyn scrape them all ruthlessly into the bin, scarcely bothering to read. I think the otherness of the past disturbs them too much: they like everything new and fresh and start-again.

The plaster walls are painted cream, not papered dark green and brown, and the paint at least does not poison you with lead – though traffic pollution may serve you worse. But very little changes in essence. Other generations lay in this same room at night and stared at the same ceiling worrying what the next day held.

In my sister Serena's solid early-Victorian house in a country town, the stone stairs from the basement are worn down in the middle from the tread of countless servants, up and down, up and down. You'd think their tired breath would haunt the place but it doesn't seem to. Serena's mother-in-law died in the room where Serena now has her office but the fact only very occasionally affects her, though she claims her ghost walks on Christmas Eve. That is to say she once saw the old lady cross the passage from spare room to bathroom, and looking twice there was no one there. Her mother-in-law left a benign presence behind her, Serena claims. When I say, 'But I have seen the ghost of the living Sebastian in his studio,' she does not want to believe me. She likes to be the only one in touch with the paranormal. She isn't.

I live in a small farmhouse which has been a dwelling for the last thousand years at least. The hamlet, outside Corsham in Wiltshire, is mentioned in the Domesday Book. Its occupant would have been fairly low down the social scale: a sub-tenant perhaps. Originally it was a single room for family, animals and servants. Then an outside staircase was built and a couple of rooms above. The families moved upstairs, the servants and animals stayed below. Outhouses were built: animals were separated out from servants. The original barn was long ago converted to a dwelling. A studio was built out the back where Sebastian now paints, in ghostly form, and I hope will again, less spectrally.

Sometimes I wake in the middle of the night, seized by the fear that he will behave like an ageing man after a heart operation, and try to change his life, and the change will include separating out from those that love him. It happened to Serena and it could happen to me. In these wakeful nights the house creaks and groans and sighs, from sheer age or from the spirits of those who went before, including pigs, horses, sheep, servants, forget the masters and mistresses. Oh believe me, we are not alone. The central heating gurgles like a mad thing at night.

But back to the young, the loving, the breeding and the present, that is to say Hattie and Martyn. Martyn, to give him credit, is more conscious of the past than many, if only as a contrast to the benign Utopia he and his friends hope to achieve. Martyn has explained to Hattie, as she sits trapped in her nursing chair (an antique, which Serena bought her as a present) feeding Kitty, that the terrace house they live in – two up, two down – was designed for the wave of Irish navvies brought in to complete the earthworks for the great London stations which served the manufacturing North, the land of his roots. St Pancras, King's Cross, Euston, Marylebone – every shovelful of earth and rock had to be moved by hand, and now forms Primrose Hill.

Hattie would like to live somewhere larger, even if less historical, but they cannot afford it and in any case, says Martyn, they should be grateful for what they have.

The navvies lived six to a room in what is now home for two grown-ups, one baby and now the maid. There is still an old coal fireplace in the top back bedroom where once, over coals scavenged from the King's Cross mustering yards, meat and potatoes were cooked. A puny extension for the kitchen and bathroom was built in the 1930s and takes up nearly all the sunless yard. Agnieszka is to have the small back bedroom, next door to the one where currently Martyn, Hattie and Kitty sleep.

There is gas-fired central heating but the gas comes from under the North Sea and no longer from the coal mines. It's cleaner, but it's expensive and Martyn and Hattie dread the bills. Though at least everyone on the way from the oil rigs of the north to the man who reads the meter – or rather leaves his card and runs – is decently paid. Or so says Martyn. Martyn's father, grandfather and great-grandfather fought for this prosperity and justice and achieved it. No one now who can't afford a lottery ticket!

Martyn has recently been asked by his employers to write two articles explaining to a doubtful public that casinos are a good thing, bringing pleasure to the people, and he has, although he is not quite sure that he agrees. But he bites back argument as he writes. There is, as always, a case for both sides and it is not sensible to overturn too many apple carts in pursuit of a principle, this being a relativist age, and Hattie not earning, and so early in what he hopes eventually to be a parliamentary career.

Morality, as Hattie recently discovered, is a question of what one can afford. She can afford less than Martyn. Even so, putting the comforter in the baby's mouth, plugging its distress, Hattie feels guilt. Guilt is to the soul as pain is to the body, a warning that harm is being done. Gender comparisons are odious, as Hattie would be the first to point out, but it is perhaps easier for men to override the emotion than it is for women.

Perhaps I shouldn't have given Hattie permission to go back to work. Along with the child-care comes guilt, in the form of another pair of hands to soothe Kitty's brow, another voice to lull her to sleep. Bad enough for Hattie to have bred a baby – and guilt is to motherhood as grapes are to wine – now she must worry about how Agnieszka will react to the baby and the baby to Agnieszka and both to Martyn and back again.

Hattie will have to develop the art of diplomacy fast. Wouldn't it just be easier to put up with the boredom of motherhood and wait for Kitty to grow up? I feel like phoning Hattie and saying 'Don't, don't!' but I desist. The girl is not cut out for domesticity. But will Agnieszka influence Kitty's character, mar her development in some way, teach her how to spit out food and use swear words? I am Kitty's great-grandmother. I worry. The guilt outruns the generations.

Learned Characteristics

Back in the sixties when we were in our early thirties, living round the corner from each other in Caldicott Square, Serena and I passed au pairs around like hot cakes. Nearly all of them were good girls, just a few were very flawed. But they all made their mark. I am sure some traces of various learned characteristics remain in my children, and in Serena's too, to this day.

Roseanna, Viera, Krysta, Maria, Svea, Raya, Saturday Sarah – all will have had some input into what they became. Ours may have been the predominant influence, but I'm sure my Jamie learned from Viera how to get his way by sulking and from Sarah how to love in vain. It was from Maria that Lallie the flautist learned to despise us all, but from Roseanne how to value and respect fabrics. Lallie may be falling into bed with a lover but she won't fling her clothes on the floor. She will place them neatly on the back of a chair, or indeed on a clothes rail. She is prepared to spend hours washing by hand, while I just bung things in the washing machine and hope for the best.

In the days of the many au pairs, I was working in the Primrosetti Gallery for a pittance, Serena was beginning to earn well as an advertising person, and George her new husband had just started his antiques shop. Serena and George lived in a big house in Caldicott Square. The girls lived in the basement, for I had no spare room for them, and though the basement was in its raw early-Victorian state, all damp walls and loose plaster, they did not seem to mind.

I have never been jealous of Serena, she is too amiable and generous for that, and takes her own position in the world lightly, thus obviating envy. She is also, frankly, fat and maintains that this is what has enabled her to survive as well as she has in a competitive world. 'Oh, Serena!' people say, 'Sure she seems to have everything: money of her own making, a nice home, an attentive husband, her name in the papers, creativity, reputation, children – *but isn't she fat!*' And they can't be bothered even to throw the barbs.

Back then in the sixties, working in advertising as she was, weighed daily by an expensive doctor in Harley Street and injected with some terrible substance made of pregnant mare's urine, or some such, plus a daily dose of a crude amphetamine, Serena was thin and glamorous enough. Then indeed, yes, I was envious. Why is it so easy for her, I'd wonder, so hard for me? But then I'd think, well, my twenties were wildly good for me, in a desperate kind of way; hers, until she took up with George, were boring and anxious.

When Serena met George around her twenty-ninth birthday, it was as if some curse had lifted and all the jagged pieces of her life so amazingly and unexpectedly fell into place.

Before that she was a hopeless misfit, suffering from what they now call low self-esteem and an over-placatory nature.

The curse moved over from her to me – perhaps this is the fate of sisters – and it was my turn to endure a decade of blighted life as a single mother, trying to bring up two children – one a sports fanatic, the other, stunningly talented but basically unfriendly. Until then, I was the one who was enviable. I was thin and she was fat.

I daresay if you add up the anxious, tearful, tormented days and nights we have had throughout life, the pair of us, they come to about the same. I clocked up a good few in my seventy-first year, when Sebastian was held incommunicado in a Dutch police cell, and later in prison, but I don't think as many as Serena did, flailing and wailing and staring into space, when George betrayed her, turned against her, locked her out of her home, around the time of her sixtieth birthday. She married again soon enough.

Martyn On The Way
Home From Work

New Century House, where Martyn works as a statistical journalist for *Devolution*, is newly built and well funded: it stands all glass, steel and shininess, in a block of small rather mean streets between Westminster and Petty France. It is pleasantly decorated and has effective climate control. There was a Legionnaires' Disease scare when the building first opened – stagnant water had been circulating in the 'veins' of the building, its opening by the Prime Minister having been delayed for more than a year – but the source of the epidemic was quickly detected and put right and only a janitor died. A Feng Shui expert was called in to help with the foyer. As a result the entrance to Starbucks is at an angle calculated to welcome customers and revitalise takings. It seems to be working. The noise from cheerful non-smoking coffee drinkers floats up the escalators until well after ten each morning: the elevators smell of hot chocolate croissants.

Each of the seven floors has a dedicated rest room for stressed staff, with a good supply of fresh towels for showers, and for a small fee pillows are available for those who need to sleep. Research shows that nothing improves productivity like the short power-nap. Since Kitty arrived Martyn has made good use of these rooms. The baby sleeps well by day but not by night, no matter how often Hattie takes her to the breast, and it is impossible for Martyn to sleep through the wrigglings and moanings of both mother and child.

As well as serving as the offices of the sister magazines *Devolution* and *Evolution*, the building houses the headquarters of three think-tanks or public policy research institutes – the Centre for Post-Communist Economic Development, the Policy Coordination of Welfare Reform Initiative, the Institute for Social Commentary – and two quangos dealing with societal management and measurement.

There has been some talk of Martyn being seconded part-time to the Welfare Reform Initiative under the new Moving and Growing Human Resources Plan, which deals with unemployment issues, but Martyn is manoeuvering so this won't happen. The pay is more, but Martyn sees his future in political journalism and indeed in politics itself. He is more likely to be selected as a candidate out of a journalistic background than from one more concerned with statistical research. He needs visibility.

Martyn is taking a nap in the fourth-floor sanctuary. It is a pale green room with pink features; rather hard on the eye but the colours are recognised to foster sleep. At home Hattie and he have strong, dark, powerful colours on the walls and they have painted the furniture red: Kitty's cot is yellow to maximise her synaptic responses. Hattie scorns the New Age – crystals and horoscopes and so on – but has a belief in the power of colours to influence mood which Martyn finds endearing. His own upbringing was so practical and no-nonsense he sometimes finds himself hungry for Southern whimsicality.

Martyn is joined by his editor and immediate boss Harold Mappin, who collapses on an adjacent couch (modelled on one from a first-century Roman fresco) saying 'they've junked almost the entire edition. Except for your *Skinflints and Killjoys* piece, which went down a treat. How can they call this living? If I don't have a bit of shut-eye I shall kill myself. Debora's wearing me out. God save us from younger women.'

There has been some policy change at the top: new health initiatives are proving too expensive for the Treasury: research is showing what Martyn had always suspected – that the more you asked young healthy people to look after their health the less inclined they were to do it: only the already ailing and the elderly bothered. The focus of the autumn issue is now to be devoted to good news rather than grim warnings. Also, circulation is falling – even the Government departments amongst which *Devolution* is read, themselves victims of spending cuts, are no longer taking the magazine.

All this Harold delivers to Martyn, who is pleased and flattered to be taken into his confidence, while arranging his pillows. More significantly still, he also says that he has changed his mind about transferring Martyn to the Welfare Reform Initiative. 'Much too dull for a dude like you. We need you in the team. What about a positive piece on the new cholesterol research? What this country needs is good news.'

'You mean something like *Why You and the Chip Butty Can Be Friends?*' asks Martyn. He is speaking ironically but Harold just says, 'Exactly' and falls asleep, not waiting for further comment, arms flung above his head like a small child.

Harold is a large, noisy, hairy man in his fifties, with shrewd eyes. His staff put it about that he is autistic, or at any rate has Asperger's: they look up the symptoms on the Internet, hoping for grounds for their belief that his communication and social interaction skills are so minimal he can be described as mad, and they can ignore him. Martyn has always got on with him perfectly well.

Martyn goes home encouraged and cheered. He walks to Trafalgar Square and takes the Barnet branch of the Northern Line from Charing Cross back to Kentish Town Station. Many a Westminster worker has taken exactly this route home to Kentish Town since the line was built, a hundred years ago. You walk a little first, both for the exercise and to save the trouble of changing at Embankment. And like so many before him he approaches home with a mixture of emotions: desire to see his family conflicting with a kind of terror that they exist at all. The waiting family is the source of all pleasure and the source of all dread. Once he was young and free: now he has obligations and must not be selfish.

If he is promoted as he can see he might well be, from editor to commissioning editor, his salary will jump by some £6,000 a year. That would mean Hattie could stay home with the baby, and they would no longer need to have an au pair. He wants his house to himself. Hattie, being flesh of his flesh, doesn't count as another person: Kitty's arrival had been an upset but she too now feels like an extension of himself, not a foreign body to be eased out.

Privacy had been dearly earned in his growing years – the lad Martyn would sit by himself in the cold in the outside loo and read, just to get a bit of peace – and not even reading had been private: you read the book your teachers said you should read and had to discuss it afterwards, otherwise you didn't pass your exams and then what became of you? To the man Martyn the idea of a stranger living at close quarters, sharing his table, sharing his television, knowing his secrets, feels nightmarish. Surely the value of money lay not in the things you bought, but in the time, space and privacy it earned for you?

At home, there was at least the peace of familiarity, although currently disturbed and messy and Hattie mad and the baby crying and no food in the fridge. But this peopled privacy was what he had chosen, and what he wanted; it was his delight. His domestic happiness was like a Russian doll, securely weighted at the base. Sleepless nights, wailing baby and wranglings with Hattie about this and that, made it lean so it seemed bound to fall, but then it was certain to bounce back again.

But now Hattie has called him on his mobile, excited and pleased, to tell him the Polish girl is already installed in the spare room – his time, space and privacy has wilfully been breached, and by Hattie, who is meant to be on his side, thinking only of her self-interest. He disciplines his thoughts. He will not think like this. All will be well. No use being a loner in this sharing and caring age. He will go home, fit in with everyone, and behave.

Martyn Comes Home To Agnieszka

Martyn is not prepared for what meets him when he opens the front door: Hattie with her wild hair in order, in a clean, ironed shirt and fresh jeans. She smiles at him as if she were happy to see him, not, as so often these days, with a complaint and an argument ready to spring to her lips. He had forgotten how pretty she is. She is wearing a bra again, so she has two separate breasts not a kind of undifferentiated flesh shelf. Her figure is back to its pre-baby state. It probably has been for months but no one, least of all Hattie, has paid it much attention.

'Kitty's asleep in Agnieszka's room,' Hattie says, 'and supper's on the table.'

It is too, and like the old pre-Kitty days: delicatessen food, no longer boiled potatoes and cheap tough chops. Lots of spoons for sauces on the table and little jars of this and that which Hattie has lately derided as a wicked waste and empty calories. But no sign of Agnieszka, who it seems is out at her belly-dancing class.

'A belly dancer! Our child is to be in the care of a belly dancer?'

'Don't be so sad and old-fashioned,' says Hattie. 'Belly dancing's in, forget Pilates. Belly dancing teaches relaxation, muscular control and a healthy mobility.'

Hattie tells him that Agnieszka hopes to become a qualified tutor: even start up her own school in London. She loves dancing. She was even in the Polish Dance Company for a time, on a day-release course during their equivalent of our sixth form. She'd been chosen over hundreds of applicants.

'I thought she was meant to be learning English over here and then going home.' Martyn is disconcerted. Perhaps Agnieszka is a figment of Hattie's imagination? Perhaps she's in Hattie's head and nowhere else? It occurs to him that Hattie's new appearance might be a symptom of a disordered mind. The madness is not in the disorder but in the order?

But the food looks good and Hattie is still smiling and the room is tidy and napkins arranged by the plates, as his mother would do on special occasions. This is not imagination. A fairy god-mother has appeared and set everything right. Martyn's mother never read fairy stories to her children as a matter of principle: '*If they want to read let them do it for themselves.*'

'But what does she looks like?' he asks. He feels that this is not a question he ought to ask, women's looks are not up for discussion, and should not be taken into account in the work sphere, but he wants to know.
'There's nothing to tell.' Hattie has to struggle for description. 'She's just ordinary. No busty beauty, no long-legged harpy. She looks pleasant enough. She has a flat tummy.

Mine isn't quite back to normal yet. I might go along to classes with her.'

'Leaving me to look after Kitty?' He speaks lightly but already he can feel himself lonely and left behind by two women.

'A babysitter can look after Kitty if we're none of us here,' she says. 'Once I'm back to work we can afford as many babysitters as we want – or Agnieszka and I could always go on different days.'

This is Martyn's moment to tell Hattie that he may well be getting a big hike in salary, and the financial imperative is removed from the issue, but he does not. If this is the new Hattie he wants her.

Martyn goes into the spare room to check on Kitty and finds her sleeping peacefully in a cot in the space between the single bed and the wall. Her hair has been brushed and lies snugly against her cheek. She is a fair, round-faced, well-filled-out baby. He loves her intolerably.

The spare room has been re-arranged to its advantage: the desk from the kitchen where it held nothing but out-of-date newspapers, run-out pens, elastic bands the postman left is now under the window, and a small bookshelf rigged up above it – *English Language for Foreigners*, *Dancing Towards Self-Awareness* and *Child Development Studies* – that one from the New Europe Press. He'd reviewed it for *Devolution* when he was in charge of the book pages. There's a state-of-the-art laptop on the desk. How has she afforded that? His own is old and keeps crashing. This one obviously functions.

Kitty's clothes, neatly folded, and all the paraphernalia that goes with infant care and has previously littered the living room, are now laid out tidily along one set of shelves. Agnieszka's own belongings seem to be minimal: he looks in the drawers and sees a few neatly folded undergarments and thin pastel sweaters. Nothing is black, nothing is fancy. Reassured, he goes back into the living room.

'We could go to bed,' he says, 'before she gets back.'
'All right,' Hattie says to his surprise and follows him into the bedroom, as if it were once again the world before Kitty, before pregnancy. They have the bed to themselves: the clouds in his head clear. He groans, she moans. In the next room, the baby does not wake. They hold each other tight for at least ten minutes before the real world intervenes.

Martyn wonders if he should tell Hattie about the article that Harold obviously wants: the endorsement of the chip butty – a soft white bread sandwich with fried chipped potatoes, well salted, for the filling – as a source of approved pleasure, the Government deciding its electoral advantage no longer lies in health and the self-abnegation that goes with it. He decides not to, because Hattie is hot on nutrition and will only bring up the subject of his father's early death and the contribution paid to it by the chip butty, and he would rather she did not. They stay in bed and are asleep before Agnieszka returns.

In the unaccustomed peace of the morning, Martyn sleeps longer than anyone else in the household. He reckons he made a full eight and a quarter hours. He bounces out of bed naked and remembers he must now put on a dressing-gown before going to the bathroom. The dressing-gown is not on the floor but on a hanger, and to hand. Putting it on adds a feeling of ritual and security to the day. He shaves. The washbasin has been wiped, and the taps polished and the little knot of hair where the basin drains has been removed, so the water leaves quickly and no soap scum or detritus is left behind. The drying washing is still over the racks in the bathroom but has been shaken out and pegged not just flung over the wires.

Martyn sees Agnieszka for the first time, and understands that to call her Agnes – which he had been planning in his head, as a last defiance – would be inappropriate. She is a careful person and needs a careful name. She smiles sweetly and with a degree of humility, and says she is pleased to meet him: 'Mr Martyn, the man of the house.'

Does he like an egg for breakfast, and if so, scrambled, fried or poached? Hattie is eating a boiled egg, the first of two, from an eggcup and not one of Kitty's plastic rings. Kitty is in her high chair, well surrounded by pillows for safety. She is trying to manage a spoon and beams at her father, her mother and Agnieszka with equal pleasure. But Martyn and Hattie are new to babies: this amiability is symptomatic of the seven-month child. Soon she will become more particular and shield her face to any other than the favoured few, and weep if presented with anything unfamiliar.

Hattie and Martyn believe they are raising an extraordinarily and peculiarly talented child, of course they do: really all they are doing is raising just another human being, but one who is going to shove them back into the past a whole generation. Already they are not the ones coming in but the ones going out.

To Kitty, hard-wired to charm and annoy in equal measure the better to thrive, her parents are the means of her survival, bit-part players in her life, grand-parent fodder for the children she will have, if everything goes right. But she does love them. She loves what is familiar and those who do her bidding.

Au Pairs We Have Known

The first of the au pairs came to us in the winter of 1963. Her name was Roseanna. In those days I, Frances, and Serena pooled our child-care resources. If my children, Lallie and Jamie, were more often in the Caldicott Square house than hers, Oliver and Christopher, were in mine, it was because that was what the cousins chose. Her house was bigger, though mine was warmer.

My house was tall and the staircase wide, only one room on each of the four storeys, and a bathroom squashed beneath the roof. Serena's and George's house was one of those late-Georgian pillared double-fronted affairs, not detached, but presenting a unified face around the Square. In those days they were dilapidated and unheated. The basements were damp because the Fleet River ran underground. My peculiar house, known as The Tower, had a curved brick façade, and was squashed in between the regular-looking buildings. Some speculative builder had miscalculated his measurements back in the 1820s, and a later one filled an unproductive gap.

Serena and George owned their house. I rented, and Serena often had to help me with the monthly payments. I sometimes resented the fact that she saw me as some kind of extension of herself, and that what was hers by right was mine as well, but at least she never seemed to expect me to be grateful. Nor did George have to be consulted: Serena earned her own money.

In those days it was assumed that the cost of child-care would be borne by the mother if she chose to go out to work, as would the cost of any domestic help needed to replace the vacuum left by her absence. It was not until the eighties that the dual responsibility of parents was taken for granted. Equality carries its own disadvantages. High-earning women today are still taken aback to discover that the departing husband is entitled to alimony – half her savings, half her earnings, half her pension. Serena was certainly astounded, thirty years into her marriage with George, to discover this to be the case.

George not only wanted to go to the arms of a younger mistress, he wanted to take Serena's assets with him. He died before the financial arrangements of the dissolution of the marriage were complete, thus saving dispute, but of course upsetting everyone dreadfully.

The cousins, in the Caldicott Square days, liked one another, which was a help to whoever was in charge of them: they were always more likely to be found giggling than fighting. Jamie, I must say, was considered by all to be something of a nuisance. He was a charming enough, noisy little boy, whom we described as boisterous but now would be seen as suffering from attention-deficit disorder, and prescribed Ritalin. Lallie was even then playing her flute, the piano, the guitar and any other musical instrument she could lay her slender hands upon. If I do not speak much about Jamie it is because these days

I so seldom see him. He lives in Timaru, New Zealand, where he runs a horse-racing casino and helps coach the local rugby team. His wife Beverley does not like him to have too much to do with me, especially now that Sebastian is in prison. Beverley is perfectly amiable, and wears enviable hats to race meetings, but finds her English relatives peculiar. I don't think she would have married James, were he not in line for a baronetcy, not that any money or property went with it. Generations of profligate sons had seen to that. But Beverley will one day be Lady Spargrove and she likes that. Inherited titles are rare in Timaru, I gather.

I married James's father Charlie more or less by accident – in the way that glamorous couples used to find themselves married in thirties Hollywood films, waking up astonished in the wrong bed with a wedding ring on their finger. We were in Las Vegas and both of us were drunk and high on God knows what. The legality of the marriage was always doubtful. I certainly almost never used the title – it seemed unfair to claim it in the circumstances, though it's understandable Jamie wanted to; he had little enough from his father otherwise, God knows.

After Curran's death and Lallie's birth I abandoned the street life for that of the artist's moll. I modelled naked and slept around where the smell of turpentine was most intense, and had fun. And I dumped the baby on Wanda, most of the time, and then all of the time, when that particular patch of life came to an end and I went off America with Charlie.

Here, for Charlie's sake, I developed an interest in pole dancing, horse racing and gambling, and ended up pregnant with Jamie. I would not have an abortion. I could see that if I did there would be nothing to stop me from falling into the chasm of total self-destruction. I was near the edge often enough. And Serena found the money to bring me back home, and eventually to Primrose Hill.

Please remember that when I left Lallie with my mother Wanda I was very young, very upset, and still in mourning for her father. I am to be excused, but all the same it is not wise to behave badly towards your children: you feel guilty all your life, and think how different he or she would be, how much better their lives, if only you had not done this, had done that. Forget the initial abandonment when I'd left her with my mother, if fifteen years later I hadn't so hated driving, hadn't been so fed up with getting Lallie to music classes and recitals against rush-hour traffic I probably wouldn't have sent her to boarding school – no matter how progressive and musical – and she wouldn't have got pregnant and had Hattie and then dumped her on me – and perhaps Lallie would have smiled a bit more during her life – but then we wouldn't have Hattie and now Kitty – and so on and so on.

New-age cosmologists tell us that there may well be, in infinity, alternative universes where the ramifications of all our actions are lived out. Stored, as it were, in some massive computer, are the other worlds in which Sebastian does not go to prison, Curran does not die, Lallie is born genial and has three babies by a banker, and for all we know we wake up in one world with the memories appropriate to the last. But I fear there are some unalterable truths: amongst them that good eventual results do not excuse bad behaviour or resolve guilt.

71

Curran. Lallie's father. I met him when Serena and I went to the Mandrake Club in Soho, back in 1953. She was twenty-one and I was twenty. Artists and poets and other bad hats sat in the half-dark and played chess, drank cheap wine and planned world revolution. She had little confidence and I had lots.

Serena met David, who had an encyclopedic memory, played the guitar and sang sentimental songs, and who having once cast eyes on her pursued her until eventually she gave in and had a baby. She declined, haughtily, to marry him.

And I met beautiful Curran, who I suppose was in his midtwenties, and played chess in the evenings in the Mandrake and flute during the day on the Underground, his Irish cloth cap on the floor waiting for loose change, until moved on by the police, which happened, he complained, every hour or so.

Curran was beautiful but perhaps a little mad. He had glossy black curly hair and a pale skin and blue eyes, and lots of cash in his pockets. I always liked that in a man. He was a favourite with the passengers: he played beautifully and I can't hear *The Rose of Tralee*, *Danny Boy* or *The Four Green Fields* without wanting to cry. The mournful, lovely sound echoed through the murky subterranean warrens, above and below the rumble of trains, singing of lost lands, lost loves. I loved him so.

He let me sit by his side on a blanket – it was the days before street people went round with dogs for company. The blanket was a McLean tartan, and from it I gathered such ineptly tossed coins as missed the tweed cap. Curran was killed in a pub fight when I was five months pregnant.

I knew nothing about his family or home, and Wanda advised me not to try and find out. Men, dead or alive, were more of a nuisance than they were worth, unless they had proper homes, trades, professions and incomes. I had the baby in a Catholic home for lost girls and left it with Wanda, and went wandering within a month of Serena giving birth to David's son and Susan to Piers's. Poor Wanda: we didn't leave her much of a life of her own.

My Labrador Hugo sleeps in a basket, on a tartan McLean rug, a direct descendent of that one long ago. Hugo misses Sebastian: so do I. He digs his nose into its hairy, familiar crumples and feels comforted, and I, watching him, feel the same. I miss Wanda, and I miss Susan, and so does Serena. I have no one to miss Curran with me. If I try to talk about him to Lallie she stops me. She says she is not interested in her origins.

Lallie was born with her father's looks and talent, which Wanda tried to tame by way of sheet music and scales, and Serena by paying the fees of a progressive school where musical talent was allegedly fostered, and where she promptly got pregnant by way of Bengt the Swede. So now we have Hattie and Kitty. Serena's lot were all boys, as if to answer back.

And now Lallie wows the concert halls of Europe, Japan and the Americas, as once her father wowed commuters on the Underground. His favourite station was Charing Cross, to which Martyn walks daily.

73

Glossing Over Inconvenient Facts

Hattie calls me. Hugo and I are watching a programme on the television. Hugo likes to watch house make-overs, when the owners go away for a time and when they come back everything is different. Sometimes they hate it, sometimes they love it. Hugo is very intelligent, and when he sees a dog on the screen he gets up and barks. Then, disturbed and uneasy, he will go to Sebastian's studio to sniff around Sebastian's old paint brushes, as if he suspects there's a rabbit somewhere about. This is a Hugo face-saving device, because he too misses Sebastian and for all he knows he's dead.

'Gran,' says Hattie, when I answer the phone. This is better than Great-Nan. She must be in a really good mood.
'You've no idea,' she says, 'how wonderful Agnieszka is. Kitty adores her. She's so competent and the house looks like a dream and Kitty is fine with her. She smiles at everyone and holds out her arms to Martyn when he gets back from work.' And she tells me that Colleen has had a pregnancy crisis and they want her, Hattie, to start again at Dinton & Seltz the following Monday.
'Isn't this rather soon?' I ask. 'Shouldn't you try this Polish girl out with Kitty for a month or so before rushing off?'

'I need the month's money. Au pairs have to be paid for. You're getting to sound so like Great-Grandmama on a bad day,' says Hattie. 'A kind of built-in doubt that anything we wanted to do could ever be for the best.'

'It's called experience,' I say. 'What about breast-feeding? Is Kitty ready to go onto a bottle?'

'It's more than time. Agnieszka says we British overdo the breast-feeding thing. She says as babies get older mother's milk may not have enough protein to satisfy their needs, especially in the evenings.'

'How convenient,' I say. She's right. I am turning into Wanda. She tells me Agnieszka plays peek-a-boo with Kitty and Kitty loves it. Agnieszka believes that little minds need as much stimulation as they can get.

'Can't you do that, Hattie? Or even Martyn? Peek-a-boo is not very difficult.'

'But it makes us so self-conscious,' she complains. 'We feel silly, Agnieszka doesn't.'

Well, what can I say? When Lallie was seven months old I was too eaten up with grief and drama to play much peek-a-boo myself. I left it to Wanda to do. And when Hattie was little Lallie left it for me to do, and I daresay I never learned because Wanda wasn't the peek-a-boo kind. Lallie was always so busy, touring, playing, recording, enchanting everyone to tears, hard as nails herself. She had elegant, orchestral boyfriends, mostly from the back rows of the strings, rather than the front row, in the same way as some film stars seem to go for the cameraman rather than the director. They don't like competition. And I can see Martyn's mother probably wasn't the peek-a-boo kind either. Too busy running out to the chip shop for a butty. Perhaps it will all be all right. Perhaps if Agnieszka plays peek-a-boo with

Kitty a family curse will be lifted and Kitty will breed a race of peek-a-boo players. All may yet be well. But I can see I too may be guilty of wishful thinking.

'Is Kitty sleeping through the night now?' I ask.
'Yes she is. And the crib's in Agnieszka's room, so Martyn and I can have some private life at last.'
'Perhaps she's feeding the baby opium?'
'That's not funny,' she says. She tells me Agnieszka doesn't believe children should be exposed to TV so she won't have one in her room, but mostly sits in her room in the evenings and studies. She did a course in child-care in Poland.
'I know about child-care in other parts of the world,' I say. 'When our Czech girl Viera was six Father Christmas came down the chimney and gave her a lump of coal instead of a present. She'd been bad: she'd wet the bed.'
'You're talking about years ago,' says Hattie, which is true enough.

Four decades back. Poor Viera, who at twenty-seven saw herself as too old to be marriageable. Her fiancé of seven years had jilted her on the eve of her wedding. She'd fled her mountain village, where Father Christmas came down the chimney with lumps of coal, because of the shame of it.
She met a young Sikh boy when she was with us and wanted to marry him. Feeling responsible, I went to meet the boy's father, a noble man in a white turban and a grey beard. He said it would be all right because they were both so dumb. They wouldn't notice any cultural differences. He was right. They lived happy ever afterwards, Viera wreathed in sparkly saris.

'You've checked she doesn't just jump out the window after Kitty falls into a drugged sleep, and earn a little extra money in nightclubs?' I ask.

That was Krysta from Dortmund. Krysta would nip down to Park Lane by night to work as a croupier at the Playboy Club. She worked a four-hour shift from one to five a.m. What did we know? We thought she must be ill, she seemed so tired all the time. Then Serena found her fluffy white cotton-tail and black satin corset costume in the wash. The black had run in the hot water and everything in that load was permanently grey. It was ages before we fired her: the children really liked her. She said her mother was so proud of what she had achieved. Black satin was a sign of status in the Bunny world. I tell Hattie all this.

'Don't be silly, Gran,' says Hattie. 'You had one bad experience. But I did check, actually. I went in to ask if she wouldn't like to watch TV with us – Martyn usually just falls asleep the moment he sits down and it would be nice to have company – and forgot to knock and she was sitting there with a book in front of her, copying notes onto her laptop.'
'What was she studying? Immigration law?'
'I don't know,' whispers Hattie. 'I'm not as nosy as you.'

She's getting quite cross with me. She likes to have my permission. She wants me to say it's okay to abandon her child to a girl she's only known for a week and came on the recommendation of Babs. I have met Babs once or twice. She is a very persuasive creature of the new female breed, glossy-haired, ambitious and slim as a whippet, but she will always have some hidden agenda or other going on. But perhaps I am being unkind. Hattie seems to like her.

'Why are you whispering?' I ask. 'Is Agnieszka listening?'
'She's out at an evening class,' says Hattie. 'I don't want to wake up Martyn.'
'And what is the course?' I ask. 'Police and the Asylum Seeker?'
'Belly dancing,' says Hattie. 'Before you say anything it is a very sensible thing to be doing. It teaches stretch, relax and control. I'm going down to a class with Agnieszka myself soon. I've got to get rid of this bulge in my tummy somehow.'
'Hattie, you're so thin a bulge in your tummy can only be a half carrot you've just eaten.'
'Agnieszka made carrot soup and a cheese soufflé before she went out, and I had some of each. And Kitty had a wee taste of both and smiled and seemed so grateful.'

She tells me Martyn went to fetch the barbecue sauce but Agnieszka raised her eyebrows and he tossed it in the bin. Agnieszka has convinced Hattie that it's barbecue sauce that has been making Martyn bad-tempered: it's almost all acetic acid and sugar.

'Carrot soup?' I say. 'Organic, I hope?'
'Of course. Agnieszka has a friend in Neasden who grows her own vegetables, and she goes over there on her days off: she says she'll bring back what she can.'
'A female friend or a male friend?' I enquire.
'I don't see what that's got to do with anything,' says Hattie. 'She didn't say. Anyway she has a husband and she loves

him very much: he is a screenwriter in Krakow.'
'What's a screenwriter doing in Krakow? The Polish Film School is in Lodz.'
'Gran, I have no idea. I don't even know where these places are.'

She tells me now that Agnieszka is to have two weeks off over Christmas to go home, leaving her with three days uncovered for child-care.

'So if you could possibly come and stay with us just to tide us over, Gran . . .'
'But Kitty hardly knows me. I've only spent a few hours with her since she was born, and most of that time she was asleep.'
'But you'll have the same family feel, and smell, and the way of handling her that I do. You're bound to. Kitty is in your direct line of descent. She won't find it strange.'

That girl will believe anything it suits her to believe, but I must say I am touched. I say I'll see what I can arrange.

'Agnieszka says it's alright for Kitty to have a dummy. The feeding and the suckling function in babies are separate. Sometimes they have enough food and want to go on sucking, and vice versa.'

It was hopeless. Hattie was beyond reason. Hugo was snuffling at the door wanting to get out, and I had been standing in the draughty hall. The mobile signal in Corsham is erratic. I said I had to go and she remembered to ask after Serena, Cranmer and Sebastian. I said they were all as okay as their circumstances would allow. I asked her if she'd heard from her mother and she said she had not. So what's new?

I did say that if she wanted to see her mother, Hattie would have to have Kitty christened, so Lallie could turn up for a photo opportunity, her face looking lovely in the candlelight with stained glass in the background. Hattie said what hypocrisy religion is: how can the baby have a christening if the parents are committed rational humanists? If they're not even married in the first place? That seemed enough for the evening and we hung up.

Child Support

As a young woman I, Frances, did not have Serena's appetite for work. I never quite accepted employment as an essential part in my life. I thought that Charlie the baronet should support me while I brought up Jamie, no matter how accidental and hurried a child he was. I was sure at the time of my first pregnancy that Curran, had he lived, would have turned up trumps and happily shared the contents of his cloth cap with me, but I daresay I was mistaken.

If you love the father of your child you feel he has given enough. If you don't love him all you want is his money. I didn't love Charlie. So I wasted time and energy, once back in London, though calmed-down, de-toxed, and fortunately having failed to contract the diseases that so often go with a young, wild life, trying to wring money out of this hapless man of my choice. I had a dream that, like me, he would wear wildness out and settle down and I would learn to love him and that we would live happily ever after. But he was away hunting game in South Africa and hadn't come home when he said he would, and seldom answered my letters.

So I set up home in The Tower with Jamie, and asked Wanda if I could have Lallie back. The ease with which she handed over her grandchild did take me a little aback. She as good as thrust the child into my arms. I had expected a struggle.

But there was always a remoteness about Lallie as if she related better to notes on the page or vibrating through the air than she did to people, as if it didn't matter to her one jot who came and said goodnight to her, which I could see might be disconcerting to Wanda. And, as first I, then Susan, and then Serena had all at one time or another handed our babies to her to look after, I could see she might simply want to get out from under.

Wanda must have felt that her own young were bent on punishing her for known and unknown crimes – perhaps for her leaving our father? I think that this indeed was what we were doing – forcing Wanda into recognising the consequences of her action, in an ongoing protest which surfaced in our almost wilful fertility and careless proclivity for sex. The trouble was we weren't just re-acting, acting out, we were acting too: we all did like sex so. And Wanda just didn't, or didn't allow herself to. What she did have was a ferocious sense of duty towards her children, which we three daughters turned to our advantage.

Once settled in The Tower, around the corner from Serena and George, and with Roseanna to help with the children, I found a job at the Primrosetti Gallery where I held the fort in the frequent absence of its owner Sally Anne Emberley. Sally Anne was a minor film star by whom a famous film producer had a child, a little boy, Lallie's age. The child was always seen as the famous film producer's son, and she by inference just a brood cow, rather than Sally Anne's son by the famous producer, but that was the way the power relations of the day went. The famous film producer at least bought her the premises and some start-up paintings, and now she ran the gallery in a lackadaisical kind of way: thus, it was assumed, he kept her occupied and out of his hair. The gallery hung the works of local contemporary artists – some of whom then went on to better things: a handful even ended up in the Tate and the Metropolitan.

People now write books about the Primrose Hill Group; lucky were those who bought their work while they could. George, who had given up painting for Serena's sake, was so dismissive of Sally Anne and all her works that Serena kept away from the Primrosetti and so missed the odd cheap Hockney or Auerbach. I once would have bought an Edward Piper but the washing machine needed mending. Sally Anne, though generous to her artists – she could afford to be – paid me so miserable a wage it was smaller even than Roseanna's. Those who work in the arts are meant to work for the love of it.

Roseanna earned £5 a week au pairing for George, Serena and me. I was paid four pounds fifteen shillings a week, without board, for showing, and even occasionally selling, paintings, doing the post, keeping the records, sweeping, dusting, polishing and cleaning the loos. I would have been better advised to train and study and get some professional qualifications, but this was the sixties, what did we know? It was the woman's role to be supported, the man's to provide, and if he failed as Charlie failed, the woman played the martyr, and I was good at that.

This tendency to martyrdom in me would annoy my mother. 'What do you expect?' she'd ask. 'Of course this Charlie of yours is not going to support you. Don't waste your time hoping. Men only support women if they're in front of their noses, filling the bed and cooking the food. I told you not to marry him.' Though at least he made an honest woman of you and you were little better than a drunken drugged-out slapper at the time, she could have said, but kindly didn't. I went through a bad hormonal patch in my early youth, or as bad as the early fifties could accommodate.

Serena, venturing briefly into London's boho underworld, picked up an adoring follower, who would be in touch with her all his life, and then hastened back home to Mother again. But I followed the lure of freedom and excess from underworld to Underground, and it took me years to get back home.

Martyn And Hattie Have A Tiff

'You can't do this, Martyn,' says Hattie. Kitty is asleep. 'You can't write an article in praise of the chip butty. You always told me it was chip butties which killed your father.'
'My God, Hattie,' says Martyn. 'You are so literal when it suits you. Try to lighten up a little.'

He's a fine one to talk, thinks Hattie, who feels she has been putting up with Martyn's super-seriousness ever since Kitty was born. It is Hattie's second week back at work. Already, to Martyn's eyes, she seems overeager with opinions and judgements. It is the pre-Kitty Hattie back again but he hopes it doesn't go too far. He realises he'd got rather accustomed, and rather to like, her dismal version of herself.

This evening both parents are home in time to help bath the baby while Agnieszka whisks up some kind of tuna and carrot pie – she uses carrots a lot: vitamin A, carotene and gentle roughage, which can go in the blender the next day for the baby's lunch. Hattie is down to one early-morning feed, which these days she even looks forward to. Her breasts no longer feel sore and exploited. She and the baby can nuzzle and cuddle each other, and make little peek-a-boo jokes together when no one is looking, and Martyn doesn't feel left out.

They have to make love quietly because of Agnieszka in the next room, but that is oddly exciting, deliciously forbidden, like the early days. Not that anyone has ever forbidden sex to either of them, on the contrary, the spirit of make-love-not-war, which so absorbed their parents' generation, no longer raises eyebrows. But in any genera-tion untrammelled love freely expressed just seems too pleasurable to go unpunished.

'But what's happened to *Devolution*?' asks Hattie. 'I thought it was meant to be a serious publication. Why are they asking you to write rubbish all of a sudden?'
'It's not rubbish,' says Martyn. 'It's good journalism. We're changing tack. We're concentrating less on what's bad for you and more on what's good for you, that's all.'
'I think you should refuse. *Why You and the Chip Butty Can Be Friends*. Everyone will laugh at you.'
'No they won't,' says Martyn. 'They'll read me, even while they sneer. Harold's offered me my own column. They really liked *Skinflints and Killjoys*. Apparently it changed quite a few minds at the top.'
'I suppose they have minds,' says Hattie. 'Where's the deep seriousness, the mission to change the world, of all our youths? Why are you colluding in this?'

Martyn confesses that the alternative to writing up chip butties and a casino on every street corner seems to be a transfer to Welfare Reform, and points out that his prospects both parliamentary and financial will be best served by his fostering his journalistic career, rather than burying himself in statistics.

'They've bought you!' says Hattie. She's wearing a red suit which Serena bought for her as part of her back-to-work wardrobe and it looks really good on her. It's Prada. Hattie has filled out just a little because of Agnieszka's dinners and breakfasts and perhaps because of the lunchtime glass of white wine she has at the sushi bar all but next door to the office, and she's stopped looking gaunt. She looks fabulous.

'I don't think you should say that,' says Martyn. 'Statistics show that the body absorbs nutrition more efficiently when it is enjoyed than when it is not. The occasional chip butty does no one any harm. On the contrary it does people good.'

'You mean it wins elections,' says Hattie. 'Particularly in the north. Northern man's body lies mouldering in the grave but his soul is withering away.'

'And I rather begin to wonder whose side you're on,' says Martyn. 'If a couple of weeks at Dinton & Seltz can do this to you, God help the working class. A literary agency is the most capitalist of all capitalist institutions. It creates nothing, improves nothing; it just passes on profit. And what is this book you are trying so hard to sell in Poland – *ShitCockPissDog!*?'

'It's a book by a man with Tourette's Syndrome,' says Hattie. 'It's done very well in North America. Tourette's is a terrible condition, and people need to know about it. The fact is, Martyn, that you're putting career above principle and you swore you'd never do that.'

She May Not Leave

At this point Agnieszka comes smiling through the door. She hands Hattie a plain skirt and jumper and suggests she changes before supper's ready so that Agnieszka can hang her work clothes before they get stained or crumpled, and says she's looked out a pink cashmere sweater and short grey skirt for Hattie for the next day.

'You don't want to wear the same thing two days running,' says Agnieszka. 'You need to give the impression you have an infinite wardrobe of lovely things.'

'Does that apply to men too?' asks Martyn.

'No,' says Agnieszka decisively. 'Men shouldn't look as if they took too much notice of their appearance: that they have more important things to do.'

'That's a bit sexist,' says Martyn, and Agnieszka looks puzzled. What can he mean?

But she is taking the tuna and carrot pie out of the oven. It is topped by a light cover of shop-bought golden, well-risen pastry. She is not against puff pastry sheets bought from the shop, but that is about as far as her approval of convenience food goes. Martyn is still bristling a little. He feels the need to appeal to Agnieszka.

'Do you think,' he asks, 'that a man's primary duty is to his family or to the society around him?'

Hattie frowns a little. This is surely too abstract a question to put to an au pair, and why is he not asking her, Hattie, not Agnieszka, but Agnieszka does not hesitate.

'They used to ask us that kind of question in school,' she says. 'The proper answer in the old Poland was the last, but now we all know better and the answer is the family.

88

Of course if you have a talent, as you do, Mr Martyn, you also have a duty to that. And when opportunities come along for the artist, it is foolish not to take them.' 'There you are, Hattie!' says Martyn triumphantly. 'I foster my creativity, while writing about the beauty of the butty and you publish help-yourself-towards-Tourette's, and at this rate we might all be able to take a proper holiday in the summer and now we can all have dinner out whenever we feel like it.'

And he laughs and embraces Hattie as she slips off her suit and puts on the old jersey and skirt. She is perfectly decent while she changes, in pants, bra and even slip, which Agnieszka seems to think all women should wear, but Agnieszka seems slightly surprised, as if she thinks Hattie should have gone into the bathroom first. Hattie feels a kind of pang: she wants her privacy back: she wants not to be observed, not all the time. But the pie, with its strange ingredients – who ever thought of tuna plus carrots plus pastry – smells delicious and she is hungry, and shakes the uneasiness out of herself.

Martyn says 'I love you anyway,' and Hattie says 'I love you too,' and they all settle down to eat. Martyn is really pleased that Agnieszka came down on his side.

Men, Women, Art, And Employment

With the coming of Roseanna to Caldicott Square, and the general easing of domestic pressure, came a stirring in me to develop a little ambition and stop grizzling about Charlie.

I asked Sally Anne for a rise – she grudgingly put my wages up to £6 a week, agreeing that really I ought to earn more than the au pair. If you don't ask you don't get, especially if you are a woman: it is also surprising how much you do get if you do ask. Serena, by then flourishing in her advertising agency, said female colleagues seldom asked for rises: they felt they could only be getting what they deserved, and management must know what it was doing. Men colleagues would go in and bang the boss's desk and make demands. Women writers, she complains, are pathetically grateful if a publisher decides to publish them: men take it as their natural right, and can be quite violent if thwarted.

Thanks to Roseanna I could now find time to look at what artists, then and now, were actually painting. The model takes a bird's eye view of what goes onto the canvas and it is a very limited eye. Being painted sucks something out of your very being – as mediums complain happens when they channel the spirits of the departed for the benefit of those still on the earth. It's an exhausting business. You are left with what's over when the essence of you has gone into the painting and the better the painter the less left of you there is. That is what makes one a pushover sexually. But now I actually looked and learned. I frequented the major art galleries and the big auction houses and the galleries up and down Cork Street and I got my eye in.

My mother, Wanda, trained at the Slade and was no mean painter herself, though so much of a perfectionist it took her six months to do one painting. But she seemed to resent my new habit of art-going: I would do better to stay home and look after the children.

Wanda thought the Wallace Collection was vulgar: all that tasteless ormolu: all those paintings in the wrong frames hung any old how. She really hated Fragonard and Boucher: though she had quite an eye for a Turner in the Tate. She wanted to be the only one to *Know*.

George was much the same where Serena was concerned. He preferred to look at art on his own, while she longed to know what he knew, but if she asked questions he became irritated, dog-in-the-mangerish, and suggested she go and have a cup of coffee in the café and wait for him there, and not talk about things she knew nothing about. She should stick to advertising. The cobbler thinks others should stay away from his awl, I suppose.

Roseanna came to us by accident like a kitten turning up on the doorstep shivering and hungry. Far from spending her time dressed in a white starched cap and pinafore and opening some grand front door to the English gentry, as her mother in sending her off had imagined, Roseanna found herself living in the household of an emigré Polish sea captain and his wife above a wool shop in Primrose Hill. She was working a twelve-hour day in exchange for her keep. She was a pretty, gentle little thing, but she was practical and determined, and worked out that if she slept for six hours out of every twenty-four, that still left her six hours' spare time. She put a card in a shop window offering her services as a cleaner. Serena responded.

Ours was not a family accustomed to employing others – at least not since the mid 1920s. In her young days my grandmother Frieda had employed a cook and a maid of all work, but by the thirties she was divorced, and off to California where only the very rich had servants. When her daughter Wanda was twenty she went with her husband Edwin to New Zealand, a pioneering land where servants did not enter into the social equation at all. After that divorce, when the all-female family – mother, grandmother, Susan, Serena and myself – came back to London in 1946, after years of war exile, the domestic structure of society had broken down. The servant class had disappeared – who would scrub other people's floors when you could get twice the money for half the work in a munitions factory? Or go into the WRENS and meet men?

The fifties stayed largely servant-free. In the sixties, with increased prosperity and in a more adventurous age, came the first flocks of au pairs, nice girls from abroad who would live in and help out. They came to learn English, and were on the whole virtuous, honest and clean and did not expect to have boyfriends or anything other than minimal wages. Since few mothers were out at work, the au pair was seldom left in sole charge. They were treated as one of the family. In certain circumstances, as with Roseanna and the Russian sea captain, the word 'family' was open to interpretation. Stories of the husband who ran off with the au pair abounded; but by and large that instinctive 'duty of care', as we now call it, towards the helpless and the vulnerable – the 'taboo' as Freud named it – was normally observed.

Today's au pair wants a sex life, proper wages, to go to pubs and clubs and occasionally classes. Her imperatives are her own: her mother will have little influence on her. She will be the product of her own generation, not the one that came before. She will come from a country further east – Hungary, Romania, Poland are current favourites – and her habits may be more unexpected; we expect them to be like ours and they are not. She will be more desperate for survival: the cultures where men looked after women are vanishing fast. If she is from outside the new Europe she may well hope to marry an Englishman for his citizenship.

It's a two-way street, of course. Many a European man searches advertisements for a bride from the Far East who will cook, clean and fill a bed in return for her keep and a little pocket money, and sit quietly at dinner parties, thinking herself lucky. Russian girls have longer legs, but are dangerous. The man will choose according to nationality rather than character.

The world manages, as Hattie has observed to Martyn, on the differential between those who have, and those who have not. There is nothing much to be done about it. But you never know. Things may change. Did not Martyn only recently remark, upon the hiring of Agnieszka, that there was a problem here? '*Is it ethical?*' Wanda's principles crop up in the oddest places. Nor can it be a matter of genetic inheritance, since Martyn is no blood relative. Perhaps Wanda simply haunts the family.

Serena has always kept secretaries and maids, and sometimes a chauffeur, but has never felt truly entitled to them. Wanda, in her nineties, was given a 'carer' by Haringey Council – usually a bewildered girl from Botswana or Zambia – who would be asked by Wanda just to sit down and read a book until her time was up, while she got on with the housework and cooking. She liked her toast just so, and her bath just so.

Susan, Serena and I, unlike Wanda, tended to put up with what we were given. We lived too much on the edge of emergency, all of us, to afford the luxury of being pernickety. This piece of toast will do: that too cold or too hot bath is just fine. But perhaps pernicketiness and employment are mutually exclusive: my mother went through only a few years in which she had to go out to work. For Susan, Serena and me it was a lifetime's necessity – though Susan's life was not long enough, I am afraid, to be able to quote it as a case in point.

But we are all of the kind who cleans up before the paid help arrives: a habit that irritates Sebastian. If I fold up his clean clothes and put them in his drawers or tuck his socks into one another to keep them in pairs, he is as like as not to toss them all onto the floor for Daphne our cleaner to pick up and sort. 'Why should you do that?' he asks. 'Isn't that what we pay her for?' Daphne, as a result, adores him, and just about puts up with me.

Sebastian is an Old Etonian and sees no need to be approved of by the servants. It was customary amongst the English aristocracy to behave as if domestic servants did not exist. Their employers would defecate and copulate in front of them, pick their noses and eat the bogeys, as if the servants were simply not in the room. They have learned better since, of course, as demand for servants greatly exceeds supply.

George And Serena's Household

The reason that Roseanna turned up on George and Serena's doorstep unannounced was that the sea captain had appeared in her bedroom and started to get into bed with her along with a group of his drunken friends. With the wife's assistance she had managed to keep the men the other side of the locked door, but with the dawn slipped out of the house, and sat on a bench on Primrose Hill, with her coat on over her nightie until she thought George and Serena might be up, and then knocked on their door. They of course took her in.

George went round to the captain's house and removed Roseanna's few belongings. The captain's wife was furious because Roseanna had walked out without notice. The captain was too hung-over to care. Roseanna slept on the sofa until the Caldicott Square tenant – a fund raiser for the ANC, one of the left-wing Jewish exodus from South Africa in the sixties – took pity on her and gave up her bed, going off herself to live with a Jamaican poet in an even damper basement.

Those were the golden days of Caldicott Square. It was a warm, hospitable, untidy household. George and Serena were great party-givers. I was included within the generosity of their household, but I did feel rather like a poor relation. They were married, I was not, or only by default. To be into your thirties and without a partner then was a pitiable thing.

One-night stands – of which there were many – too seldom turned into lasting relationships. The men were rarely there the next morning, and if it was their place they would expect you to go before breakfast. Breakfasts between strangers were embarrassing. Those doe-eyed blank-faced girls of the sixties were as unhappy as they looked, in their tiny pointed victim shoes.

But George and Serena had somehow found each other. It was fairly obvious to me that George would spend the occasional night with some other woman – he would return home in the early hours saying he'd 'fallen asleep on the sofa' or some such, and Serena always chose to believe him. She never could bear too much reality, and the more fiction she wrote, the less she could.

She would suffer agonies while waiting for him to return, but she was easily reassured. And she would on occasion find herself in the wrong bed, those being the sixties, but she never counted that as infidelity. It was just something to do while waiting for George's love to resume.

Bad Chianti in wicker baskets was giving way to an acid Muscadet: it was not until the arrival of non-European wines in the eighties that the ordinary drinking stuff actually began to taste nice. But Serena would take her Berry Brothers catalogue and order the great clarets of the fifties and the sixties, Lafites, Latours, Margaux, for next to nothing: bottles which if only she had put down would now be worth hundreds, even thousands, and down the gullets of the appreciative and the non-appreciative alike they would go.

Serena was on the whole one of the non-appreciative, though she tells of a time in the late seventies when, hired to write the love story of JFK and Jackie, she was researching their old haunts with a couple of TV producers, and struck one a blow in the name of good wine. The producers, Vietnam veterans, quarrelled a great deal, and would stop the car and throw punches at each other. Once the one who did the driving had his glasses broken, the other refused to drive, she couldn't, they had to resume their journey with a man so short-sighted he failed to see red stop lights. The producers added a fictional baby and nanny to their expenses and charged for overnight stops at Hyatt Regencies, when actually they went to Holiday Inns. When, at a restaurant in Hyannis Point they ordered a bottle of '62 Chateau d'Yquem which the waiter said was the last not just in the restaurant but in the whole United States, they just slugged the transcendent liquid down their throats, she got to her feet and gave one a right hook. Europe's honour was at stake. They came to heel after that. The programme was never made.

The size of the Caldicott Square house was increasing. George decided to build an extension to his town house and restore and damp-proof the basement and incorporate the coal hole, down which once the Victorian coalman had poured his sacks of filthy, shiny coal, the better to house Roseanna, a piano for his talented niece Lallie and a proper bathroom. Hitherto the bath in Caldicott Square had been in the kitchen, and had a wooden lid which served as a sideboard. Before the bath could be used kitchen utensils and foods would have first to be removed, and space found for them elsewhere. In the early days Serena bathed the babies in the kitchen sink.

As Serena's income increased, the bath moved to a new bathroom, the space it left was filled by cupboards, a dishwasher was installed, washing could be done in a washing machine and not at the launderette. The house-front was painted, windows replaced, woodworm removed, even the basement was dug out and converted to a perfectly acceptable bright habitation.

But Serena's income did not come by accident; it did not fall like manna from heaven, it had to be earned, and she had to go to work, and while she worked much of the child-minding was given over to the au pairs. And the au pairs produced Lallie, and Lallie and I (mostly I) produced Hattie, and now Hattie and Agnieszka will produce Kitty and which of them will play the greatest part in the production who is to say.

Hattie At Work

Babs is in trouble. She is in floods of tears. She can't work, she can't think, she can't even answer the phone. Her seductive eyelids are swollen and sore. She is one of the most beautiful women Hattie has ever known: they worked at Hatham Press when they were both starting out in publishing. Babs was then a rather gawky girl with a fleshy face but now she has turned into something controlled, shaped, sculpted and exquisite. Hattie uses her arms for balancing when she walks, for lifting babies and embracing Martyn: they're usually covered to protect her from cold and the exigencies of life. Babs goes sleeveless, in the confidence of her perfect body, her unlumpy upper arms. When she gesticulates it's not just with her hands but with her arms as well, so white, smooth and infinitely sexy. Since she married Alastair the Tory MP, who has inherited wealth, her clothes have been perfect, lovely, designed by fashionistas so remote and grand you hardly see them in the newspapers; though sometimes she descends to Harvey Nichols and can be seen vanishing into a changing room.

Hattie is rather surprised that Babs still seems to regard Hattie as her best friend. What does one so extraordinary want with something so everyday as Hattie? But she does: she's nice. Envy her as you may, Babs is still nice. And actually even in the month Hattie's been back at work she too has begun to look a little more grand and groomed. She's had a hair treatment or so and her eyebrows shaped, and her nails are growing.

But today Hattie, who does Foreign Rights, is feeling a little frazzled. She has to keep running in next door to look after Babs and calm her down. In the meanwhile Hilary Renshaw who shares Hattie's office is taking Hattie's phone calls and Hattie is not sure that this is a good idea. Hilary seems to think that, though she does English Language Rights and Hattie does Foreign Rights, the latter is subsidiary to the former, though actually the two women have equal status. Hattie gets paid less for the moment but that's because of maternity leave and the pay structure, not that her job is less vital to the agency's interests: indeed, she expects within six months to out-earn Hilary.

Hattie is expecting a call from Warsaw: she does not want Hilary lifting the phone and doing something stupid like closing a deal Hattie does not want closed, not yet: because Hattie is pretty sure the Warsaw publishers are prepared to offer more if pushed, and she plans to push. Hilary is stuck somewhere in the past and believes that the former Soviet states have no money: Hattie knows that their playing the poverty card no longer works: publishing in Poland is booming. Agnieszka has told her so.

Neil Renfrew sits at a great oak desk on the top floor and presides over all that goes on below: film and TV agents, literary agents, fiction and non-fiction, processing what comes out of the heads of those strange people, regarded with mixed awe, disparagement and merriment, as 'the writers'.

The writers sit alone at computers all over the land, mining the insides of their heads for treasure, sometimes finding some, mostly not. The agent must persuade publishers, film-makers and newspapers that the gold is not fool's gold but the real thing. Just sometimes it is, but there's no knowing in advance. Gamblers all. Hattie will soon have to talk to Neil Renfrew about the delineation of responsibility, if she can ever get in to see him.

Dinton & Seltz occupy the whole building and will soon have to move to bigger premises or buy the one next door, or somehow split its operations. Too many people work in too small a space. Unlike Martyn's office this one is old, old, old. The building dates from the end of the eighteenth century, when it was built as a town house for a wealthy rural landowner. The rooms are high and gracious – until you get to the servants' floors, which are mean and pokey. Computers, files and telephones sit oddly within the building, and no matter what kind of furniture they try it never looks right. The place seems to be waiting for something which will never quite happen. A lift shaft built fifty years ago makes the stairs and corridors, once so gracious and airy, feel crowded and wrong. Health and Safety will soon be after them, worrying about fire exits and wheel-chair ramps. Neil's new office, set back from the street frontage so it can't be seen from below, is a mere five years old, and won its young architect an award or two. It only just passed Planning.

All twenty-eight women on Dinton & Seltz's staff and a percentage of the seventeen men are a bit in love with Neil who is good-looking and usually tanned from a recent holiday. He is happily married, goes sailing at the weekend and comes back to make decisions others shrink at, which is why he is in charge.

Harold at *Devolution* belongs to the old school of idiosyncratic bosses, who rule by a kind of wild-eyed individuality and the making of unreasonable but often inspired decisions: Neil, of a younger generation, knows his management procedures, plays no zero-sum games, and likes his staff to be in a win-win situation.

Hattie responds to a plaintive cry for help through the office walls: Babs has run out of tissues and can't leave the office to find any because her nose is running, so Hattie fetches them for her friend. Babs would do the same for her. But still Hattie doesn't want to be away from her office too long because of the expected Warsaw call, and the fear that Hilary will mess things up half on purpose, half unwittingly.

Hilary has been with the agency twenty-seven years and must be the oldest woman in it. She wears tweed skirts, cardies and pearls. As nuns devote their lives to Jesus, so Hilary has devoted her life to Dintons. She has no children. The betting is that she's still a virgin, though some say she had an affair with Mr Seltz, long deceased. The phone goes but it's Babs again. Her period has come on early because of all the upset. And she'd so hoped she was pregnant. She daren't stand up because she's wearing a white skirt and it's stained and will Hattie find her some sanitary towels and another skirt, size 6, quick, quick.

Babs's problem is that she has been having an affair with a young TV producer, Tavish, who came in six months back to film the office at work for a BBC documentary. Hattie has never seen him, but Babs has described him, and Hattie rather imagines him to be like the grandfather Curran she never knew, the street singer with the McLean blanket who ran off with Frances, procreated Lallie, and died.

Babs, for all her beauty, loves Tavish more than Tavish loves her. Lots of women in the office have affairs, but seldom claim to be in love. It's seen as a rather stupid, dangerous state for a woman to stoop to: if women weep it's because of some frustration at work, or a fertility problem, or some callous remark from a partner, but on the whole at Dinton & Seltz it's a *'women have died and worms have eaten them but not for love'* kind of office culture.

Babs is now apparently above all this; she lives on some entranced, old-fashioned plane. She is in love, thoroughly seduced, those white, white arms longing to embrace one man and only one, and he the wrong one for her career, her future, and her marriage.

What's happened is that Babs sent a compromising email intended to be picked up by Tavish at an Internet café and it went to her husband Alastair by mistake. You press the wrong key and your life falls to bits. *I love you, I love you, I love you, see you at the café same place and he's away at his beastly constituency so I can stay the night.*

Babs realised within seconds what she had done and took a taxi home hoping to delete the message before Alastair got back, and would have suceeded, only his secretary was working on his computer, saw the word 'constituency' and forwarded it automatically. Or so she says. Babs says she thinks it was done on purpose.

'She never liked me. She kept telling Alastair how much I was spending on clothes so it didn't get mixed up with party expenses, but that was just an excuse. What she didn't understand, those kind of people never can, was that the more I spent the happier Alastair was. It turned him on. Something had to.'

'Well,' says Hattie. 'No such thing as an accident. You must have unconsciously wanted Alastair to know. The guilt must be tremendous.'

'A bit of guilt is really good for one's business acumen,' says Babs, who means one day to take over Neil's position. 'It doesn't half help negotiate deals. You get mean and twisty and love secrets, and having something over other people. But now Alastair says he wants to divorce me and I can't afford that.'

'But mightn't that be a good thing?' asks Hattie. 'Then you'd be free to go off with Tavish.'

But Tavish has gone back to his wife and children in Scotland, not even waiting to find out if Babs is pregnant or not. They hadn't always used a condom, there hadn't been time, it had all seemed so important and urgent, and Babs didn't like messing herself about with chemicals, implants or metal coils. Anything foreign you took into your body could do you harm. She'd made the mistake of telling him she loved him and that drove men away, everyone knew except her, apparently.

She, Babs, was just an innocent. Babs had hoped to have a baby by Tavish and pass it off as Alastair's. She was thirty-nine and the biological clock was ticking. How lucky Hattie was to have a baby, and a job, and a husband who wasn't boring. The trouble with Alastair was that he was an old fart, landed gentry, and made her feel stupid because she hated horses and although he was no good in bed had an eye for girls and had started groping Agnieszka so Agnieszka had to go. Not that she, Babs, minded all that much. 'All that carrot-pie stuff: one got so sick of them.'

'Hang on a moment,' said Hattie. 'You didn't tell me anything about this. I thought Agnieszka came to me straight after she'd left the triplets in France?'
'She stayed with me a couple of weeks when she had nowhere to go,' says Babs. 'She was looking for a permanent job. She made all my new curtains and put them up for free. It would have cost thousands to have the shop do it.'
'So why did she leave Alice? I thought it was because of her English classes.'

Babs tells Hattie that Alice's partner Jude, father of the triplets, had pinched Agnieszka's bottom and Alice had seen and told him it was up to him, either Agnieszka went or he went, and while he was deciding Agnieszka said she had better go for the family's sake.
'She came to me in tears that same afternoon,' says Babs.
'Poor Agnieszka.' says Hattie. 'Alice should have thrown Jude out.'
'I'm not so sure,' says Babs. 'Sometimes you just run into women like Agnieszka who want to destroy every marriage they encounter. Once they've got rid of the wife they lose

interest. My therapist says it's Oedipal. They're in love with their fathers and hate their mothers.'

Hattie decides Babs is talking about herself and not Agnieszka. Babs is projecting her own guilt about Tavish's wife and needn't be taken seriously. Martyn can be trusted not to fondle, pinch or otherwise molest a woman just because she's in his house.

'You're so lucky having Martyn,' says Babs, and Hattie is quite sorry for her.

'Well, you've got Alastair,' says Hattie. 'And if you take my advice you'll do what you can to keep him. And that doesn't include trying to pass off another man's child as his. Be glad that it's gone.' She speaks a little peevishly. She wants to get back to the office.

'My life has just fallen to pieces,' says Babs. 'I'd like a little more support. You've got very odd since Kitty was born. I don't want condemnation, I want pity. I probably don't even have a husband any more: you've got everything and I've got nothing. Whoever thought it would end like this?' And Babs snivels some more, as if exhausted with the effort of thinking about someone other than herself. 'Please Hattie, do something about the skirt, just don't make me sit here.'

Hattie remembers there's a kilt hanging up in one of the cleaners' cupboards, left over from the Christmas party which had a Celtic theme. Hattie hadn't been able to go to the party because she was too big with Kitty to move. She fetches it for Babs, and Babs wriggles out of the skirt and wades into the kilt. Babs tells her to throw the white skirt away because it's going to be irredeemably stained but Hattie thinks probably Agnieszka will be able to save it. Hattie can hear the phone ringing in her office and Hilary picking up.

'I need Alastair's money,' says Babs. 'And I like being married to him. We had dinner in the House of Lords the other day and I was the best-looking woman there by a long way. And I do want a baby. But I just don't want it to have Alastair's paunch or thick neck or piggy eyes. I want a baby with Tavish's eyes who'll look up at me and adore me. I love the way little Kitty looks at you, Hattie. She worships you. That's what I want.'

She is in tears again. She looks terrific in the kilt if you ignore the state of her face. The kilt would look dreadful on most women but Babs has the long legs and small bottom to carry it off. Hattie wonders what the tartan reminds her of and remembers it's like the blanket Frances keeps in Hugo's smelly old basket.

'I always get like this when I'm having a period,' says Babs, cheering up quite a lot. 'I expect Alastair will calm down. He usually does. But if Tavish has gone back to his wife who can I have a baby by? I expect Neil has quite good genes. Do you think he would be interested?'

Hattie goes back into her office and Hilary says, 'I just had a call from Jago at Javynski in Warsaw, which you weren't here to take. Too busy gossiping with Babs. They want to change the name of *ShitCockPissDog!* to *Another Way of Crying*. They say it translates better. So I said that was okay.'

'But the whole point,' protests Hattie, 'is that the book's about Tourette's Syndrome? I had enough of a struggle with the author as it was. He wanted just a line of asterisks and stars and shout-marks on the jacket, and his name, but I said you had to be able to read a title in order to talk about it on the radio and he eventually took my point. He's not easy: he's never going to accept *Another Way of Crying*. And really, Hilary, it's a decision I have to make, not you.'

'We really need to get this sorted out,' says Hilary. 'With the best will in the world this doesn't seem to be working out between us. Perhaps we should go and see Neil and see what he says.'

'I'm easy,' says Hattie, without the gravitas Hilary would have liked. 'I think that would be a good idea. Get the air cleared.'

'So you're off now,' says Hilary, as Hattie searches for her trainers, the better to stride off home. She can walk it in twenty minutes. But they are under her desk where she's pushed them, and she has to get down on her hands and knees to retrieve them.

'I'll be staying until about eight,' says Hilary. 'There is so much to do. Couldn't you stay on until I go through the emails with you? Or is the baby waiting to be bathed?'

'My emails are up to date,' says Hattie, snappily. 'And the Poles are an hour later than us. They'll have closed down for the day. I'll call Jago's in the morning and we'll talk more about the title and the money.'

'I completed the deal,' says Hilary, 'I thought you understood that. I agreed we'd change the title and the money they offered was fine, considering the risks they were taking and their own financial situation, which is pretty dire. I can't go back on the deal now. And *ShitCockPissDog!* is simply not the kind of book this agency, which has quite a literary reputation to maintain, should be taking on. *Another Way of Crying* is a much more informative title anyway.'

'We'll get Neil to sort it out,' says Hattie, as calmly as she can.

Hilary's hair is thinning. Hattie feels almost sorry for her. She dabs a little scent behind her ears, to show that she is young and carefree. She doesn't normally wear scent but Agnieszka gave it to her. It's called Joy and is described as the most expensive in the world, so Hattie supposes it to must be okay. It was apparently a leaving present from Alice when the family went off to France. But Agnieszka isn't a scent kind of person, so perhaps Hattie would like it? You can't keep scent too long or it goes off, and the neck of the bottle, pretty though it is, gets sticky and gathers dust.

So now Hattie keeps it in the office and if she remembers puts some on. Hilary sniffs the air when she does and gives some variation or other of 'Good Lord, are you wearing scent? I thought *au naturel* was the thing these days: pheromones and all that.' So Hattie, regrettably, does it all the more.

Now Hattie calls by at Babs's office and asks her if she'd like to share a taxi home but Babs says she has no home. Hattie doesn't pursue the matter. She does indeed want to get back for Kitty's bath time. Now she is away from Kitty she feels the physical absence of her more. It is as if a part of her is missing and she needs to be reunited with it quickly.

She lopes home on well-cushioned feet but when she lets herself into the house and sees Kitty sitting well propped by tidy cushions in her high chair Kitty hides her face and cries.

A Good Au Pair And The Promise Of Life After Death

Roseanna had trained as a shop assistant in Austria, and it seemed to be in her very nature to fold fabric and arrange clothes and objects neatly on shelves. Clothes were colour-coordinated, and plates stacked in exact size order. Like Agnieszka she brought order wherever she went. The children, under her care, were groomed and clean, their hair cut and their nails clipped. As George filled up her basement room with chests with missing handles, tarnished silver, torn canvases, so Roseanna busily polished, repaired and nurtured them, as unobtrusively as she could, because George did so like things to stay as they were (not so much objects as 'happenings') in preparation for their departure to George's emporium.

The only time Roseanna's courage failed or her temper snapped was when we all went on a camping trip to Brittany. That was at a time when the English saw virtue in living next to nature, crawling face down in the wet grass into green canvas one-person tents, cooking baked beans and sausages in a tin can over a Primus stove. French camping was a very different matter: their tents were big tough bright orange stand-up affairs, supported by metal struts of great complexity, within which you could hold dinner parties: the smell of pounded garlic wafted over the camp sites of the French. I think it was the humiliation as much as the discomfort that made Roseanna burst into tears and stamp her foot, thus astonishing us all. We packed up at once and travelled home early to running hot water and dry beds.

As we lived through them, those days when the children were small seemed trouble enough: looked back upon they were a delight. We were young: energy abounded: change was always around the corner: we thought we knew better than our elders and our children had not started to argue with us. If they were in danger we tucked them under our arms and walked away. Later they made their own decisions as to where danger lay, and the girls said 'oh Mum, don't be silly, you can trust me' and when the boys said 'ha ha, I'm just running down the road for a fix' you didn't know if they were joking or not.

Serena somehow juggled work, motherhood and wifedom. I juggled motherhood and work, and found that difficult enough. I missed the permanent companionship of a man in my bed, the familiar warmth on winter nights – I am sure marriages lasted better in the days before central heating – but I could see the advantages of a single life.

Bliss it may have been with George in those early days, though later, with her worldly success, it was all to turn sour, but he was not an 'easy' man, even by the standards of the times. He would control her by withdrawing his approval: days would go by when he sulked – seldom for anything she did, but for what she *was*, frivolous, untidy, ignorant of art, buying too many shoes, too much bound up in her family. Things she could do nothing about – being too ready to forgive, or too little interested in politics, too like his mother. Anything would do, I sometimes thought, as a stick to beat her with – then, as she and he suffered, her whole house became sad, friends avoided them, the children whickered and wept and caught colds. It was as if a cloud passed over the sun. Then it would clear: George would be himself again.

Roseanna went home to Austria as soon as she had her English proficiency certificate, which took over a year, leaving a friend, Viera, in her place – the one who was to marry a Sikh boy and live happily ever after. Roseanna wrote to Serena and George, and to me, for years: gradually we drifted into mere card exchanges at Christmas and then finally silence, after the manner of these things. She married and had children, I think. She will be well on in her fifties now but I can still see her quiet, sweet, pretty face, and the skill of her hands as she beautifully if obsessively washed, ironed, folded every piece of available fabric. I suppose it is possible that she has died – forty years is a long time, even in this healthy age – but I don't want to consider that.

Serena reports a classic near-death experience under anaesthetic. She travelled along a warm dark corridor towards a great light, and from all the way down the corridor doors opened and people appeared, friends and family – not exactly people in flesh and blood, more their spirits – encouraging her on. Some were still in the world: some were not. There was a feeling of great love and warmth, understanding and welcome. 'Roseanna was there,' she said, 'and Austrian Viera

114

in her sari, and all the people who have ever helped in the house. Wasn't that strange? Even Mrs Kavanagh the cleaner with her hairy warts and straggly hair, and her tales of how she tied her little daughter to the table leg and made her eat from the floor when once the child used her fingers not her knife and fork. (*Eat like an animal, get treated like an animal.*) She was only three.'

'I expect Mrs Kavanagh thought she was doing it for the best,' I said, 'though I never liked leaving Jamie and Lallie in her care. You were always more sanguine than me: you thought Oliver and Christopher would be all right. But I'm glad to know that even the worst of us can be forgiven.'
'Everyone was there,' promised Serena. 'We were all part of the same thing. Part of the one-ness, I suppose, though I hesitate to use so new-age a term. The wholly bearable lightness of being. And then I had to come back, it was not my time, and I was so disappointed. But I haven't been afraid of death since.'

But my father died, and Wanda died, and Susan and George died, that I know: it is to be expected by the time you get to your seventies that your circle will be somewhat diminished, but all those girls who came to us and were part of our lives, and ours of theirs, what happened to them? Do they talk of us, as just occasionally we talk of them when someone like Agnieszka turns up and stirs the pool of memory? Will we all be together in some pleasant afterlife of the kind Serena describes? I think that can only be some excitation of the brain as the result of anaesthesia: I do hope so. I don't want to meet my second husband, who had hammer toes and whose name I forget, in the afterlife.

Preserving The Peace Of
The Home

Most men behave well enough when they are in a position of authority and responsibility. A good modern family man, husband or long-term partner, will not let his sexual fantasies turn into reality. He may dream of the busty Macedonian au pair who bends over his chair at breakfast time, or of the pretty hands of the Irish girl who hands him his car keys when he has lost them, but he will wake with a start before consummation occurs. Self-interest is at work in both master and mistress. He does not want trouble: he does not mean to foul his own nest. She wants someone to share the dreary tasks of housewifery and child-care, so they can concentrate on higher, lighter and brighter things.

Martyn wants to think about the role of gambling and the food people want to eat, but kills them if they do, in the new society he hopes for. Hattie wants her writers to get a fair whack of the deal in all non-Anglophone territories, and to get Hilary under control. These are things Agnieszka either can't or doesn't want to do. What goes on in Agnieszka's head is not quite clear at the moment to her master and mistress. They prefer to ignore tiny minor signs, like the matter of the screenwriter husband in Krakow, which does not quite ring true, and the reasons she left her previous employment, which begin to seem slightly other than they had believed. Her future plans are a little obscure – is it belly dancing in London or midwifery back home? – but really what they hope is that she will never ever leave.

And surely, in any case, unless the mistress of the house is singularly unpleasant or plain, she will be preferred to the maid. The mistress, being in a higher social and financial category, is likely to be brighter, have more energy and better looks than does the help. The maid is likely to be younger – but only in really frivolous men will that be any particular inducement to infidelity.

But certainly any woman who invites a younger one into the house should beware of two things: a girl of the kind to inspire romantic love, a poetry reader, say, fragile and beautiful, or one who feeds upon the protective instinct of the male by turning up to work with a black eye and tales of boyfriend cruelty. The master may feel the need to go to her rescue and that can become difficult. Happily for the mistress, low-born maids seldom inspire romantic love: that happens in fairy tales, when the prince marries the dairy maid, or in novels like *Pride and Prejudice* in which little Miss poor-but-quirky Bennett snatches Mr Darcy from better-born, better-heeled Miss Bingley.

True love needs its inducements. George did not marry Serena until she was making good money, though I never

117

say that to her. We are talking about forty years back and she still believes it was love at first sight. And as for riding to the rescue of a damsel in distress that is not so common as it was. The Benefits Agency and support groups take the place of knights in shining armour. Why should the latter bother?

Hattie is wise, all the same, to have done the choosing. When the man hires female help another element becomes involved. She is the slave he brings back from battle: she is the booty of war and her body is his by right. As it is Agnieszka becomes Hattie's maidservant, and her loyalty is to the one she first set eyes on, in this case the female mistress, not the male conqueror. Hattie abhors biologism – indeed, both she and Martyn laugh heartily at the absurdities published in the name of science in *Devolution*'s sister magazine *Evolution* – and I don't put any of this to her. She would scoff.

But so far, so good, for Hattie and Martyn, and for baby Kitty, who loves routine and the calm presence of Agnieszka, and tends to love most the person who puts food into her mouth and makes her comfortable and plays peek-a-boo. Bath times are all right, with parents present: it's more fun, but they get soap in her eyes, and let her slip beneath the water so it panics her. She prefers Agnieszka.

Dream On

I meet my grand-daughter Hattie for lunch at a Pret à Manger in the Gray's Inn Road just round the corner from her office, and she's looking wonderful: everything shines, eyes, hair, nails. I am pleased to have so splendid a grandchild, and think I've not done so badly after all. She talks non-stop about Martyn's job, about Babs's crisis, about Hilary at work – they are still waiting to see Neil – and the problem with *ShitCockPissDog!* and its difficult writer, and takes a breath and puts her hand on my arm – she has been to a manicurist – and stops mid track and says 'Gran, I'm sorry, it's all me, me, me, isn't it, I'm just so full of everything all of a sudden. Having been nothing, nothing, nothing since Kitty. How are you and how is Serena and Sebastian and prison and everyone?'

And I tell her and she shows real interest and I think again how lucky I am. Poor Serena only has boys: she will never experience the down-pull of the female generations through the mitochondrial line. It will continue down from Frieda, to Wanda, to me and Lallie and Hattie and Kitty, and if Kitty produces a girl to her: and through Susan to Sarah, and down to Sarah's two girls – but with Serena's branch it stopped. She had only sons. It's nice to feel sorry for Serena

119

sometimes. But there is something bothering Hattie, there's something wrong, I know it.

She tells me.

It's the way Kitty burst into tears when Hattie came into the room after her difficult day at the office, her anxiety to get home. How Agnieszka had been so understanding, and said to take no notice; babies do go through a phase of this when they meet strangers. Just a week and it will be over.

'You're hardly a stranger,' I say. 'You're the mother. How dare she say a thing like that! Even if she thinks it she shouldn't say it. Of course you're upset.'
'She's not English,' says Hattie. 'It's only a question of communication. She got the wrong word for stranger. I don't know why you're so against her. You haven't even met her. It's just that Agnieszka's with Kitty all day and I am not.'
'That's what happens when someone else looks after your child,' I say.

I'm a one to talk. Roseanna, Viera, Raya, Annabel, Svea, Maria, girls unlisted and unlimited, all looking in their time after Lallie. Lallie grown and giving birth to Hattie at sixteen.

Who looked after Hattie when Lallie played the flute? I hardly know. Lallie wasn't speaking to me at the time. I'd given her another stepfather, the one before Sebastian whom she resented greatly. I don't have all that good a memory of him, either. He was a writer and we lived in the country and Lallie disapproved. I remember his sandals more clearly than anything else about him. He didn't believe in socks. He had hammer toes with dirty nails, but he had a good literary reputation.

It only lasted three years, and being free, I found myself looking after Hattie again. A woman with a small child does what she can. I have known women get married just to get away from their mothers, their children, their therapists, their jobs – just to have the excuse: '*I can't look after you in your old age, your illness, your art obsession, your desire to know my inner thoughts, to get up at six every morning to improve an employer's profits, whatever – I AM MARRIED. I have another duty now.*'

'What I don't understand,' Hattie says, 'is that she still stretches out her little arms to Martyn and smiles when he comes in. He doesn't get the tears. Why should I be the stranger and he not?'

She bends over to put half her avocado-and-watercress salad on another plate, to relieve herself, I suppose, of the burden of looking at it. She really does have anorexic tendencies. I am glad to hear about Agnieszka's carrot pies and their pastry crusts. Men from various corners of the room are staring at Hattie. I have a vague nostalgia for the days they would stare at me. I am conscious, as Hattie moves, that she's wearing scent. It's not something we do in our family. Scent suggests that people are trying to hide the fact that they haven't washed lately. Wanda told us this, and no one had forgotten it.

'Are you wearing scent?' I ask.
'It's called Joy,' says Hattie. 'It's very expensive. Only a little bit.'

'No wonder Kitty cries when you go near her,' I say. 'All the proper mother smell, the milk smell, is covered up. It's not you she doesn't like, it's the bloody scent.'

I say a stronger word than bloody. Another customer looks up from her sweet red-pepper soup in surprise. I am a bit diaphanous today: that is to say I have a pink-grey chiffon scarf floating round my neck. I am wearing a pale pink suit. I have a good figure for a woman my age, so long as I look at myself full on not sideways. My hair went white overnight, shortly after the departure of the man with the hammer toes. Since then it has been a joy to look after. Just dunk and go.

I look rather like my mother at my age. Wide eyes and high cheekbones. I hope I have a jollier temperament than her. I certainly have a more forceful vocabulary. Hammertoes had a taste for swearing: a habit picked up by the upper classes in the sixties from the working class, with which I in turn have been infected. Hattie is silent for a little. She does not tell me that Agnieszka claims that Alice gave her the scent. She has not told me that Babs has implied that Agnieszka left her last job rather fast, and not on Joy-giving terms. Hattie does not know that soon Agnieszka will start to appear in Martyn's dreams.

Hattie and I kiss each other formally when we part. One, two, three, cheek after cheek after cheek, the French way. I don't know how these habits have arisen. Once people shook hands, rather lightly and formally: now lips touch cheeks. As if we're all trying to get into one big bed together, demonstrate that no one's afraid of catching anything. Which we are.

Martyn Is Alone With Agnieszka

Next day when Hattie is in the office she gives Babs the bottle of Joy. She does not tell Babs how it has come into her possession. She does not want Babs's comments, she just wants not to waste anything so expensive. She tells Babs, truthfully enough, that Kitty doesn't like it.

'I wonder if I really want to have a baby,' Babs says. 'I don't want not to have one but then I think of the reality and my heart sinks.' Alastair has taken her back, on condition that they start a family. He has shown her pictures of himself as a child, and as a young man before his neck thickened, when he was really not so bad looking.

After that Kitty does not cry any more when Hattie comes near her but beams and smiles and cuddles, and has learned to say 'mama'.

'I told you it would be all right,' says Agnieszka. 'I told you it was just a stage they all pass through. Something about finally cutting the metaphorical umbilical cord.'

Her English is getting really good. She goes to two English classes a week, and one belly-dancing class. Two evenings

123

a week Hattie and Martyn like to go out to friends or to a restaurant dinner, two days a week they stay home and just recuperate, and sometimes Agnieszka joins them in the living room and sometimes she studies.

One evening Hattie goes off to join the belly-dancing class in Camden Town. The class runs from eight until nine o'clock. The approach is dismal. The police have moved the drug dealers and addicts up towards Kentish Town but the sense of graffitied peril and grimy chaos remains; she has to pass groups of hooded boys, who fortunately seem more engrossed in their affairs than hers. She hopes that will still be the case when she emerges. Before the lesson itself she is sold some rather lovely Egyptian scarves, belts and skirts which she does not need, and is then taught how to separate out her belly from the rest of her and how to move the hips to aid the movement of the stomach. It is rather nice and makes her feel quite sexy and free. The teacher, who is large and has a lot of belly which she moves round most dramatically, probably thinks Hattie is anorexic.

Agnieszka was originally meant to come with Hattie and introduce her to the teacher, and Martyn was going to babysit, but she has to revise for her latest English proficiency exam, and Martyn has some more research to do into the fat content of beef-burgers, the better to argue that they're good for you.

Martyn and Agnieszka are alone in the house. Hattie does not let herself even think about this. Even if a scrap of what Babs said was true, Martyn is no Alastair. Alastair is an unreconstructed dinosaur from the old school: Martyn belongs to the new world, and though his grandmother would have assumed that a man and a woman alone in a house could only lead to one thing, sex, that is hardly the case today.

However, at about half past eight Agnieszka comes into the living room, she and Martyn have a break from their studies and a cup of coffee, and the subject gets round to belly dancing. Martyn remarks that Hattie seems to have scarcely enough stomach to train, and Agnieszka says oh, that makes no difference, and she pulls down her jeans and her skinny jersey up to reveal a firm, hollowed white midriff, which she proceeds to make shift from here to there and there to here. He can see the muscles move beneath the very fine pale skin. It is perfectly decent: Agnieszka shows little more belly than many a teenager at the office with a gap between hipsters and T-shirt, but Martyn has to go into the kitchen for more coffee to hide the beginnings of an erection.

Sheer force of will brings his body back to its senses, and he goes back to find her jeans and her sweater meeting again, and says perhaps he'll go down and meet Hattie out of the class, since it sounds like a low-life area. Agnieszka says it is a bit, but it has never bothered her: she studied Aikido in Poland and it's a skill which stops one being nervous in any city in the world. Perhaps Hattie should have classes too?

Martyn goes down to Camden and meets Hattie as, flushed and pleased, she leaves the class. He can't tell her about the incident with Agnieszka; how could he possibly? He is convinced in any case that Agnieszka acted without seductive intent. She is oddly innocent, with her grave face and her short upper lip and her straight no-nonsense hair. It is he who is at fault.

Later, much later – when he has had rather a lot to drink with his boss, celebrating his new promotion at *Devolution*, where *Burgers and other Delights of the Flesh* went down very well with its singular mixture of serious research and lively presentation – prompted by Harold's usual bawdy talk, Martyn describes some exotic dreams which the belly-dancing incident has sparked. In which the au pair comes closer and closer to him with her bare tummy, and he is in bed with Hattie and the girl gets in too, and he is immensely relieved when he wakes up, with a start, just before consummation, to find it hasn't happened in real life. (Harold tells Hattie and Hattie tells me. Harold – and his staff may be right about marginal autism – doesn't understand quite the effect this information will have on Hattie.)

Martyn compensates, when Agnieszka is out of earshot, by finding fault with her work: saying to Hattie that he's sick of carrots, complaining that the girl's careless and has put the black and white clothes in the wash together (actually it was Hattie but she doesn't own up), or has tidied away the *New Statesman* so he can't find it. This is mostly to reassure himself and Hattie that his relationship with the maid is perfectly in order.

Another Country

Martyn has his dreams, I have memories. The past is another country, but there are no children there. We look at it through adult eyes.

But we three girls in the days of our teenage! The word had not even been invented. We were not a market. We had nothing to spend. We had two sets of clothes: one for school and one for out of school. Two pairs of shoes, one wet and one drying. Clothes were meant to cover and disguise growing bodies, not display them. No doubt there were paedophiles around but no one had heard of them. Certainly girl children did not dress to tempt, deny and defy men as they do now. Chance for us would have been a fine thing. Our hair was caught at the side with a metal clip to keep it out of our eyes. It was the most unflattering style that could be devised.

I was rebellious. I refused to have my hair cut by my mother, I wanted to grow it long like Veronica Lake's in *I Married a Witch*. I refused to believe that just because Veronica Lake's hair was smooth and silky mine could never be like hers. There was a terrible scene once when I was ten. Wanda seized my head and chopped away at my hair. I grabbed the scissors and stabbed her bottom to make her stop. Susan and Serena were traumatised. I was so ashamed of myself I let Wanda cut my hair thereafter, whenever and however she wanted.

Wanda, well read and informed, able to quote large chunks of obscure poetry at the drop of a hat, impressed us girls greatly by her ability to grasp abstract notions and fling them in the air. The pity was that since she had never been to school she took authority over-earnestly. We lived with her anxiety. If we walked on the grass when a notice said 'Keep Off' she wasn't angry: she suffered. She gave us a stern heritage and a clear eye, and if anything later drove Susan mad, she being less devious than Serena or myself, it was our mother's conscience.

I went through one of those patches, between fifteen and eighteen, when hormones take over from reason and girls can take to drink, drugs and sex. We'd left New Zealand and come to London on the first boat out after the war. Wanda had inherited just enough money to pay the fare over for herself, her mother Frieda, Susan, Serena and me, an all-female family. Now there was nothing left.

My sisters settled into their new penurious life in London well enough, studied, passed exams. They did mostly as they were told, biding their time, curbing their opinions, waiting to grow up. I didn't. I was too angry. My mother had taken work as a live-in housekeeper – she had no real source of income until Serena grew rich – and had somehow to house and support us. Just as our au-pair girls once did, and now Agnieszka, she took refuge in some other woman's more comfortable home and did the dirty work in exchange for her keep and a few pennies. Thus necessity makes servants of us all, or used to.

This was in the late 1940s, just after the war; and the drink was rum and cider, the drugs were unsophisticated – Benzedrine mainly, army surplus – and the sex, though plentiful, was straightforward and mostly in the missionary position. The body was still the temple of the soul. That there were such things as blow jobs did not enter our young comprehension. Sodomy was unthinkable. Pornography no doubt existed but not any we had ever seen. Brief flares of love and emotion, translated into lust, could lead – if you were me – to one-night stands in shoddy hotels with exciting strangers, but seldom down alleyways on your knees in exchange for money. By the mid-fifties all that had changed. Everyone knew everything.

But as the forties turned into the fifties our home was in a basement flat, dark, damp and with barred windows, beneath the grand house where my mother was the servant. I was humiliated. I thought that to live in such a place was beneath me: I missed my father. I thought my mother had no business taking us away from him, making him lonely, so that he had married again and started another family as if his existing daughters didn't matter.

I rejoiced in my hatred of my mother and played truant, went to nightclubs, stayed out all night, sold myself for pocket money if I needed to buy clothes; left school early with no exams, worked as a (bad) waitress and a (worse) cleaner, got myself pregnant with Lallie by way of the vanishing Curran, gave birth to her in a Catholic home for unmarried mothers where they made you scrub stairs because it was good for the stomach muscles and your soul. Then I handed the baby over, on and off, to my poor mother and went on my adventures again.

I drifted into the world of the arts. I liked paintings and artists and the smell of oil paint turned me on, though like Serena and unlike Susan I couldn't draw to save myself. I turned myself from an artist's moll into an artist's model, was painted by William Gear, RA, and others of note. Joe Tilson painted my teeth. My face and my body appear on various gallery walls and versions of me I have quite forgotten turn up from time to time in retrospectives. But finally, after becoming something of a legend – I was quite beautiful, I think, and must have been very bright for a bad girl – I was shocked into some kind of sense.

I moved in circles which brushed up against Christine Keeler's. Stephen Ward, who befriended us all, killed himself when accused of living off immoral earnings. He was drawing me the week before he chose to die. Ward was a nice, foolish, proud man, a talented osteopath, a good portraitist, hounded to his death by the newspapers. We weren't immoral, we girls. We were just having a good time and he helped us. But we got too near the centre, and it had to be stopped before the scandals touched the really powerful.

Through these connections I met, ran off with, finally married and had a baby, by Charlie Spargrove, playboy and baronet. Out of the frying pan into the fire, though he didn't have an artistic bone in his body. Las Vegas was wilder and nastier than London. So I took the baby home to where it would be safe.

I had stopped hating my mother. I could see that a woman had to do what she had to do. I think I married Charlie to stop Wanda worrying about me, and to bring us all back by virtue of his title into that class of Old Etonians and Royal Academicians into which my mother had been born, and from which the family had been untimely flung by war and divorce. I can think of no other reason for my having married him. Why I'm so beastly about poor Beverley, Jamie's wife, I don't know. She is no less of a snob than me.

And Serena did the same, and became famous, just to ease Wanda's pain. And between us we have ensured that our children and our children's children join the world that she so nearly lost for us, and Hattie can find her level wherever she goes.

My poor mother! She had schlepped us virgin girls across the world from New Zealand, after the war, in the hope of recovering for herself and her daughters the bright, intellectual life of the kind to which she was born. Instead she found herself working as a housekeeper, with one wayward daughter, me, one who was seriously withdrawn, Susan, and one frivolous chatterbox, Serena; all clever and talented, but with no apparent prospect of making a success of their lives, and no context for herself in the shabby post-war world to which she had returned. She was too ashamed, I think, to take up the threads of the old life. She could not bear being pitied, or being seen as déclassée, or having to be grateful.

And, as one by one her daughters handed over to her their unplanned and unfortunate babies in full confidence that she would look after them, she blamed herself. She should not have returned to England. She should have somehow kept her marriage together and not let her husband divorce her. Had she only stayed in New Zealand, Susan would have turned into some kind of functioning poet, Serena would have been a farmer's wife, and I might have stayed on the rails and married someone with a regular life and income. Serena and I would reassure our mother in our later years – *see, you did the right thing, we turned out okay* – but she never quite believed us.

Susan, my elder sister, was the most beautiful of us three girls. She was dark-eyed and pale-skinned, quiet, grave and slender: Serena had a tendency to fat, thus shielding herself from painful nerve-endings which she maintained were on the outside, not the inside, of her skin by reason of some accident of birth. Her teachers complained that she talked and giggled too much, and never appeared to do any work at all. She would come second, or third in the class, whatever that class happened to be, dunces or high flyers, as if aware that to be unnoticed is safest while you bide your time to grow up. Do too well too young and the Fates might notice and push you under a bus.

I think that I always put out more pheromones than the other two from the beginning. In the hot New Zealand nights, in the year before we left for England, Susan would study astronomy and look at the stars, Serena would do her homework, and I would lie awake, fingers in my private parts, thinking how extraordinarily wonderful it would be to be married and have some man lying in the bed beside me every night, *every night*.

It was on that sea voyage to England that I lost my virginity to the ship's purser. I was thirteen and he was twenty-four. We had some excuse. The ship's engines had failed, there was a force nine gale and forty-foot waves. The stewards were going round with those calm yet panicky expressions you see on the faces of cabin staff when there's a real likelihood an aircraft won't make it. (I have seen it twice and that's more than enough.) The purser, single-handed, was trying to swing out a lifeboat: white water surged over the rails, dark blue water towered above. I was trying to help him – he was very good-looking, and had brass buttons – and he kept telling me to get off the deck and back inside but I was too fascinated by the majesty of the sea and the way the foam was swirling over the decks, and indeed the purser, to be much interested in survival. Boldly and abruptly he tried to push me back inside with his body. As in the meeting of Hattie and Martyn, physical proximity worked its own magic. He was angry and I was defiant – it was like the moment with my mother and the scissors.

Before we knew it we were writhing together in the shelter of one of the great phallic ventilation funnels those old ships sprouted from their decks. His thing hurt when it went in, but I didn't look, I didn't care. I had no idea what these 'things' looked like and I didn't want to know. We could feel the engines thrumming back into life below, and the movement of the ship as it slowly headed back into the waves and we were saved. I think to this day it was I and the purser did it. The sacrifice of virginity is not without power. For the rest of the voyage we pretended we did not know each other.

I felt very fond of him though, and when the nightmare voyage ended, and he was shaking hands with the departing passengers, he bent – he was very tall – and kissed my cheek. My mother was outraged. 'You're too young,' she said. 'You're only a child. The way he looked at you! What am I going to do with you?'

But she had no idea of what had happened and I certainly wasn't going to tell her. I never told her a thing if I could help it. I knew in advance whatever it was she'd tell me to stop doing it, so why bother.

Susan began to menstruate on the voyage; she was the eldest, but the slowest to mature – something, I believe, to do with body weight. Both Serena and I were substantial: Susan was wraith-like. The ship's surgery held stocks of sanitary towels, which were innovative, and of which they were very proud. (Before that it was customary to use 'rags' – folded strips of cloth which like hankies had to be washed out and re-used.) By today's standards they were primitive. They would shred into little balls of scarlet paper when one walked – we girls would walk behind one another on the deck discreetly following the trail and picking them up for each other. It was rather a relief when the supplies ran out and we could return to rags.

Frieda, my grandmother, who was with us on this voyage and was made miserable enough by the fact that we slept in dormitories, row upon row of tiered iron bunks down in the hold, with diarrhoea and conjunctivitis rife – there were 2,000 of us on a ship which carried 150 in peace-time – thanked God that she was beyond reproductive age. I of course, like Serena, still bleed. We have HRT now and neither of us ever observably reached the menopause. But neither do our limbs break or our libidos fade away. Oh fortunate generation!

Agnieszka And Martyn Go Shopping

Agnieszka has been with Hattie and Martyn for three months. Kitty is nine months now, and well into what Agnieszka refers to as the oral stage. Her course in child development was run on Freudian lines. When Kitty gets cross with an object she can't quite control and tries to bite it to bits with her tiny new teeth – she already has two at the bottom and two at the top – Agnieszka observes that Thanatos, the death instinct, is surfacing in the normal way. That's impressive. But then she says 'just as well breast-feeding is behind us', which annoys Hattie. Us?

Kitty has been making 'ma-ma-ma' noises at Agnieszka, and Martyn says jokingly to Hattie: 'You'd better be careful or she'll begin to mistake Agnieszka for Mummy. Pure self-interest on Kitty's part. Agnieszka is a long name for a baby to get its head around. You should have gone for Agnes.' This makes Hattie crosser still.

Martyn is feeling mean because Hattie has been late home once or twice lately, staying on at work to keep up with some promising new openings in the Ukraine, and what with Agnieszka having to go off to classes, he's had to bath Kitty by himself and she played up. Also Hattie stayed on a little after work to have a celebratory drink with Colleen, who has just had a baby boy and come in to the office to show him off. Colleen asks if Hattie and Martyn will come to the christening and Hattie says yes of course she will, though it's years since she's been in a church and Martyn probably never has. But she liked singing hymns at school.

The sight of Colleen's baby, oddly enough, has made Hattie feel quite broody. She'd like a little boy but it's out of the question; she's got more than enough on her plate as it is. She'll tell Martyn about the christening later. In the meantime he needs soothing. Placatory as ever, she points out that at least Kitty said da-da-da before she said ma-ma-ma, and Martyn should be pleased to be the first parent claimed. Then Agnieszka interjects and points out that that da-da-da always comes before ma-ma-ma: this is normal in infant development. The hard sounds come before the soft. Hattie is seized by irrational anger. She wants Agnieszka out of her life and her baby back.

She also knows that on this Saturday morning, when she and Martyn are still drinking their freshly roasted newly ground coffee, and the low late-autumn sun is shining through the windows – which Agnieszka cleaned a couple of days back – the girl has already cleared and re-stacked the dishwasher, run round to the dry-cleaner, hung Martyn's suits in the wardrobe, changed and dressed Kitty and checked for nappy rash (just a patch showing after a couple of nights being bathed and put to bed by Martyn) and cleaned Kitty's ears out with a cotton bud. So she bites back irritation. Kitty is going to be very pretty, everyone agrees. She has great big blue eyes and is very smart and happy. She sits in her high chair and bangs her cereal with the flat of her spoon and Agnieszka says calmly and reasonably 'don't do that, Kitty,' and Kitty just doesn't. There is no way Hattie can do without Agnieszka. It's too late.

Great-Aunt Serena rings to ask how everyone is doing, and if there are any problems with this month's mortgage. Hattie says no, everyone's managing very nicely now Hattie is back to work and when she gets her rise in six months' time things will be better still. She has an office of her own now: she had been sharing with a rather difficult older woman called Hilary but it's all been sorted out.

'Hum,' says Serena. 'You have to be careful of older women. They haven't survived for nothing.'

'Oh Good Lord,' says Hattie, 'there's nothing tooth-and-claw about where I work. It's all publishing and agenting.'

Serena, who has published thirty-two books, laughs a little hollowly. She asks Hattie about the baby, and Hattie, ashamed now of feeling so mean about Agnieszka, lists the girl's accomplishments in the last two hours.

'A dream,' she concludes.

'Sounds a bit dreamish to me,' says Serena, 'but she shouldn't really be using cotton buds. Take them away from her. If you use them in baby ears they can puncture the membrane. Just wipe the ears out with a soapy cloth, and be careful to dry the folds behind them.'

Serena is full of advice, about everything from how to cure thrush, how to survive a divorce, how to write novels. She feels that if she knows things others don't it is her duty to

pass them on. Many of her sentences begin with 'Why don't
you –?'

Hattie passes the advice onto Agnieszka, and Agnieszka
snaps back that everyone uses baby buds in Poland and so
far as she knows there's no particular problem with deaf-
ness in the population. Hattie is startled. She has not known
Agnieszka react like this before. Agnieszka sits down with
a noticeable plonk rather than her usual graceful glide and
buries her head in her hands. She is crying.
'I am all alone in a foreign country and no one cares about
me. My husband will find someone else if I am away so
much. I had the letter from him which I did not like. If I
could only telephone more but it is expensive, and I cannot
use your phone.'

Martyn comes in carrying Kitty on his shoulder, finds
Agnieszka in tears, hears what she says, and is mortified.
He says it is sweet of Agnieszka to worry about the cost
but she really must phone her husband whenever she wants.
'But Serena may be right about the cotton buds and a flannel
being best,' he adds.

Hattie is grateful for this last at least. She realises that Martyn
has managed both to placate Agnieszka and please her, and
feels a pang of sheer pride in him. He is developing a real
talent for managing other people. She was already feeling
bad about the phone. Babs had advised Hattie to tell
Agnieszka that she must ask before she phoned abroad: but
Agnieszka surely deserves to be able to run her emotional
life with some kind of privacy, and Martyn realises this too.

Martyn has taken to wearing contact lenses since his promotion to Assistant Editor and Hattie notices that he has beautiful blue eyes, and wonders why it has never occurred to her before. Perhaps there just hasn't been the time. Circulation of *Devolution* is picking up after only two issues which feature the new thinking, and Harold says Martyn's article on junk food, *Fancying a Little, Gaining a Lot*, made a big contribution.

'You have to entertain as well as instruct, or you go to the wall,' Harold says, and Martyn clearly has a knack for doing just that.

Martyn is Hattie's protector and her strength, her ally and her friend. He looks very good and handsome and positive, and his cheeks are filling out from carrot and tuna pie and the other delicacies which turn up upon the family table. Agnieszka now serves borscht, a kind of beetroot and sour-cream soup which is strange and delicious. Kitty is allowed a spoonful every now and then. It is important to stimulate a baby's palate with new tastes. Agnieszka also produces boxes of chocolate-covered prunes, which her husband Aurek sends through the post; they look uninviting, but taste exquisite.

If Kitty hadn't been born, if Agnieszka wasn't around, they could go to the bedroom and make love, or even right there upon the sofa as once they had. But this is now and that was then and that is that.

Usually Hattie and Martyn go shopping on a Saturday morning, which is more fun now there is a little money to spare. Agnieszka babysits. They look round the markets and check what's new in at the organic food store. But today she has manuscripts to read and so Martyn was going to go alone.

'Tell you what, Agnieszka,' Hattie says, 'why don't you go shopping with Martyn and I'll look after Kitty? You need to get out of the house more. All you ever do is work.' 'I go to belly dancing,' says Agnieszka. 'That's frivolous. Frivolous is a new word for me I like very much.' And a smile breaks through and she looks really pretty and grateful.

Martyn looks slightly put out but says: 'Yes, why don't you? Come too, Agnieszka. Though it's rather dreary. I'm only after oolong tea which means going in the Chinese supermarket direction.'

So Agnieszka and Martyn go shopping, not to the trendy market, but along dusty, dirty streets, where wandering drug addicts shake their fists at the sky. At home Kitty is tetchy and troublesome and has to be jigged about and entertained so Hattie doesn't get much work done.

Babs rings. Hattie had a drink with her only yesterday, along with Nisha, who's now covering the Indian subcontinent – books are still mostly pirated, but responsible publishers are beginning to translate, and even pay – and who has just joined Dinton & Seltz and needs to get to know everyone. Babs has news. She says that she is indeed pregnant, the non-pregnancy was a false alarm, and it's Tavish's baby, and now what is she to do? She and Alastair have been really trying to conceive but she's sure it's Tavish's. In the old days she could just have covered up the dates and had an early baby but in these days of scans you can't do that: babies are really and truly monitored before birth. She sounds panicky.

Hattie has a terrible feeling that whatever she suggests Babs in her current mood will do. So she says, 'When in doubt do nothing,' and then, 'Let's talk about it on Monday,' though Monday is packed with meetings, and *ShitCockPissDog!*'s writer is now annoyed with her because someone should have told him in the first place that the title was unfortunate. He wants to be represented by Hilary, not Hattie, abroad as well as at home. Had he not definitely told Neil that the Tourette's community have to be taught what's offensive and what isn't, through behavioural psychotherapy? No one but Hilary, he complains, had bothered to point it out to him. Babs tells Hattie she's beginning to think the Tourette's is a sales gimmick anyway, the writer fears he's going to be exposed as a fake and is getting cold feet. Babs has a way of compartmentalising her problems which Hattie rather admires.

Hattie expects Martyn and Agnieszka to come back any moment, but by midday they are still not home. She would like to be out with Martyn. They spend little enough time together as it is. Why on earth did she suggest Agnieszka went with him? Why does Agnieszka have to be kept happy at all costs? She goes into Agnieszka's room and looks around. She has been too honourable to do this before. There is an official-looking letter in a brown envelope from the local educational authority, opened for some time from the look of it. She takes it and reads. What has she come to? The letter is more of a form than a letter, in the smudged dark ink and cheap paper of officialdom. It is from the registrar of a further education college saying Agnieszka has missed so many classes she has been removed from the tuition roll. 'There is a very great demand for places and such measures are sometimes necessary.' Hattie puts the letter back in its envelope just in time: Martyn and Agnieszka are struggling in the front door with a brand new very expensive stroller. It is bright red and pink, stuffed and studded and truly beautiful. Hattie is outraged. She should have been there with Martyn buying that for Kitty. 'I couldn't help it,' says Martyn, 'we saw it in the bicycle shop and I couldn't resist it. There was a sale. Only £220, reduced from £425.' £220 – it's madness. What's he thinking of? *Fancying a Little, Gaining a Lot*? The opposite is true.

'What do you think? Agnieszka said it was just right for Kitty. Properly sprung and with good back support.' He sees Hattie's face and looks worried, and realises he's done the wrong thing.
'I wished you'd been there with me, darling, so we could have bought it together, but I just couldn't bear anyone else but Kitty to have it, so I went ahead.'
'That's okay,' says Hattie and goes back to her manuscripts and sulks, but not before seeing Agnieszka and Martyn look at each other as if Hattie had rained on their parade.

She does not tell Martyn about the letter from the college. She's too cross with him about the stroller. She remembers the pleasures of sulking when she was a little girl and Lallie would go on concerts and leave her behind for Frances to look after. 'But I'm grown up now,' she thinks. She wonders what Agnieszka does when she says she's at English classes and isn't. But perhaps she's just switched courses and is at another college anyway? If Hattie tells Martyn he will make some kind of fuss and upset everyone again. Hattie doesn't know what to do next, and remembering her own words thinks, *When in doubt do nothing.*

She goes into the kitchen and helps Martyn and Agnieszka unpack the day's goodies, with little cries of appreciation and delight, and Kitty makes little cooing noises in the background. Really she is the best baby.

Ordinary Women

I, Frances, get a phone call from Serena. We speak to each other, I suppose, once or twice a week. It's very agreeable to be in close touch with someone who has known one all one's life and still puts up with one. This is not necessarily the case with husbands. I have nothing to say to Charlie Spargrove, though we exchange Christmas cards and once, way back, when our son Jamie was attacked by a crazed horse and ended up kicked almost to death in Timaru hospital, he did call me and tell me, and asked after my welfare in kindly and forgiving terms. Beverley had been in touch with him first, not me, of course; I'm only the mother. Charlie has the money and the title. Charlie these days owns a racing stable and has two grand-daughters who used to be sweet little pony-club things but whom I now see in the gossip columns waving their long legs about and giggling drunkenly. I expect they'll grow out of it.

But I was the one who flew out to be with Jamie then, not Charlie. Charlie just wanted to be kept informed. By the time I had made the journey Jamie was sitting up in bed, still much-bandaged and attached to drips, but cheerful and about to go home. He had always been a terrifically healthy child: I thought of the early days of his upbringing, and decided that Serena and myself, and Roseanna and Viera and Maria and Raya and Sarah and the others whose names I can't remember, had done a pretty good job on this stranger. We must between us have managed to feed him on something other than fish fingers, chips and peas. I think Beverley hoped Charlie would fly over, not me, not the mother-in-law from hell with her multitudinous husbands, disreputable past and gossamer scarves.

The in-between husband, the sandalled writer with the hammer toes, prefers not to speak to me. I feel quite amiable towards him, but he is still sore and ruffled. I don't know why. I neither asked him for money, nor tried to take the house. I just packed my bag and left, moved by that odd despair and panic women sometimes get – if she does not leave now there will be nothing left of her. She will be a shell, with nothing inside. A black dead mussel on a rock by the sea, its shell thickened by parasite barnacles, opened and empty but for a strand of slimy seaweed drifted in. It's a terrible vision. He doesn't beat her, or make her life a misery, she cannot explain the urgency to her friends: he is just wrong. It is dangerous. He is stealing her soul. It is an urgent and irrational feeling but one which needs to be respected.

I daresay men feel it too, which is why they too will leave suddenly one morning and not come back. They haven't gone to a mistress, they have just gone. It is something to do with sharing a bed, the way two people merge with each other in front of the telly, by the kitchen sink – it can make you panic, and rightly. Anyway, I walked out on

146

Hammertoes like that and upset him badly, and my name, I hear, is never mentioned in his house. He married again, perfectly happily, to a lady script editor who could help him on in his career.

Indeed, apart from the years when I pestered Charlie to help with Jamie, I have never expected financial help from men. I am too like my mother to enjoy being dependent. I remember her dictum – that men offer money and support to the woman in front of their nose: in the bed, at the stove, with the children. '*Out of sight is out of mind.*' That's why divorce laws exist. Because men and women take so different a view of what is right and natural. I have accepted lots of money from Serena over the years, but she's my sister. If she thinks what's hers is mine, I'm truly grateful and truly glad. And I define my life, as she does hers with me, over the telephone and now through email too. We get to see each other every month or so. She complains she writes so much fiction she can hardly remember who she is: she says I help her keep a sense of identity. I just like chattering and so does she. Neither of us shows any signs of losing our marbles.

When we lost Susan to cancer – and it was as if a limb had been chopped off from the all-female family body, tightly interwoven as Wanda, Susan, Serena and me – we clung together as if only thus could we keep our balance. When between us we took over Susan's three children, that served us as a kind of prosthetic limb with which we could get by. We were at least balanced again. When Wanda died I thought, at last she is free of the anxiety which crept out of her into all our veins: I am happy for her. Perhaps she should have done more to save us from it, but for all I know

I too have passed anxiety on, down through the mitochondrial line. Lallie is riven by anxiety before performances.
Perhaps Hattie just pretends to me that she finds the world
a controllable place, free from surprises.

This morning we talk about Hattie and the new au pair.
Serena had called Hattie yesterday morning and been briefed.
We talk about cotton buds and baby ears. Serena asks me
what does this Agnieszka look like, and I say oddly enough
no one has bothered to say. They just list her achievements.
She must be a kind of ordinary-looking person.

We go through lists of ordinary-looking people we know
who have broken up marriages. There are quite a few of
them. It is not necessarily the ravishing beauty who runs off
with other women's men. Sexual desire is not as compelling
a motivation as one assumed when young. The wit, the soul,
the politics, the ability to play the piano well, anything, even
the plainness, can turn out to be the seductive factor.

Beware most of all the spare woman at the dinner party,
with lowered lids, quiet and sweet, dressed like a country
mouse: those eyes can open wide, hungry and inviting while
the hostess is not looking. Like Ann Footworth, who was all
of fifty-five when she ran off with Serena's married publisher.
Ann was his dull secretary. His wife Marjorie took pity on
Ann, she was so much alone in the world, and asked her to
dinner – and it ended with Marjorie herself standing outside
the publishing house throwing stones and shouting abuse up
at his window, while he cowered under the desk with Ann,
until the police were called and took the wife away. And no
one forgets T. S. Eliot's wife, the one he put in a lunatic

asylum, who poured melted chocolate through the letter box of Faber & Faber.

But that was rather rare and special. In the old days, we agree, men just had affairs and said they would leave home, but very seldom did. It was *'wait until the children are out of nursery school'*, and next thing it was GCSEs, then AS levels, then A levels – and then *'until they've finished college'*. It takes until then for her to realise he was probably never going to leave his wife and join her. And then the wife has a late baby and of course he's been sleeping with her all the time. Women believe what they're told if they want to enough. (I think of Serena and George.)

We fear Hattie may have inherited the tendency to believe what she wants to believe, not what's under her eyes. But then so many of the young do. They have been brought up on a diet of too much fiction, film, TV, novels – and they believe they are heroes and heroines of their own lives and everything will turn out well. What is worrying is that this Agnieszka may not share this delusion. She will have grown up with less fiction than we in the West: novels will have been in shorter supply, the TV will have been devoted mostly to exhortations or national folk dancing. She will know the world is hard and earnest and will behave accordingly. On the other hand, had Hattie and Martyn engaged an English girl she would have come with a weak superego, sat around in fast-food outlets feeding the baby with burgers to keep it quiet, or in the café in the supermarket teaching the toddler how to drink bright pink fizzy juice with a bendy straw. I've seen them.

It is true, we agree, that men have been known to leave their wives for the mistress the day the children's A-level results come through. That happened to Grace: Grace and Andrew the accountant were in the middle of their summer holiday in a *gîte* in France when the message came that the youngest had got three starred As, and Andrew just walked out the door and never came back. He joined the waiting mistress, the one Grace didn't know about, holidaying, until then on her own, in the Bahamas.

If that sort of thing happens far less nowadays it is because everyone is so guilt-ridden and self-conscious they can't have a sexual relationship without thinking it's the real thing and confessing all: scarcely are they out of the wrong bed than they're determined to make it the right one and planning a divorce. All the parties involved talking about *authenticity of feeling* and agreeing that for the sake of the children everyone must be amicable and always come to Christmas dinner. And the children with another set of step-parents to take on, and the busiest Christmas Days ever, partners and children flitting here and there. Then the cycle starts again. The registry offices are full of people marrying second, third, fourth wives only because they've been taught that secrecy and lying are bad (*inauthentic*), and a flicker of feeling is registered as life-long emotion. Good Lord, in sexual matters secrecy is the only way society survives. Serena and I have really got each other going.

At least when I left Hammertoes, I remind her, I didn't leap straight into someone else's arms. It was a year or two before Sebastian turned up, and very worrying ones too. I hate being without a man; I remember those early days back in

Caldicott Square as part golden, but part alarming and despondent, when I had nothing and Serena had everything and I was cleaning the Primrosetti Gallery floor. But that may just be habit, and my generation. Since Sebastian's been inside I've managed to get others to fit the garage door, plaster over the cracks in the bedroom ceiling, indeed have the whole place redecorated, pictures re-framed, settee re-upholstered. Sebastian did not like having workmen in the house. He felt it was a householder's job to do these things – every man his own plumber – but he just never got round to doing them.

'But what will he say when he comes out?' asks Serena.
'He won't notice if the workmen aren't still there,' I say and we laugh.

She says Sebastian and George had a lot in common. I ask her if she misses him and she says yes, of course: the longer people are dead the easier it is to remember the good times rather than the bad. But she still gets a pain in her stomach, and another one as if her heart was splitting when she thinks of his affair with Sandra, the rather plain and ordinary girl he left her for. Twelve years later and she's still recalling incidents: the way he must have mocked her behind her back, took her round, all unknowing, to see the flat where his mistress lived – the betrayal and cruelty of it, when all she had done was love him.

'Hang on, Serena,' I say. 'You had affairs too.'
'They didn't mean anything,' she says, and then has the grace to laugh.

151

Some flashy men rather like ordinary women, we agree. The ones you might think would have some glamorous trophy wife hanging on their arm occasionally go for truly dowdy partners, little brown mice who when it comes to it are bullies, requiring men to zip up their dresses and fetch their handbags which they could do perfectly well themselves; who occupy the moral high ground, reproach men for political incorrectness, put hands over their glasses and say 'you've had more than enough'. We decide such women make a man feel secure, back in the nursery; only a step away from Miss Whiplash, with her high heels and whip, but socially acceptable.

We get back to Martyn and Hattie, and we think their partnership is sound enough, and Agnieszka is probably the treasure they think she is, and we just a pair of sceptical old biddies. We have noticed, though, that since Martyn got his promotion and Hattie went back to work, he and she no longer have their long tetchy conversations about politics and ethics, but talk mostly about food, strollers and cotton buds. Perhaps with prosperity principle goes out the window: perhaps ideas need a background of poverty if they are to flourish. Comfort and lack of conviction go hand in hand.

We quote Yeats, as our mother Wanda would have. That rough beast slouching towards Jerusalem, waiting to be born. We shiver.

'*The best lack all conviction*,' says Serena.

'*While the worst are full of passionate intensity*,' say I.

We both wish Hattie and Martyn would get married. Not that we have set them much of an example, doing it so often. They must look at us and think why bother?

'The reason our generation used to get married,' says Serena, 'was that it made it less likely the other one would get away. We couldn't take the risk.'

'But everyone's so interchangeable these days,' I say, 'it hardly matters if they do. Lose one partner, find another.'

She tells me not to make such sweeping statements. People probably suffer as much as ever. I say not. If they have an uncomfortable feeling they go to a therapist and get it ironed out.

'At least,' I say, 'you and I will have to settle for what we have: it's pass the parcel. Cranmer for you, Sebastian for me. The one we were left with when the music stopped.'

'Speak for yourself,' says Serena after a long pause.

Chocolate-Covered Prunes

Agnieszka hands round another box of chocolate prunes. They've come through the morning post, rather squashed together in their royal blue and gold cardboard box, and slightly melded together but at least separable. She won't let Kitty have a taste. She says prunes are 'too severe' for baby digestions.

When Agnieszka has finished handing round the prunes she washes her hands and takes up her sewing again. She is putting a button back onto the waistband of Martyn's best trousers. It seems a little personal to Hattie. There's something intimate and slightly seedy about the white banding that strengthens the flies of expensive-label suits: jeans just have zips and one button and that's that. But it's good to have the mending done. Agnieszka is using a thimble which seems to fascinate Martyn. He hadn't even known what it was for, let alone called, until now.

'So everything's okay with your husband now?' asks Martyn. 'The supply of prunes is flowing once more?'

Agnieszka giggles and says her husband's little friend has

been fired anyway, and she will be going home for Christmas as planned. Martyn asks if he can help arrange her ticket, but Agnieszka says no she can do it through a travel-agent friend she knows in Neasden.

Kitty is asleep in her crib. Agnieszka keeps a firm routine. Nothing must disturb it. Some of Hattie's friends take their babies along to dinner parties: this shocks Agnieszka greatly. They should be sleeping peacefully in familiar cots. As for toddlers playing under the table when adults are eating: she'd have the parents put in prison if she could.

The three of them sit in front of the television with the mute on, waiting for some bearable programme to start, when the sound will go up again. They feel like a family.

'I'd imagined Aurek worked from home,' says Hattie. 'Most of our scriptwriters do. Sitting in an attic writing films which'll one day make him famous? And either you'll go over there and be a midwife, or he'll come over here and you'll run belly-dancing classes. Isn't that the plan?'
'So many plans,' says Agnieszka. 'So many choices. Aurek drives for a bus company by day. In the evenings he writes. We both work hard. In Poland that is not unusual. The girl I didn't like was one of the conductors. A really cheap dyed blonde who chewed gum. She was stealing from the passengers. Can you imagine? A little skilled pick-pocket as a bus conductor?'
'I didn't somehow picture Aurek as a bus driver,' says Hattie, taken aback, and Martyn shakes his head slightly. Hattie's snobby origins are showing.

'In Poland we earn a living how we can,' says Agnieszka. 'The road sweepers are trained accountants, the station porters are doctors. There is much training and little work. That is the legacy of the Soviet Union. And that is why I am here, looking after Kitty, not at home.'

Hattie feels a little cheated. A bus driver! She has been misled. There's been no mention of the mother or the sick sister lately, either. Hattie has checked Agnieszka's post-office savings book. She saves: she does not spend. There are quite a few thousands in it. Once you secretly read someone else's letter there is no end to what you may go on to do. Sometimes Hattie even slips into Hilary's office if Hilary is out of the building and runs through her emails. But Hilary seems to be behaving herself. Her favourite Internet sites, according to Google, are mostly to do with Tourette's and dating agencies. Poor Hilary!

'It's hard for writers here too,' says Martyn.
'True enough,' says Hattie. 'People can spend years of their lives writing a book and then not be even able to sell it.'
'Then they are fools,' says Agnieszka, briskly. 'But I like Aurek to be writing a film script because it keeps him out of mischief in the evenings. One day he will finish his script and we will get married.'
'I thought you were married already,' says Hattie and even Martyn looks startled. 'We are married in the eyes of God and our friends,' says Agnieszka. 'That is all that matters.'
'But you told us you were married,' Hattie protests. It's one thing to offer free phone calls to Poland for a husband, but for a boyfriend it doesn't feel right.
'You two live as if you are married,' says Agnieszka, 'but

you are not, so you know how it is. A certificate makes no difference, except to immigration authorities.'

And she hands round more chocolate prunes, though it means she has to put down her sewing. She offers to make hot chocolate for everyone. She is very good at hot chocolate. She uses cocoa powder which she boils with sugar and water in the bottom of the pan until the starch is cooked and only then pours on hot frothy milk. Martyn's cheeks are positively plump these days, and Agnieszka has been out with Hattie and together they bought Hattie some size 10 skirts, though the size 6 blouses seem still to fit. Breast-feeding has altered her shape. Perhaps she didn't stop gradually enough: she had to take pills to dry up the milk.

Hattie has given Agnieszka a couple of dresses which no longer seemed to hang properly on her. Agnieszka doesn't wear them in the house – she says she doesn't want Kitty getting confused – she puts them on when Kitty is asleep and before going to classes, if there are classes. But she goes out with exercise pads and textbooks and comes back with them so to think anything else may be paranoiac.

But while Agnieszka is out in the kitchen Hattie can't help saying:
'That's a bit unsettling. Perhaps she goes out to visit a boyfriend and doesn't go to classes at all?'
'Well,' says Martyn, 'it wouldn't be the end of the world if she did. She does her work perfectly well.'

But Hattie is still not reassured. She wants Agnieszka to give Kitty all her emotional attention. Looking after Kitty can't

157

be just something Agnieszka gets paid to do: it needs to be her life's work. But Hattie can see she's being absurd. If Agnieszka has a boyfriend then at least it's unlikely that she will make a play for Martyn, or Martyn will be tempted to make a play for her. She is shocked to find such a thought even crossing her mind. It's primitive.

While they are dressing Kitty one morning – Agnieszka puts on one sock, Hattie the other: it's a game Kitty loves – Hattie asks casually after Agnieszka's Christmas travel arrangements, and Agnieszka looks sad and says she won't be going to Poland after all. Her mother and her sister are flying out to live with her aunt in Sydney, where the climate will be better and the medical care is very good. They have got residential visas on compassionate grounds. She will miss going home to see her friends and the rest of the family, but her boyfriend will be coming over to see her instead, just for a few days. So she'll only need to take one week off after all. Hattie says boldly that the boyfriend can stay with them if they're stuck, though they'll be rather crowded. Kitty's cot can go into hers and Martyn's room for a change. But Agnieszka says it's okay, they can go to her friend in Neasden where there's more space.

Hattie calls up her grandmother and says the child-minding emergency is over: Agnieszka's holidays will coincide with Dinton & Seltz's Christmas break, and it is agreed that everyone will go down to stay with Serena for Christmas. Cranmer will cook some wild Christmas dinner – he disapproves of turkeys, but likes to bake hares and ducks and pheasants alongside each other in the Aga, so the tastes mix and meld; there will be a Christmas tree which Kitty will love, and a good and flavoursome and more spacious time will be had by all than it would at Pentridge Road or Frances's cottage.

Coming Over

Serena calls me up and tells me she has a gap between deadlines; she can make time for a visit to Sebastian; will I come with her? She'll get the tickets. We can go club class and stay at the Amstel Intercontinental which Serena says has all the trimmings, and she's been around a bit.

I point out that the Bijlmer has to have at least three days' notice but she says she's already called them up and wheedled them. She's a known visitor and they have stretched a point, we can both go, and we're on the list for Friday. A limo, she promises, will take us from Schiphol to the prison, wait the two hours it takes to get in and out of the place, and take us back to the Amsterdam Amstel.

The visit itself is one hour – the rest is gruesome formalities, which involve finding names on lists, identification checks, on-the-spot photos, a lot of clanking doors, scanning irises, taking off shoes and belts for inspection, the inside of your mouth looked into to see if you have drugs stashed in a false tooth, finding out how to work the lockers into which all portable belongings must be placed, and waiting for the prisoner to be located and brought forward into the falsely cheerful room in which visits are conducted.

I expect the whole world to be like the Bijlmer most of the time, that is to say tiresome with only occasional bits of it easy, so life falls into place in the pattern of my expectations. Serena has higher hopes of destiny so it obliges. If I call up the Bijlmer Visitors' Programme I sound whiny and cry and nothing happens: it will be decided I have given too short notice for a visit. Serena is game for it all; she just bounces in and gets her way.

After the visit, which will be emotionally exhausting, and I will cry a little, and Serena will bounce, for this is my husband, not hers, though she is fond enough of Sebastian to visit him as often as she can, why then we will retire to the Amstel and its glories. And I will be glad she did not listen to me when I said, 'Oh no, I can get there and back by easyJet within the day; honestly, Serena, it's easier. I will meet you there.'

True, once we are in the Amstel we will probably not have the freedom to open the windows, since it is the tendency of too many guests to jump out of them; and we will be observed and talked about behind our backs by waiters and chambermaids, and the limo driver will tell everyone where we have been, but we will not be locked in, and out of the windows we will see the canals of Amsterdam and the plane trees that line them, and be conscious of history and of civilisation working slowly ever forward towards a destined future.

We will not have to look out at concrete and wire and grey depression – it's the ugliness of prisons that most depresses – or hear nothing but the sounds of clanging gates and the clatter of boots on uncarpeted floor, and the distant sound of a hundred televisions tuned to different stations, and the sudden echoey shouts and odd yells of the mad and almost mad.

Rather, we will listen to the sound of Vivaldi from the TV as it welcomes us with our names – *Welcome to the Amstel, Miss Hallsey-Coe*, and *Welcome Mrs Watt*. It's almost as if the TV itself knew and recognised and cared about us.

Today, after the visit to the Bijlmer, a bellboy carries two of Sebastian's paintings – oil, stretched canvas but without frames – up to our suite. The prison generously allowed us to take them out. We get a glimpse of them when we are going in, and are told we can take them with us when we leave. They have no doubt been inspected and screened for drugs. Such traffic can be outwards as well as inwards. One painting is of a black bed against a plain grey background. The other is a pink plastic moulded chair against more grey. These from Sebastian, who normally does riotous landscapes when he's miserable and bold colour-field work when he's cheerful. The paintings come as a surprise: I think I like them.

'All I have to look at seems grey,' says Sebastian, when he tells me during the visit that the paintings can come out even if he can't. 'It's all I can paint, and a few objects inter-rupting it. I think my sight memory must be going.' I remind him that Van Gogh painted a good chair or two.

'Not moulded plastic,' says Sebastian, rather crossly.

He has another year inside to go. He looks pale and depressed and shifty-eyed. He says everyone gets to look like that because they're always looking over their shoulder. Serena says later that the paintings look like Dutch Interiors, and we laugh a little nervously, because so they do. They're detailed and careful. I won't try to sell them in the gallery: we'll keep them for his next exhibition.

'Tell me,' asked a suspicious immigration official at Schiphol airport the other day, putting up my name on his screen, 'why do you keep making these short visits to Amsterdam and back?'
'I go to visit my husband in prison,' I say.
'Good for you,' he says and smiles in the most friendly fashion, and I am touched, and feel less disgraced.

If Hattie were in my place she would have to say, 'I go to visit my partner in prison,' and it wouldn't sound nearly so good. But of course she never would be in my place.

Suspicions

Babs has decided she can't have the baby when she's not sure who the father is. She has opted for a termination which Alastair doesn't know about. Hattie hasn't told Martyn because Babs has sworn her to secrecy, and because Martyn might just think it was his moral duty to tell Alastair what was going on.

Hattie is horrified to realise that flitting into her mind and out as fast as she can push it is the realisation she doesn't really want anything to stand in the way of Babs's termination. If Babs has the baby she might try to poach Agnieszka back. But that surely is being absurdly paranoiac. Agnieszka is an au pair; Babs can afford a pukkah nanny. But Hattie can see that if she is to offer proper advice to Babs she will have to work hard at being impartial, and not let self-interest stand in the way of duty to a friend. 'Oh Babs!' she says. 'That's a terrible decision to have to make. You've got to be sure that's what you really want to do.' She is pleased with her own moral rectitude.

Hattie has been out with Martyn to buy a ring. Now she is working they can afford one. Not an engagement ring, not a wedding ring – she gets furious when Martyn suggests it – just a ring to celebrate the fact that her hands are white and smooth and no longer red with housework and eczema-pitted from washing-up liquid. The ring is perfectly simple, costs about £100, and goes upon the middle finger of her right hand. Her promotion hasn't come through: Neil says he has to get the paperwork together, but Hattie need have no worries it's on its way.

That evening, when Agnieszka is out at classes, Hattie notices an unusual stamp on some wrapping paper which has been torn up and thrown in the bin. It's the rather inadequate packaging which went around the squashed box of choco-late prunes. The stamp is large, pretty and unusual. A rim of flowers surrounds a painting of an old monastery. 'UKRAINA', it says.

Hattie puts the paper back where she found it. Well, she thinks, Aurek could have gone on holiday to the Ukraine. A busman's holiday perhaps. Where exactly is the Ukraine? She is not sure. She looks it up on the Internet. No, it is not in the European Union. Warsaw's just a little way from the Ukrainian border. The bus route might even take Aurek daily from one nation to the next, though there would be an annoying wait at the border. Or perhaps they just let buses through automatically? It's not as if anyone was at war. Aurek, giver of prunes, posted the parcel in one post office rather than another, that's all.

Hattie goes to find the box, and sees that the allegedly 'Polish' chocolate prunes, posted in the Ukraine, come from the Czech Republic anyway. Supposing Agnieszka is lying when she says she comes from Poland? What difference does it make? Well, if she was born in the Ukraine she will have to have a visa. Does Agnieszka have a visa? Possibly not. Possibly Agnieszka is an illegal immigrant. Does she care? It would not be good for Martyn's political career should the matter ever come to public attention. But perhaps it won't, and in the meanwhile Kitty's growing curls down the back of her neck. Miniature reddish ringlets. She will have Hattie's hair.

Hattie decides, no, she does not care. Agnieszka's national status is Agnieszka's business. No, she won't tell Martyn. What you don't know you can't mind. If she hadn't seen the stamp she wouldn't now be worrying about these imponderables. Rewind, rewind, rewind, erase, delete.

Meanwhile, in Martyn's dreams Agnieszka looks less of an abstract version of the household help, and more and more like the real Agnieszka. It doesn't stop there. One night she comes towards the bed where he lies with Hattie. She wears no clothes. Her little breasts bounce. She picks up the ring which Hattie takes off before she goes to bed and slips it on her own finger. Even in his dream he can tell it is the third finger of the left hand. His mother wore a wedding band, his father did not. His father thought rings for men were dangerous, they might catch in machinery. His father had known it happen and the firm concerned would not pay compensation. They claimed if employees wore rings it was at their own risk, and the Courts backed them up. Martyn realises he is awake again. What is the matter with him? He turns towards Hattie and strokes her thigh and she sighs and almost without waking opens up for him. It is Hattie he loves, and after Hattie, Kitty. The rest is nothing.

They have to be quiet, because Agnieszka is just the other side of the wall, but they're used to that.

Frances In Love

Something quite extraordinary and unexpected has happened. I am in love. It is absurd and ridiculous and to the young will even seem rather revolting, but nevertheless it has happened. All the old signs are there, the sense that you are breathing some different, fresher air, that the trees and the leaves and the clouds are involved in some cosmic, hilarious game which suddenly includes you, the intimation of infinite possibility, the awareness that you are only fully alive in the loved one's company – trust and doubt, fear and conviction, all mixed up together and exhilarating. It would be pathetic if it wasn't mutual. But it is.

Not that the word 'love' has passed between us: it is too easy a word, and wrongly used so much of the time. He hasn't said so, I haven't said so, we both just know it. He seems to assume I will live with him for the rest of our lives. He doesn't know how old I am: he has not asked and I haven't told him. Nor do I have any idea how old he is. It seems irrelevant. He is grizzled, like some bear, that I do know. He comes from Canada, also like a bear. He is not like anyone else. He is larger, for one thing. Six foot four, I would imagine and wide with it. He lumbers. He fills my small gallery with his presence. I am afraid if he moves something will break. I have some nice spun glass pieces on a display table, and they are fragile. Sebastian started out at six foot but age and trouble have taken away two inches at least. I am five foot four and on a different scale from him, so I don't think the detail of me is particularly noticeable to this bear, which is probably helpful.

His name is Patrick. He is of Irish extraction. He emigrated to Vancouver in the fifties. He made a fortune logging in Canada. He owned and destroyed probably as many trees as Susan could see stars when she looked through her wrongly focused telescope in those last days in New Zealand, while Serena studied, and I played childishly with my private parts and longed for this man of all men, it now becomes clear.

He tells me he lives in a log cabin but I think he probably overplays its loggishness. He also seems to have a palace in Italy which houses lost children. I think he feels bad about all the trees he has cut down, and now that he is bored with the business, and anyway the government is taking too much interest, he tries to make amends, but he would not dream of saying so. He is not the kind to talk about his feelings or expect too much respect for them. They are his own: he will put up with them.

He came into my gallery in Bath at eleven o'clock on Tuesday morning and tried to buy it. Not just the paintings but everything, buildings, fittings, fixtures, goodwill and all. He said he was bored with trees, nature's handiwork, and wanted to look at paintings, man's handiwork. And woman's too, he added, looking at me sideways in case I was a feminist sensitive. He was quick, very quick. He knew what went on in the world.

He liked Bath: a noble city. If he bought he would hang the paintings of local artists for free. I am reminded of Sally Ann Emberley and her film producer and how everyone laughed. Perhaps the world has grown up and no one will laugh.

He proposes to buy me out lock stock and barrel for £550,000. That would certainly get Sebastian and me out of trouble. He was very precise as to the sum. It was just about its market value: he was giving nothing away. He sat there in my gallery and made these extraordinary propositions, and broke the chair he was sitting on. It was a ridiculous spindly thing.

We talked about our life and loves and fortunes through lunch and through tea and on to supper time when he looked at his watch at seven o'clock and said it was late and he would be back in the morning. I locked up and he helped with the grille and he walked me to the door of the Royal Crescent Hotel where he was staying and sent me home in a taxi. In a perfect world he would have seen me home but it is not a perfect world: he sent me home.

I told myself the man's mad, and who could live with such a talkative man, and anyway I was Penelope to Sebastian's Ulysses.

He was there when I opened up, soon after ten. He said I was ten minutes late and that was no way to run a business, he'd better buy it from me and then I could stroll in whenever I liked. I said no. He went on talking until eleven o'clock, twenty-four hours after we'd first set eyes on each other, when he said 'that's enough talk' and stopped and we just sat there and I pottered and saw a few customers, none of whom bought anything, and he watched me and occasionally smiled and I thought who could live with such a silent man? Already we had assumed that 'living with' was an option.

He had been married once: she had died. That was twelve years ago to the day. That, he thought, was appropriate mourning time after a marriage of thirty-two years. This man made instant decisions. 'This is the day!' and it was. 'The tree will fall that way!' he'd cry and point and they'd jump and it would, and just as well or they'd all be dead. That I suppose is the art of successful logging. That and jumping from trunk to trunk as the logs tumble down the river to the port. He had a limp in one leg and a crook in his arm from being crushed between floating tree trunks.

And he'd walked into this small art gallery in Bath and seen a woman with white hair in a Pre-Raphaelite cloud, and a good figure, and gauzy scarves, and just assumed she had been sent to join his life because the time was ripe. Why me? I have no idea. Were we *meant*?

Something else extraordinary. You know I said he was of Irish extraction. He told me about his brother Curran who had died in a pub brawl way back. He'd been a great musician with bow and fiddle. Patrick himself had gone off to Vancouver and made a fortune. The brother had gone to

170

London and sung in the Underground, Charing Cross Station mostly, and died. A strange world, he said.

Yes, I said, a strange world, and I was so frightened I refused to see this Patrick the next day or the next or the next. I cannot bear the patterns life makes, so that nothing is ever over. Do I have to tell Lallie she has an uncle? 'I don't think I can find the time to see him,' is all she'd say. 'I have a concert.' She moves in this world of liquid sound: it doesn't seem to have much to do with the rest of us.

I take it back. I am not in love. I have been shocked back into sanity. I am Sebastian's wife and that is how I will stay. I am so sorry, everyone.

I did take his card, though, as I sent him on his way.

Agnieszka's Passport

Christmas has come and gone. There were twenty-three round Serena and Cranmer's table; crackers, jokes, and gifts around the Christmas tree, and every bed and sofa in the house occupied. Martyn feels less out of place than once he did. He'd begun by finding Hattie's family noisy, self-opinionated, socially suspect and wholly out of touch with reality. Serena's money has cushioned the lot of them and made them soft. Now he feels he is one of them: he would like to be married and have more children.

He would like to have a family wedding with Hattie in a white dress, and speeches, but he can see this is out of the question. Want must be his master, as his mother was fond of saying. '*Want this, want that. Want must be your master.*' Martyn's mother came from a Catholic background, and Martyn's father was an atheist and went to his own wedding in a state of protest, refusing to join in the prayers, kneel or sing the hymns, though putting on the bride's ring and allowing himself to be blessed. So the Arkwright family story goes.

Martyn is staying late at the office. It's a Friday night. This month's issue of *Devolution* goes to press in a couple of hours. He is re-writing a colleague's article on Europe. There is no time to ask the colleague, Toby Holliday, to do it himself. Toby is one of those writers who deliver at the very last moment and then switch off their mobiles in case they are asked for re-writes. If the article goes to press with unapproved alterations Toby will storm about and shout and demand that someone's balls become garters. In this case it will be Martyn's balls, but Martyn has no choice, the responsibility rests with him: Harold has gone on a two-week 'sabbatical'. Toby's piece is a eulogy to the New Europe, which is fine – *Devolution* is pro-Europe in word, thought and spirit – but needs to be done with more subtlety or the text just becomes laughable. Martyn is racing through the lines, changing words like 'total' to 'somewhat', 'fabulous' to 'pleasing' and 'triumph' to 'positive outcome'.

Martyn calls home to say he will be late and Agnieszka answers with her soft familiar slightly exotic, slightly accented voice. Whenever he hears it he thinks of the muscles working beneath the soft thin skin of her belly, and has to blot the image out. No, Hattie isn't home yet and Agnieszka needs to get to her English class. Kitty is bathed, in bed and asleep. But of course she'll stay until someone gets back. Luckily he hears Hattie come in to the house with her normal 'Oh my God, am I late again?' and can get back to his work with a clear conscience. 'Europe's post-Christian society' becomes 'Europe's multi-faith community'.

If Harold would only put the paperwork in hand to get him some more money – Martyn is after all effectively doing Harold's job – they could afford to let Agnieszka go. The trouble with Agnieszka is that she's always so much *there*. He likes her to be there in one way, but he also doesn't like the shock of pleasure when he hears her voice. He is confused. He really would like to be alone with Hattie sometimes. And of course with Kitty. But if Hattie not Agnieszka were to look after Kitty, Kitty would soon stop being a contented, non-crying, routine-adapted baby and turn into the bundle of demands and reproaches of the kind his friends spawn, and there would be no domestic peace anyway, and Hattie would become argumentative and mean again. So Agnieszka will have to stay.

Meanwhile, at home in Pentridge Road, Agnieszka has left for class wearing Hattie's dress, the red silk one which now sits too tightly on Hattie's hips but looks really good on Agnieszka. Martyn won't be back for an hour or so. Kitty is sleeping soundly. The baby likes her new stroller and it can be made really safe against wind and weather by a transparent plastic screen; this is just as well. Agnieszka thinks that rain needs to be ignored, and babies need fresh air and that changes of temperature do no harm. The winter is setting in and Hattie's instinct is to curl up under duvets and turn the central heating high, but Agnieszka thinks it's healthier to put on an extra layer of clothes and allow the body to adapt to the weather, rather than trying to adapt the weather to the baby.

The house is quiet and still, and very neat. Even the pot plants seem to have been trained to grow straight: so many offshoots this side, so many that. Hattie goes into Agnieszka's room. Kitty is lying on her back in the cot, asleep, bathed, pink and clean, little arms flung upwards in trust. Hattie decides to look for Agnieszka's passport. She wants to *know*, exactly what she is not sure, but she wants to *know*.

It is not in the drawer of the bedside table, not in the chest of drawers, not in the plastic folder marked 'Documents' – which mostly has membership of belly-dancing clubs and store loyalty cards and application forms for English classes folded neatly inside – it is under the mattress. Well, you're not going to lose it there, are you, especially if you're the one who turns the mattress.

It's a dark red document rather larger than the neat European one, positively handsome and proud, with a gold saltire crossing through the cover and words in Cyrillic script. Hattie opens it, and there is a photograph of Agnieszka, quiet and demure. What it reveals about her Hattie cannot say because she does not read Cyrillic script. She knows enough to tell that this is not a Polish passport but somewhere further east, outside the European Community. She imagines it will be the Ukraine, because of the stamp on the packet of chocolate prunes. She sees nothing that looks like an English stamp inside the document, that might go with a visa or work permit.

Hattie decides it's of no account. Hattie is on the side of the dispossessed, of asylum seekers, of victims everywhere. It was how she was brought up. She will defend Agnieszka to the death, or certainly from the Immigration Office. She knows Martyn will too, though she won't tell him about the passport, as she didn't about the Ukrainian stamp. He might start making a fuss. It is simply unfair that to be born five miles the wrong side of a certain border – it could be as little as a yard – can make a difference to where a person works or lives. She slides the passport back under Agnieszka's mattress and makes herself a cup of really strong, really black coffee. Agnieszka doesn't approve of coffee because of the caffeine but Hattie thinks she will treat herself. It is really nice to have the house to herself.

Then the phone rings and her peace is shattered. It's Babs in a state of hysteria. What shall she do? To terminate or not to terminate? that is the question. Babs is thirty-nine. If she doesn't have this baby perhaps she can never get pregnant again.

'You didn't have much trouble this time,' says Hattie.
'But that was an illicit affair,' says Babs, and she tells Hattie that women are much more likely to get pregnant if they're not meant to be doing it. Something to do with excitement and emotional upset and eggs dropping down the Fallopian tube. It's why rape victims get pregnant more than the national average for reproductive intercourse.
'That may be too much information,' says Hattie.

Babs complains that Hattie is very bad at thinking about what she doesn't want to think about, and that the likelihood of eggs dropping when she's with Alastair is rather small. She's very fond of him, he'll make an excellent father – but he's no egg dropper, and he's bound to want her to stay home with the baby and proper help is so hard to find. Then Babs asks Hattie how she is getting on with Agnieszka and Hattie says just fine. Babs says, 'Of course I may have imagined all that stuff about her playing footsie with Alastair under the table,

I was in such a state at the time. Have you noticed how easy it is to suspect others of doing what one's doing oneself?'

'What, playing footsie with your lover under the table?'

'It did happen once or twice,' Babs admits. 'While Tavish was editing the film. Alastair asked him round and it would have looked suspicious for me to turn him away. That was why Alastair got so upset. His own dinner table, that sort of thing. But he's all right now. And I do owe the poor man something.'

'Probably you do,' says Hattie. She can tell which way Babs's mind is going. If she does have the baby she will try to bribe Agnieszka to come to her. Babs has unlimited money and a splendid house. Hattie hopes Agnieszka would be loyal, but you never know. So she just says Babs had lots of time to think about it, and Babs says, well, no, at three months the soul comes in and then it's too late, after that it's murder.

'I beg your pardon?' asks Hattie, surprised.

'The doctrine of ensoulment,' says Babs. 'I was brought up a Catholic and the soul comes in at three months. President Bush says it comes in at conception so there can't be any stem cell research, but I don't think that's true. Alastair thinks Bush is right, and we've had terrible rows about it. So whatever's done must be done secretly. You don't have to have a paternal consent form these days, do you?'

'I don't know,' says Hattie. 'But if Alastair thinks it's his and asks for a DNA test and goes to the Courts to stop you I daresay he could.'

'Don't go there,' says Babs and Hattie agrees it's best not to. Babs clicks off.

Hattie goes and looks at the sleeping Kitty. She thinks of Wanda and Lallie and Frances and Serena and it seems a great shame to cut off a branch from the tree of life, Agnieszka or not. She calls Babs back.

'Babs,' says Hattie bravely, 'I think you should go ahead and have the baby.'
Babs fails to realise the degree of self-sacrifice in Hattie's decision.
'It's all very well for you,' says Babs. 'All that childbirth stuff's behind you and you have Agnieszka, and you never worried about clothes or how they looked. I can't talk now. Alastair has just come in.'

Hattie hears Babs welcoming Alastair home, with love and effusion.

Animals

While Hattie and Martyn were at work one day, Agnieszka heard something scratching and miaowing at the front door and opened it to a kitten. Now the family of four, Hattie, Martyn, Kitty and Agnieszka, has another member, Silvie. Hattie calls Serena, excited and pleased.

'Somehow it closes our family up from beneath,' she says. 'Now there's someone younger than Kitty. I've always wanted a cat. It's so pretty and funny and hides and springs out at you, bounces on all fours in the air as if it thought it was a lamb, and I'll swear it makes jokes.'

Serena remarks that spare stray kittens used to be a commonplace but what with the animal centres providing free neutering they have become quite a rarity in London. She hopes they've put cards in newsagents' windows to the effect that a kitten has been found and Hattie says actually not. Agnieszka loves it so. Agnieszka had a cat like that back in Krakow and it makes her feel at home.

Serena calls me up to report the conversation with Hattie. 'I'm really surprised, Frances,' she says. 'Once Martyn and

Hattie wouldn't have dreamt of not at least *trying* to find the rightful owner, no matter how cutesy the creature was. What's happening to them?'

'Keeping the au pair happy,' I say, 'has become one of their major concerns. All morality vanishes.'

I ask Serena what kind of kitten it is, and when she says from what she gathers it has long silvery hair, a flat snub nose, a squashed-up face and big round orange eyes, I say, 'That's a Persian and they're expensive. What's more, they use litter trays not the back garden, they leave hairs everywhere, they're not very bright and will probably give Kitty asthma. A pity they called Kitty what they did, in the circumstances. Didn't they think that one day they might want a cat?'

I point out that confusion between maid and mistress is bad enough but now there will be confusion between child and pet as well. Those coming to the house for the first time will assume Sylvie is the child and Kitty is the animal. I warm to my theme.

Kitty will no longer wake to birdsong, I say, just the yowling of cats in the dank backyards of Pentridge Road. I am really quite cross. I am a dog person. I also know quite a lot about cats. Hammertoes' mother bred Persians. Going to visit was an ordeal because of the smell, and the hairs, and the sense of living amongst aliens if there were more than three of the creatures in the room at any one time. Which there would be, and in various stages of pregnancy and moult. The only time I really warmed to Hammertoes was when he once said to me sadly of his mother, 'She loved her cats more than me,' and I had that rush of concern

180

common to wives, when they want to make up to their husbands all the bad things that ever happened to them, and which almost amounts to love. But it didn't last long enough, I'm afraid. It wasn't true love. I just made more bad, or baddish, things happen to him. He grew depressed after I left and no one wanted his scripts.

I call Hattie on Saturday morning and say, 'I hear you've got a cat,' and she can tell from the sound of my voice I am not pleased. 'Don't give me a hard time, Great-Nan,' she says. 'It's only a kitten. She's so lovely and such fun, and Kitty adores her. I know all that stupid stuff about song-birds and eye disease but she's very healthy and there aren't any birds round here anyway.'

I think about Sebastian, where no birds sing, and marvel at how people make prisons for themselves when there's really no need.

'Agnieszka says she's about three months old,' says Hattie, 'which is just right for a new kitten. We've taken her to the vet and she's had all her jabs, and Agnieszka combs her every day.' I hope she is trying to reassure herself or me, but decide it's just me.
'And there wasn't a notice up in the vet's about a lost Persian kitten?' I ask.
'No,' says Hattie flatly.
'So long as Agnieszka stays,' I say, 'it won't be too bad. But what happens if she goes on holiday, or leaves, or starts her belly-dancing school or her midwifery course?'
'I think Agnieszka is very happy with us,' says Hattie. 'She says we're the kind of family she never had.'

'Isn't she supposed to have a husband hiding somewhere, and a mother and a sick sister?'

'I don't know why you're so against poor Agnieszka,' says Hattie. 'There were communication problems when she first came to us – the husband isn't a husband but a boyfriend, and that sort of thing, and he's a bus driver as well as a scriptwriter, and he's coming over here to live as soon as he's sold his script which means Agnieszka can go on working for us for ages. You know what selling scripts is like. Kitty will be old before that happens.'

'Easier in London than Krakow, I imagine,' I say.

'As for the mother and the sister, they've emigrated to Australia,' says Hattie. 'Things don't stay static in the outside world,' she adds, suggesting (perhaps) that I'm too old ever to be au fait with what goes on.

'Did you meet the boyfriend when he came over for Christmas?' I ask.

'No,' says Hattie, 'because he missed his flight, there was a bomb at Heathrow and flights were cancelled. We'd gone down to Serena's by the time he turned up. And he left before we got back.'

'The busman's holiday being over. The friend in Neasden with the carrots goes on being real, however,' I say.

'She doesn't grow carrots any more,' says Hattie. 'There is such a thing as the rotation of crops. The ground needs a rest, and she doesn't believe in artificial fertilisers.'

'Carrot fly can be quite a problem,' I say, 'especially if you don't like to use insecticides.'

I don't know why I am hopping mad with her, but I am. Then she says she has to go, Agnieszka is putting lunch on the table. It's the nearest I've ever got to actually having a row with her, and I couldn't for the life of me tell you what it was about.

I phone Serena. She suggests I come over for lunch. I say I can't because I'm in the gallery, and she's a forty-minute drive away. She asks how many customers I have had in today, and I say only two and they were 'just looking' – times are quiet – but one punter is definitely in the market for a William Bates print at £750 and will decide tomorrow. Serena says put a note in the window saying '*Gone to Lunch*', which is nothing but the truth, and come on over, so I do. Most of my clients are regulars, and have my mobile number anyway.

Serena is better at animals than me. After she moved to Wiltshire with George the family had a smallholding. They kept Soay sheep – seven of them, small, neat, deer-like creatures whose native habitat was the Scottish Highlands. They had an elaborate family structure – top ram, second ram, favourite wife, second, third and fourth wives, grandmother. They lived in the acre field next to the farmhouse and stood upon a mini Primrose Hill in the middle of the field, made from grassed-over stone rubble from old farm buildings and soil from where space was made for the underground septic tank. Top ram would stand proudly on the summit, the others ranged behind. Top ram had impressive, strong and curly horns; second ram's were feebler and smaller as befitted his lack of status; first wife preened and primped, second, third and fourth sulked; grandmother was allowed to tag along.

After that Serena and George accumulated geese, hens and ducks, and at one time fattened and ate – with great reluctance – two pigs. They had three dogs and two cats and at one time tropical fish. When they needed to go away together, I would be asked to come and live in and 'look after the animals' and such children as were still at home. And I did, but never with great enthusiasm.

Serena had a late baby with George just after they moved out of London to the country: it was if the house was waiting to be filled. The new baby cemented the relationship all right – but the cement was not necessarily what George wanted. He'd rather have freedom and flexibility. He was fifty-five by then and had had enough of children. She was forty-six. She asked her doctor whether it was safe to have so late a baby, and he said his mother had been forty-eight when he was born and age had nothing to do with anything. So that was that.

Like so many city dwellers in the panicky early seventies, George had wanted to get out of the city – the nuclear threat was building. OPEC had got its act together, the price of petrol was approaching 50 pence a gallon, there'd been a three-day week – during the course of which productivity paradoxically increased – and a firemen's strike – again, the number of fires reported was cut by a third – and rumour had it that ration books were being printed.

And as Serena had observed to George's fury, in Harrods' hosiery department there were only two shades of tights on sale. Mention of Harrods always infuriated George, as it does Martyn today. Same fury, against the capitalist evil, against sumptuary sin. The wish was to be associated with the wretched of the earth not the rich and powerful. A Harrods bag was seen as an offence against humanity, and

Serena had quite wilfully got herself a Harrods account card. Hattie, having more conscience than Serena, would not dream of owning such a thing, even if her credit rating allowed her to.

George had fled to the countryside, to Grovewood, a farmhouse, still with its old barns and chimneys as in a child's drawing, creepered and rose-covered, an ideal home set amidst open fields. Serena had followed him. It made little difference to her whether the desk she wrote upon was in the town or in the country. But it was nice if it was not whipped from under her pen and sold to a stranger. That was less likely to happen now. George wanted to give up the antique business, live next to nature, own and till his own land, have animals, start painting again – and where George went Serena would go too, without argument. She wrote, and the cheques flowed in.

He had just not expected, any more than she had, to have another baby. It meant for George the end of a peaceful daydream of rural life. Now it was all bottles and breast-feeding and baby chatter and another round of au pairs and household helps. There was Maureen Parks, the seamstress, who came in to turn the sheets sides to middle, and ended up dressmaking for Serena, as talented as anyone you would find at a Paris *couturier*. There were the country girls, busty and dumpy, Mary, Judith, Anne, Jean – local girls with local foibles, which included pederast boyfriends, kleptomania, narcolepsy – let no one think the countryside is less eventful than the town. That has never been my experience, nor Serena's. She and I both live in small towns now, not open countryside. This way you get a kind of median existence, the synergy of boredom and too-much-happening divided, flickering from one to the other.

None of the Grovewood animals were truly sought after: no one went out of their way to assemble them – they just turned up, like Sylvie. Animals are often rendered homeless – owners fall ill, die, get put in prison, run out of money, run off – and what happens next is usually the blow to the head, the bag in the river, unless soft-hearted people like Serena and George come along. The old lady who owned the Soay sheep died; a local farmer rounded them up – no easy matter: Soays like to run, and run fast – and dumped them in the Grovewood field, with a brief instruction as to how they were to be fed. They needed sheep-feed daily, and salt licks.

The bustling hen-house started with two miserable hens rescued from a battery farm – sold off to passers-by as a profitable alternative to slaughtering. They lived at first in the back of the garden shed, terrified of light, suffering from agoraphobia, but eventually ventured out, and became brave, bold and bad-tempered, as if they were feminists trying to make up for their years of oppression. George brought in a cockerel, to return them to their natural state, and sure enough they turned into little bustling chirpy broody things, who quickly produced a new race of chicks. So a proper formal hen-house had to be built. Then it seemed only sensible to add extensions for unwanted geese, found wandering, or the ducks who just flew into the pond one day, and stayed.

Poor little Sylvie, I must not be so resentful of her. I wouldn't mind a puppy, but Hugo wouldn't like it. Serena has no animals at all now she's with Cranmer. Cats make him sneeze: dogs are a millstone. He is quite right. But ties, Serena argues, are a good thing. After the children have grown there has to be some shape to the day: animals provide it. Dusk comes, and the poultry has to be bribed or cajoled into the hen house for fear of the fox: food has to be put out in rain, hail or blizzard. The animal feed we fetched in sacks from the warehouse through the eighties, and put out morning and evening in the troughs, we later found out was foul stuff indeed. We thought it was innocent grain meal, but it turned out to be laced with ground-up animal corpses.

A new regulation came into force. Sheep had by law to be dipped once a year: thoroughly doused, heads under and all, in a strange dark-metallic, bluey-green liquid provided in big cans by the Ministry of Agriculture, to prevent scabies and parasites. We couldn't easily herd our half-wild creatures into a truck, to take them down to the official dipping centre, so we doused them ourselves. That is to say George dug a pit, lined it with concrete, poured in the mixture, got friends and family to catch the sheep one by one – four people and one dog to do each – and bring it to George who would hurl it into the pit and push its head under with a pole. There was a lot of splashing and shouting and cheering and the sheep would emerge shaking and furious.

We would come over from twenty miles away, Sebastian and I, to help with the catching. George wore thick rubber gloves, but took very little notice of the skull and crossbones painted in red and black on all sides of the cans. He did not believe officialdom ever knew its arse from its elbow, and he was more right than we believed in those blithe days. The silvery-blue pool was almost neat organophosphates: it lay open to birds and bees, foxes and voles, until George got round to draining it and hosing it out into the water-table.

Serena sometimes claims that it was contact OPs which drove George mad, damaged his heart, rendered him paranoiac, so that she his own wife became a focus of hatred not love and ate away into his moral being, so that finally he chose a mistress over her. I am not so sure. He was fairly difficult even before the OPs got him, though I daresay they didn't help.

I sometimes dream of that oily pool in the field at Grovewood, silky, dangerous and still, surrounded by green fronds, nettles and cow-parsley. Hattie dreams of it too, but at least I never let her go near it. I was responsible enough for that.

The Christening

Colleen's baby Deborah is christened. Hattie calls me and reports on the ceremony. 'It was so pretty,' she says. 'The priest held a candle and the baby watched it: its little face glowed. I'd forgotten how small really little babies are: just tiny scraps of life. Kitty's getting so heavy and sturdy.'

'Martyn went with you to a christening?' I ask, surprised.

'Yes, he did,' she says, as if this change in his habits was of no account. 'Agnieszka said Colleen's baby was too small: the water from the font would be icy cold, but for once she was wrong. The baby didn't cry one bit.'

'Perhaps someone boiled a kettle in the vestry and added that,' I say, wondering why Agnieszka had gone along too. But perhaps just to push Kitty in her stroller.

'That doesn't sound very blessed,' says Hattie, shocked. Atheists are easily shocked when the religion of others is at stake.

'I daresay it's the thought that counts,' I say. 'Did Agnieszka enjoy the ceremony?'

'I think so. Kitty did. She gazed at the candle as if it were meant for her. But then Agnieszka was holding her. If it's me she just wriggles and dickers.'

'I expect you still smell of mother's milk,' I say, 'and she wants to get at it.'

'I don't want to hear that, Gran,' she says.

I am in her good books. Promoted from Great-Nan! She's happier now she's back at work. She doesn't feel the need to be mean any more. When Sebastian gets out I wonder if he will be called Great-Grandpapa, as a special treat – a final acceptance of him into the family after twenty years – or at least Great-Grandpa, and I certainly hope not Great-Gramps.

I am still reeling from the advent and disappearance of Patrick from my life. I may not have been giving my granddaughter the full attention she needed. More warning bells should have sounded in my head at what she told me next; not that I suppose Hattie would have taken any notice.

'Agnieszka did something so strange and wonderful,' Hattie says. 'She took a piece of fern from the vase of flowers, and washed its stalk carefully and pinned it to Kitty's dress before we went along. It's an old Polish custom. It signifies rebirth.'

'But it wasn't Kitty that was being christened,' I say. 'It was your friend's baby.'

'I thought it was charming, and so did Martyn.' Martyn thought it was charming: he who so loathes superstition?

But Serena points out to me later that people who loathe things a lot can suddenly find they love the very same things a lot. It is not necessarily undue influence from Agnieszka. More likely it is simply a mild occurrence of a process Jung

called enantiodromia. It is St Paul on the road to Damascus
when a light falls from Heaven and the persecutor suddenly
becomes the Christian. We wonder if Martyn the severe
rationalist will turn into Martyn the new-age guru and
laugh and decide it is unlikely, but he will have to be
watched.

Hattie chatters on about the christening and Father
Flanahan, who was married: I said I didn't know priests
could be married and she says yes, if say they're married
Church of England priests who convert to Catholicism on
matters of principle – like the women-priests issue – they
can keep their wives. She, Martyn and Agnieszka and
Father Flanahan had a conversation about this outside the
church, after the ceremony. Martyn said he found all this
a tiny bit hypocritical, but Father Flanahan didn't seem to
mind.

'He seemed glad to talk about it,' says Hattie. 'How he
talked and talked, and Agnieszka said she'd like to come
along on Sunday mornings to Mass, if that was okay with
us. We said, of course. What else could we say? You can't
stand between people and their religion, can you, not even
if you didn't know they had any, and had been brought up
in a Communist country?'
'No,' I say. 'Not at the expense of the ironing.'
'The funniest thing happened,' says Hattie. 'Father Flanahan
asked Agnieszka when she and Martyn were going to bring
the baby down for a proper christening. He'd just assumed
she was the mother, because she was holding her.'
'But you put him right?' I ask, and Hattie says, well actually no, it had all been rather awkward, as well as funny.

'I think Martyn was a bit freaked by it. He said to Father Flanahan probably the more married priests in the Church the better, because there'd be fewer bishops abusing little boys, and I had to hurry him away.'

Hurrying Men Away

If Serena kicks Cranmer under the table to stop him saying the wrong thing, when she thinks he's on the point of making some social gaffe, or they've stayed too late, or he's totally ignoring some plain woman on the other side of the table, he just asks loudly why she's kicking him under the table. So she's given up, and when it comes to it the gaffe is usually less than she assumed.

Cranmer is younger than Serena by a couple of decades, and our generation's convention that you never discussed religion or politics over dinner is out of date and dull. What has replaced it is a new way of avoiding social embarrassment: so long as people of the same religious and political views gather together with others of like mind, and outsiders are kept out, why then existing opinions will be reinforced and social discourse will be agreeable. Guests can discuss anything over polenta or venison soup without fear of any unpleasantness.

You do have to be more careful, of course, who you invite with whom: the host and hostess can be relied upon to grit their teeth and put up with other people's views, but the same cannot be said for guests. All right for Babs and Hattie to be thick as thieves at the office, and Hattie has met Alastair on occasion, in his home, and Babs has met Martyn when he called by, but a dinner *ensemble* would be out of the question. Alastair's on the right and Martyn's on the left, and never the twain should meet. They have no desire to change their point of view.

Cranmer's also very much to the right in politics and I think Serena is drifting there too. She says reason is on his side, if not sentiment. I stay with the artists, who never notice anything that's going on anyway, but by their very nature are on the left, and believe in the brotherhood of man and the abolition of Third World Debt. Who even when they are shut up in prison like Sebastian, with murderers, rapists and con men, who express themselves only through oaths, shouts and threats – *'who are you looking at then?'* – still believe that human nature is innately good.

On the whole, Serena maintains, women long for everything in the social and family world to be nice, for everyone to get along and love one another, and then surely all will be well. It's catching: in the new feminised world men begin to feel the same. At Business School the focus is on elegant win-win strategies: zero-sum games are out of date. Harold will somehow forget the papers that deal with Martyn's new post, but will speak highly and publicly of his abilities. Hattie hasn't yet actually got her rise, though no one says an unkind word and she is obviously promoted in terms of what she's responsible for. Babs is lost in an emotional muddle, but still hoping to upset no one. Only Hilary manages a nasty thrust or two, and she's of the old world.

Serena complains that aspiring writers these days get rave rejections: half a page enthusing about the submitted manuscript and only then the: 'But I'm sorry, just not for us.' Just let's all get along and empathise with others, and upset no one or it will end in the Twin Towers. Martyn gets in his dig about the bishops, and Hattie has to hurry him away. She too likes things to be nice.

In my early years I did little hurrying men away. They stayed, I went. It was the same with Serena, as she passed from home to home and bed to bed, either because we had been thrown out or couldn't bear to stay. Longer than a weekend's residence was unusual. Someone's wife or permanent girlfriend was always coming home: or we had deadlines to meet, children to collect. Artists who painted me would want me to stay until the portrait was finished, but after that they moved on briskly to the next subject: and I'd pack up and go, out of the bed and onto the bare splintery boards of some studio floor, with its battered kelim rugs and oil-paint smudges; and the man still lying in the unkempt, often none too clean bed, his head already filled with visions of beauty other than mine.

'In the beginning I used to tot up the number of men I'd slept with,' Serena once said to me, 'until I grew ashamed, and began to forget the names. I used to think you did not know what a man was like until you had been to bed with him, but I soon came to realise you'd never get to know him anyway, so that should not enter into your calculations. Not that there was ever much calculation: lust and love were motivation enough: alcohol loosened restraint – self interest did not enter in.'

We agreed that Wanda, though so frugal sexually herself –
going, we reckoned, at least fifty years without a man, from
her forty-fourth year to her ninety-fourth – had somehow
given us the idea that if a man wanted sex it was unkind
and mean-spirited not to let him have it. And that to make
emotional demands upon a man was somehow demeaning.
You must not manipulate others. You must go along with
what they want, because they probably know best and
anyway you have better things to think about.

Wanda spent years writing a book in tiny, tiny handwriting
about the nature of the aesthetic experience and its relation
to religion. My niece has it now, the papers yellowed and the
edges ragged, tied up in a bundle with old-fashioned string,
in a box under her bed. Perhaps someone one day will have
the courage to take it out and inspect it. It may contain the
world's wisdom, who is to say? I would not be surprised.

We talk about driving. Serena is a nervous driver and has
been since her divorce from George. When she lost her faith
in the destiny which had brought them together she also
lost her faith that she would never be involved in a traffic
accident. She began clipping kerbs and not knowing when
to overtake. She has become an even more nervous passenger
than driver. Her first husband's driving techniques come back
to assault her as trauma in her later years – he liked to
frighten other drivers by overtaking on bends in his souped-
up little Ford Popular, and teach others not to tailgate by
slamming on the brakes.

Serena relates how George once went down a motorway at
120 miles an hour, with Cranmer following in the car behind.

She was Cranmer's passenger. At the time she thought George was trying to compete with Cranmer as a rival: now she thinks George was simply trying to get away from her, not be associated with her, source of his guilt, the well-known writer and the publicity that went with her. The fact was that George had become so reluctant to be seen in public with her that 120mph was nothing. She is becoming distressed, as we still do when she talks about George, and our conversation is fifteen years on after that particular motorway incident.

I veer the subject round to less painful topics. We talk a bit about how if you ask men not to go so fast they go faster, especially if you are married to them. You remind them of their mothers, with their '*don't do that, darling!*' I drive with easy confidence, except in London, where I keep looking in my back mirror, as country drivers do, and am terrified and confused by what I see behind me. How to make sense of all of that stirring, heaving traffic, with no one's bonnets pointing in the same direction? Outside London it's just fine: you sit in the driver's seat and go, or sit in the passenger seat and hope the driver doesn't ask you to navigate.

We agree that men travel fast and nervously towards any social engagement, and more slowly on the way back. They head out as into battle, while the women prefer to appear on the step composed and unflushed, as at a Victory Ball, with their pulses beating at the normal rate.

We further agree that Hattie and Martyn's determination not to own a car for the sake of the planet shows their nice natures but not necessarily their common sense. They have worked out that it is cheaper to take taxis than to own a car, but the inhibition against taking taxis is very great, and until lately, anyway, Martyn's feeling that to take a taxi is prohibited other than in dashes to the hospital or the slower progress to a funeral has been catching. Serena sometimes laments that if only she had all the money she had handed over to taxi drivers, since her psychoanalyst suggested to her that she was entitled to take taxis and she became an almost fanatical hailer of cabs even for the shortest journey, she would be unassailably wealthy.

We talk about Agnieszka at the christening and how the priest mistook her for Kitty's mother and Serena says, 'The au pair's up to something but I don't know what.'
I say that when the maid is mistaken for the mistress it is time for the mistress to ask the maid to leave.
Serena says: 'She may not leave.'

The Boss Comes To Dinner

Well, not exactly dinner, which sounds too candlelit and formal, and the kind of thing they do in Islington, but 'round for a meal'. Harold lives with Debora, who is as right-thinking a person as her partner. She is a contract lawyer for the Welfare Reform Initiative – not a very exciting job but one that is exacting and responsible. They do live in Islington, not through any choosing of their own, they claim, but sheer happenstance. Debora is thinking of having a baby and would like to take a look at Hattie's before she takes the plunge. She has had very little contact with babies to date, and although Harold has two boys from an earlier marriage they are now grown up, and have nothing to do with their father since they took offence at his leaving them when they were sixteen and seventeen.

This estrangement from his children is a source of some distress to Harold, but not a great deal. He views himself and his life with a kind of bemused detachment, as if actually it wasn't much to do with him at all. If Debora wants to have a baby he will go along with it, and try and get it right, and he even plans a newspaper column in which he will chart the course of new fatherhood at a later age. It is not quite right for *Devolution*, though a year or two down the line who can say?

It is a long time since Martyn and Hattie did any entertaining, but now Martyn does not hesitate when Harold says, 'Debora would love to come round and talk babies with Hattie sometime.'
'Why not come round for a meal one evening,' he suggests. 'Tomorrow's good.'

Hattie thinks it is a good idea too, though she is finding work quite exhausting: not that she seems to get much done, just that everything seems to take so long. Pointless emails spawn exponentially, no one ever calls back when they say they will. She and Hilary have been separated, so at least now she has an office of her own, but this means she can no longer keep an eye on her colleague. Once the division between domestic and overseas rights has been blurred, which it was with the Tourette's writer, Hilary could start poaching Hattie's authors. But it's obviously a good idea to have Martyn's boss to dinner, and she can be sure Kitty will look adorable and stay asleep during the meal, and Agnieszka can do the cooking.

Hattie wonders briefly whom to ask as well – Babs and Alastair obviously won't do for political reasons, and she can't ask Neil and his wife until she and Martyn are way up the wage scale and better housed. Being Serena's great-niece might help them up a little on the social ladder but Hattie is not naive enough to think that this will totally compensate for other factors. It is probably more useful to have Martyn's father, the electricians'-strike martyr, as a deceased father-in-law, than Serena as a great-aunt. She could mention her mother Lallie the internationally famous flute player, who is well-enough known in musical circles, but literature and music, like literature and politics, do not necessarily overlap. Moreover, she prefers not to think about her mother if she can help it. It sets off too many complicated emotions. Lallie is too strange and remote a creature to seem like true family: Hattie is closer to Frances.

Besides, Hattie is proud. She would rather be taken at her own valuation: that is to say, not as someone with impressive relatives, but as a lively and competent publishing executive, who may have a child but has a supportive husband and reliable child-care as well and will one day qualify as a fit hostess for Neil and his wife, but not yet. She seems to remember, in any case, that Neil is off again to the Bahamas.

She could ask Frances, but whoever asked their grandmother to parties? And Frances is bound to talk about Sebastian, and her views on drugs will be too naïve for comfort: Frances would probably argue that all controls be taken off all drugs, including cigarettes, and the market let go free. From the sound of Debora she will think weed is okay, but tobacco evil. So Hattie will play safe; it will just be herself and Martyn, and Harold and Debora, and of course Agnieszka.

Hattie really looks forward to meeting Debora and showing off Kitty and is pleased that Martyn invited them, even if he did so without consulting her, and at so little notice. She has a meeting with Hilary at five thirty – Hilary always sets up in-house meetings with women colleagues last thing, allegedly just to catch out those who are hurrying home to children – but Hattie will boldly cancel it, and get back home early.

She will serve *moules marinières* followed by light couscous, then just cheese and biscuits and fruit. Hattie talked it over with Agnieszka in the morning. She will do the *moules marinières* and Agnieszka can do her special chicken couscous with marinated vegetables of which they have all become fond. Agnieszka looks a little doubtful and suggests to Hattie that instead of *moules marinières*, which can be acidy and is rather obvious and takes a long time to prepare and you have to be so careful to discard any shells that are open, she does *coquilles au gratin* – scallops with breadcrumbs, cheese and garlic, put under the grill for just a few minutes – so Hattie can pay proper attention to her guests. Hattie thinks this is a very good idea.

On the day of the dinner party (or shared meal – 'just to talk about babies') Agnieszka does the shopping, and buys fresh scallops from the fish stall in the market. The shellfish are truly beautiful to look at, but Agnieszka has not bought them opened, cleaned and laid out prettily on their shells, with that strange orange segment – actually the scallops' sexual organs – settled in neatly next to the white flesh: but still alive, and in their shells. Agnieszka has done this for the sake of 'freshness'.

Hattie gets back from work at six thirty – Hilary managed to keep her late after all talking about another novel which one of 'her' writers, Marina Faircroft, real name Joan Barnes, had rather oddly sold to several foreign territories herself, so it was a moot point whether the writer was 'hers' or Hattie's. Hattie had no problem with Marina's being Hilary's, but Hilary wanted to talk about it at length, and has called Marina at home, and then everyone had to wait for Marina, who has just run to collect her little girl from Guides, to call back and confirm it was all right by her.

Now Hattie realises that she has to open the live scallops, separate flesh from shell, clean them, and cook them, wondering the while at what point of the process life leaves their little bodies.

Agnieszka is still getting Kitty to bed. She calls Hattie in to read a bedtime story, which Agnieszka chooses, and strikes Kitty as rather mystifying since it is so full of words rather than pictures, and Kitty keeps looking for pictures which aren't even there.

Meanwhile, Agnieszka stirs up a couscous, cooking it in a stock she made earlier in the day, and adding chicken and her marinated vegetables, which Martyn and Hattie know quite well by now, and approve of. Hattie is left with the scallops: how they resist her every attempt to open them: she slips a knife between the flanges of a shell and it opens fractionally only to clamp back down upon the blade of the knife. She tries to get it out by twisting and the knife breaks and she is lucky not be blinded. There is a nasty black pouch which is some kind of gut. The large private parts, or whatever they are, cling to both top and bottom shells. How to separate them? She has to consult the Internet where fortunately some kind person has provided written and illustrated instructions as to how it's best done.

By the time Hattie's cleaned three of the scallops, and there are twenty-two to go, and has not even begun the cooking process, let alone prepared cheese, onion, garlic or breadcrumbs, she hears Harold and Debora come laughing and talking into the house with Martyn. They go through to the living room where Agnieszka, already changed, wearing Hattie's red dress and lipstick, has the table laid and the candles lit and is arranging flowers.

It is Agnieszka who takes Debora in to see the now sleeping Kitty. Little cries of Debora's appreciation come from the open bedroom door, which is nice, but Hattie is pink-faced from frustration and inadequacy. She is still in the jeans and T-shirt she now automatically changes into when she gets home from the office. She'd wanted to receive Harold and Debora looking at her best, not at her worst. It is the pre-Agnieszka days back again, when nothing was ever ready and nothing properly done. Her period has started, which is a relief, because she understands why the office was being so trying, but a nuisance because she has a pain.

'And you must be Agnieszka,' says Debora to Hattie, as she comes by the kitchen. Debora speaks most civilly, as one does to a servant, conscious that they are not in a position to change the nature of their employment and like all vulnerable creatures must be treated well. 'Your fame has spread far and wide. I hear you're a brilliant cook.'

'Actually,' says Hattie, 'I am not Agnieszka. I'm Hattie, Martyn's partner and Kitty's mother. I am so pleased to meet you.' And she offers a red, raw, scratched and fishy hand.

Debora is mortified and offers to help with the scallops: an offer Hattie gratefully accepts. But Debora insists on wearing rubber gloves and is even less effective at opening, knifing and cleaning than is Hattie: the shells snap shut and trap the rubber ends of the fingers, and Debora realises with a little cry of horror that the creatures are still alive.

Family and guests end up without a first course at all, going straight to the couscous, which is delectable so everyone is happy, discussing the extension of the anti-fox-hunting bill to include angling, and what's to be done to avoid cruelty to lobsters, scallops, oysters, mussels, and so on, and at what stage human responsibility for the well-being of simpler organisms stops. All agree that the chicken they are eating, being organic, lived a good life and a full life, just one that was cut short. There is much laughter. But it is some time before Hattie can join in with a good grace: she would like to blame Agnieszka, but can't really since Agnieszka was only following the basic rules of the household, which was always to buy foods as little packaged and pre-prepared as possible.

The talk settles on Debora's dilemma: to have a baby or not to have one? It appears her desire to be a mother derives from a feeling that she owes it to the cosmos to spread their genes: she and Harold together would surely produce a baby which could run the WHO or Oxfam. With Debora's logistic skill and Harold's compassion – even Harold begins to look a little embarrassed – they would surely produce a baby that was both brainy and beautiful; theirs would be a designer baby as nature meant it to be, rather than thanks to tinkering in a laboratory.

'It may not be quite like that,' demurs Hattie. 'What comes out comes out.'
'If it's God's will,' says Agnieszka, 'we have to accept it.' It's about all she has said all evening. The candlelight flat-

ters her complexion and she speaks softly and sweetly. Conversation stops flowing for an instant, and then resumes. 'If she were otherly-abled,' says Debora, 'we'd still love her, wouldn't we, Harold? We wouldn't shirk our responsibilities.' Harold says the baby has a fifty percent chance of being a boy, and Debora looks quite put out.

'Oh, I don't think so,' she says. 'I'd only have a girl.'

But on being asked why, she just says she's the kind of person to have daughters. Anyway, Harold already has two sons.

'The point is,' says Martyn, 'this ideal baby doesn't exist yet. It's all in the head, and if you keep it like that much longer you won't have one at all. You know how female fertility drops after thirty-five.'

'The same blunt fellow as ever,' says Harold, a little stiffly. 'It's what we admire in you.' Debora is thirty-six.

Hattie, to cover the gap, says she hopes Kitty at least inherits some of her mother's talent, and when asked who her mother is, mentions Lallie's name. Debora looks blank but Harold reacts. Harold's parents were concert-goers and interested in the world of music. Hattie is gratified, and would say more, but Martyn now wants to talk about his father's adventures in the Communist Party, and Debora wants to talk about herself. Debora wins, because she is the boss's mistress. Debora says that – taking everything into consideration – she may not after all be quite ready for a baby, and Harold, perhaps thinking of his column, looks vaguely disappointed, but also relieved.

Hattie, who has had quite a few glasses of wine – Agnieszka does not drink – launches into a passionate defence of motherhood, and how it need not interfere with a career so long as a woman gets herself organised, but her voice drifts off as she sees both Martyn and Agnieszka looking at her in a puzzled way. The red silk dress, now decidedly too small for Hattie, stretches over Agnieszka's fine bosom, a magnet for male eyes, and indeed Debora's and Hattie's.

It occurs to Hattie that perhaps Agnieszka has had a boob job but that is obviously out of the question – where would she have found the time? Then Hattie realises it's just a rather efficient uplift bra, and is probably one of Hattie's own, because she can just see its distinctive red strap when Agnieszka clears the plates. It was a gift from Serena and fabulously expensive: Serena says it's what she would like to own if only she had the figure and youth for it, which she hasn't. So she bought it for Hattie.

But it is pleasant just to sit there and have someone else clear the plates, and bring out the cheese. Martyn makes the coffee.

While Agnieszka and Martyn are both out of the room fetching and carrying, Harold says to Hattie: 'Brave of you to have her in the house. The inspirer of dreams.'
'I don't understand you,' says Hattie. She doesn't think she likes Harold very much. He smiles as if he was agreeable and sighs a lot as if he was sensitive but he is sexist and spiteful. 'Agnieszka comes to Martyn in his dreams,' explains Debora. Hattie doesn't think she likes Debora very much either. Hattie hopes she will have a lot of trouble getting pregnant. Then she is ashamed of her thoughts.
'How could you possibly know that?' she asks.
'Because Martyn told Harold and Harold told me,' says

Debora. 'Office life and pillow talk. You know what it's like. If I ever have an au pair I'll make sure she's as plain as a toad.'

'Plain ones are the worst,' says Harold. 'Never think you're safe. Don't you worry about Martyn, Hattie. When you dream, you don't do.'

Hattie wonders why they are trying to upset her, and decides they are jealous because she is happy, and they are not.

'Like suicide?' says Debora. 'Those who threaten it don't do it.'

'Statistically speaking you're wrong there, Debora,' says Harold. 'Those who threaten frequently do.'

Martyn and Agnieszka bring in the cheese, and some green-tomato chutney which Agnieszka has brought back from her friends in Neasden. Martyn runs his hands over Hattie's shoulders as he passes the back of her chair, and Hattie is comforted. It has not been an easy evening.

When they are going to bed that night Hattie says: 'You shouldn't have said that stuff about infertility and age.'

'Why not? It's true,' says Martyn.

'I think it touched a nerve,' says Hattie.

Martyn puts on the pyjamas that Agnieszka has laid out for him.

'It was rather odd, not having a first course,' he says. 'That didn't help. I hope they didn't find it too strange.'

Hattie says: 'It was Agnieszka's fault. She bought live scallops, not cleaned ones. I think she knew what she was about. She loves to show me up.'

And Martyn says: 'Now look, Hattie, don't take your failures out on Agnieszka.'

Cooking Disasters

'I don't like the sound of this,' says Serena. 'Not just that Martyn's loyalties may be getting confused, but that Hattie should report that remark to you.'
'It's in the nature of women to report the bad behaviour of men to other women: *he did this, then he said that, I can't stand it a minute longer.* They don't expect to be taken seriously.'

Serena agrees that it is certainly safer to report one's wrongs to other women than to men. She tells me how recently she was sounding off about Cranmer to a male friend and months later when she saw him again he said 'thank God, you two are still together – I thought you were splitting up', and she couldn't even remember what the quarrel had been about, except she had been very angry at the time. What woman ever can remember? Unless of course, Serena observes, it concerns some act of infidelity, where the female memory seems to be more tenacious than the male. She is of course talking about herself.

More than ten years now since George died, and she remembers those quarrels, those insults, those tears, as if they were yesterday. We are coming up now to the anniversary of his death. Serena tries to keep the memories and images out of her head, she says, but they keep coming back. Today she chooses to remember the latter days of the marriage and George saying, as he carted her off to a new-age therapist – whom she hadn't until then realised he was seeing – 'She'll soon tell you a thing or two about yourself and your behaviour': and how she was bewildered, thinking, 'But I love him – why does he seem to hate me? What have I done but be myself?' She knew George was depressed: it was cyclical and left to itself would soon clear up. The depression showed itself as hostility to her, but it would pass. It had before: she must sit it out and wait for the good days to return.

Dr Wendy Style, the new-age therapist, who had already read both George and Serena's astrological charts and come to the conclusion they were totally unsuited, pointed out that both of them could live perfectly well without the other. George had agreed. This had left Serena open-mouthed while in the consulting room and gulping with tears on the drive home to Grovewood, but George was unmoved. She could not live without him, but it appeared he thought he could live without her well enough. Only later did it occur to her that this was the way he had chosen to tell her that the marriage was over. He had lacked the courage himself. Break the bad news by fax, text, email – or therapist, that's the post-modern way. Scraps of the past, gathered together, distorted and handed over.

But have some sympathy for George. He had had a minor heart attack, been told by his doctors to make major life changes, been directed to a therapist who told him that to survive he must 'cut the ties that bind', and was doing for once in his life what he was told. If his therapist said his wife must go, so that he could live healthily, breathe properly, think high thoughts and find his destiny as a great artist and a spiritual leader, he would believe her.

His paintings, it was true, and whatever his personal problems, were getting better and better. They were rich with colour: he painted flowers, fish, landscape, as if he owned them, had thought of them in the first place, almost indeed, as if he were the prime creator. They had an astonishing intensity.

Today they sit in store, gaining in strength, waiting purchasers. Some paintings lose power after the death of the artist: some seem to gather it. George's do. Until his split with Serena I hung them in my gallery and they sold fast and well. Out of loyalty to Serena I took them all down. Now she is with Cranmer she will not have one in her house, but she pays for their storage and there is talk of George (posthumous) and Sebastian (imprisoned) having a joint show in London, which she will encourage her children to organise.

In those early days Serena thought of therapists as wise, good, people who knew the rules for successful living. She thought Dr Style must know what she was doing, and when she suggested Serena move out to give George 'space', that's just what Serena did, out of Grovewood to a cottage a quarter of a mile down the road. In other words she did what no woman in difficult circumstances should do – left the matrimonial home. She would still slip back into the house though, at night sometimes, and into George's bed where he seemed glad enough to see her.

But reports came to her that a woman in a straw hat was in the habit of sitting sketching in the side garden which she and George had made, her stool set up in the shade by the fish pool with the antique fountain which never worked, being one of George's. This was the very pool, Serena was fond of telling me, where every year she would help tadpoles on their way to frog-maturity out of the water onto rocks to take their first breath.

Who could this young woman be? Friends told her. She was called Sandra. She had been in George's life for years: Serena found it hard to believe. She started divorce proceedings in the hope of bringing George back to reason, in the spirit of 'now see what you've made me do'. But all she had done was play into his hands. He answered with divorce proceedings of his own. Well, he would. He had someone else waiting and he (and Sandra) wanted the house and a generous stipend from Serena. And Serena had technically deserted him, an ill man. She'd behaved like an idiot. I don't remind her of this. Better to take her side, and wait for the fit of distress to pass. She has Cranmer now, at her side. I don't have Sebastian.

The fit doesn't pass. She tells me again, as she has told it many times before, how she shrieked her distress down the telephone, one Sunday lunchtime, after George had locked her out of her house, and he and Sandra had asked 'friends' round, who came willingly, and he sat with Sandra, at her dining table, with her children, and the friends who had betrayed her. And how George just waited for five minutes and then said, 'I have switched the telephone onto the loudspeaker. Everyone in this room can hear you and your ravings.' She put the phone down, she tells me, and sat on the edge of the bed staring into space for four hours, unable to move. They had been married thirty years. Her table, her pots and pans, her dishes, her friends, her children. Her husband.

I make her tea and Marmite toast, and she cheers up. I like it that she's come to visit me – more often it's I who go over to her and Cranmer. But with Cranmer there she can't go on and on about George the way she does when we're alone. He would be hurt. He thinks George is safely in the past, and if Serena were more like me so he would be.

It's Sunday: the gallery is closed. We're in my crowded little cottage, all mullioned windows, chintz chairs and steep and narrow stairs, and she can't sweep around as she likes to do. If she does she'll break something. Sebastian and I are used to it, as people who live in small spaces quickly become, but Serena's rooms at home are high and wide. The mid-Victorians were expansive in their buildings, full of aspirations for the future. My predecessors in this house were peasants, who huddled against weather and dark, misfortune and pestilence.

I can see that if Patrick had come to the house that evening it would have seemed far too small for him, used as he was to Alaskan forests and Italian *palazzi*. The only square inches of unoccupied space are in the studio where Sebastian worked, built as an extension out the back, which is high and spacious enough. And I couldn't have asked Patrick there in case the ghost of Sebastian materialised.

Serena's car will collect her in three hours or so, she says. She asks for more Marmite toast and I give it to her. Her chauffeur wanted to go into Bath with his wife to shop, she tells me, so she obliged him by asking him to drive her to visit me, though I think her real reason is just to talk about George when Cranmer isn't there.

Serena maintains today that as George grew older he also grew out of his mind. Many men do, in my experience. Life does not come up to their expectations: they grow older, and disappointed. At fifty they realise others have passed them by, made more money, won more respect. Their sexual drive fades and the self-esteem that goes with it. They take to litigation and shake their fists at other drivers.

It's not exclusively a male trait. As women behave more and more like men, deny the physical distinction between female physiology and that of the male, take testosterone to make them assertive, defy their menstrual cycle, regulate their moods with drugs (doctors' or otherwise) and join the career stakes, so will the same thing happen to them. They will sue for sexual discrimination, become aggressive on the road. It is more fun and rewarding than being timid and obliging.

Debora, from what Hattie tells me, is on that particular road. Live like a man, suffer like a man. Come fifty she will be bored by her career, will have failed to become managing director, write a novel anyone can remember, will have a niece and nephew or so to buy presents for if she's lucky, not if she isn't. Christmas dinner will be in an hotel with ageing friends and false jollity.

A man in a similar position is at least likely to have a wife and children tucked away in a nice home, and can fall back upon their company and care in his old age.

I asked Wanda once why she thought this was, and she said women spent so much time combing their hair, deciding what dress to buy and taking pills for their period pains they had no time to attend to their emotional lives. Like it or not, they were ruled by that hole in their middle, as my father, a doctor, once described the womb, which caused all kinds of trouble unknown to men. And if they get rid of it, perforce or by choice, they tend to get old before their time.

Serena will have none of this gloomy talk today, unless it relates to her and George. She says I take an unbalanced view of women: they are people too, not just bundles of oestrogen. That it's even worse to see someone in an old person's home who has children who never come to see her, and the humiliation that goes with that, than someone childless who has a good pension. The armchairs will be better, the carpet less smelly. She says the sum of human happiness over a life adds up to what it will: some women prefer to take it at the end, some at the beginning. Some find fecundity to be a blessing, others a curse.

I don't tell her about Patrick's eruption into my life and out of it so fast. I will in good time, but it's too recent an event for me to have absorbed properly. And she'd probably only say, briskly, 'Just as well, there'd be hell to pay when Sebastian comes out, and who needs it at our age?'

And if I said 'but it was Curran's brother', she'd probably have reacted as I did. It's frightening when you realise that the circles of acquaintance and event that you thought were safely in the past turn out to be still circling and whirling and touching, coming nearer and bouncing apart like atoms in an overheated molecule.

I'd say 'but it's Hattie's great-uncle we're talking about', and she'd say Hattie has quite enough troubles and obligations at the moment, without having a great-uncle to add to them, especially if that great-uncle were to turn into yet another step-grandfather. Kitty's great-great-nunky. Kitty's great-gramps. Yuk.

We speak of cooking disasters and humiliations we have known. We decide it has got far more difficult than it ever was to produce a meal acceptable to others. Not that it was ever easy. When Serena ran off from a husband back in the fifties, a friend of his – who ran a shop in Bounds Green, she remembers that detail – said, she heard, when told of her departure, 'just as well, she was a lousy cook.' She has not been past Bounds Green since and not remembered, and been ashamed.

She remembers the meal she cooked for that husband fifty years ago. She remembers toiling away making mushroom soup out of real chicken broth, and a beef casserole, hoping for approval. She would have done better, I say, those being the times they were, to have opened a can of soup and added croutons, and roasted a chicken, both these recognised at the time as celebratory foods. She hopes that it was the friend's taste that was at fault and not her cooking.
'I'm sure it was that,' I say.

I remembered the lemon veal roast which I had made in the tiny kitchen in Rothwell Street, for George and Serena and a new male prospect of mine. I grossly undercooked it, so nervous was I, that it was interlarded with sheets of uncooked fat. Serena and George loyally ate theirs, but my suitor left his on the side of the plate and when he called next day to say how good the dinner was, and how pleased he had been to meet my interesting family, and could he take me to the theatre at the weekend I said sorry, I was going away for six months.

These days I tend to serve baked potatoes and chicken and salad if anyone comes round. If the guests are in any-way special I bake the potatoes in the Aga, otherwise one goes for speed, not quality, and it's seven minutes in the microwave.

Hattie's young, and has ambition and energy on her side, so if someone suggests that *moules marinières* is dull and scallops are better, she believes them. Still, nothing venture, nothing win. It didn't work, but good for her.

Hattie phones again in the afternoon, after the car has come to collect Serena. I ask her how Agnieszka is, and she says Martyn is giving her a lift to the church so she can do the flowers for Father Flanahan. Agnieszka seems to have given up her vegetable-growing friend in Neasden, and is now taking an interest in local parish matters. Hattie is all for it.

'Agnieszka is in a strange country and must sometimes feel quite lonely. And it's good that she wants to integrate.' She seems to have either forgotten or forgiven Agnieszka's involvement in the scallop incident. I ask her if Agnieszka

wears her own clothes or Hattie's to go to church, and
Hattie says:
'Don't be so bitchy. Actually, she's wearing my jeans because
I can't get into them any more. But her own T-shirt.'

I can hear her munching. I ask her what she's eating and
she says a carrot and hazelnut cookie, made by Agnieszka.

Agnieszka And The Internet

'Babs,' says Hattie to her friend and colleague, the next morning at Dinton & Seltz. 'I've got to tell you what happened. I went into Agnieszka's room last night when she was at belly dancing, and opened her laptop. It came on by itself and it had porn all over it. Real hard core: girls with big boobs doing all kinds of things to one another, and three men to one girl, that kind of thing, all in garish colours, leaping around as if trying to get out of the screen. And Kitty was sleeping in the same room.'

'I don't suppose Kitty could make sense of it,' Babs says, 'even if she woke. Once that sort of thing gets onto your screen it's almost impossible to get rid of it. It surfaces unasked.'

'So you don't think I should ask Agnieszka about it?'

'I shouldn't think so,' says Babs. 'She'd only be embarrassed or take offence and leave, the way she left Alice.'

Babs is buffing her nails. She is not suffering at all from morning sickness: she has an elegant little bump between her short cropped jacket and trousers, just where the merest, sexiest sliver of naked skin appears if she stretches up her arms, well-contained and disciplined by good muscle tone.

Not for Babs the all-over swelling which afflicted Hattie when pregnant with Kitty. It occurs to Hattie that Babs has sold her soul to the Devil. Babs has now decided with Tavish that no mention will ever be made of the paternity of the coming child: it will be attributed to Alastair, who is already putting his name down for good schools. She doubts that she is the only one in whom Babs has confided her secrets. Hattie has already told Martyn. But somehow Babs will get away with it. Luck will be hers because she assumes it will be.

'But won't it be obvious from the scans that the date isn't right?' asks Hattie. Babs assures her that Alastair is not interested in medical matters, and she'll be lucky if he so much as takes her to the hospital when it comes to the birth. She may have to call a taxi. Hattie says she rather wishes she had done just that when she went into labour with Kitty. Martyn quarrelled with the ambulance men about the quickest way to get to the hospital. The ambulance men had warned the hospital that there was an agitated father on his way and fifteen minutes after Hattie was in the labour ward Martyn was still arguing the toss. A kindly nurse assured Hattie that this kind of thing was not all that unusual. Anger is a great cure for fear. Kitty appeared feet first and Martyn felt this too was somehow the hospital's fault, and felt it noisily. All the same, everyone lived.

'Men!' both agree.

Babs and Hattie talk about a new woman writer who has written a brilliant and saleable book but has the bulging eyes of a fish and the double chins of a bulldog, and wonder who best to send the manuscript to for possible publication – an all-woman publishing team or one dominated by men? They decide she will get better treatment from the men.

Hilary calls through to Babs's office and says she picked up Hattie's phone because it was ringing and ringing and had been left unattended, and that the au pair had apparently been trying to get through to Hattie. She'd suggested to the au pair that if there was a panic she should call the father: in the current climate surely the father was as significant a parent as the mother. She personally thought it was a bit much that firms should give paternity leave as well as maternity: those who chose to be childless were discriminated against. All these new government initiatives just added up to extra holidays for a few for which the taxpayer paid. But Hilary was talking to thin air.

Hattie was on her mobile, outside where the reception was good, calling home. Martyn answered. Kitty was fine, playing happily in her playpen, it was just Agnieszka who was in a state. She'd had a visit from the immigration authorities, and was in tears. No, Hattie need not come home. It was certainly inconvenient, but *Devolution* could manage for half a morning without him: they'd agreed before Kitty was born that they'd both do equal parenting, and this surely was it. He was halfway through an article on Religion, Ethics and Politics which didn't have a single funny line in it, and he was glad enough to leave off.

Hattie said she was coming home anyway: she'd had such a fright about Kitty that she felt quite sick and trembly. She goes back inside to gather her things and change her shoes, and finds Neil looking particularly suntanned and equable in her office – with Hilary, who is leafing through the papers on her, Hattie's, desk.

Hilary says, 'Home emergency, I take it. But we really do need to get at the German contracts. I can't find them in the file. You know, the ones for Miss Fishface. Neil isn't inclined to let them have the rights, but apparently you've started negotiations.'

Neil protests that it might be wise not to call the client Fishface behind her back, in case she accidentally does it to her face one day. Hilary says haughtily, 'I am not as stupid as you think, Neil.'

Neil came into the office as Hilary's junior and now runs the place. It is Hattie's opinion that Neil is intimidated by Hilary, and Hilary despises everyone who has worked for Dinton & Seltz since the days when she was old Mr Seltz's protégée, and had, or had not, carnal knowledge of him across the big shiny desk.

Neil just says the German contracts can wait well enough until tomorrow, Hilary. 'You'd better get back home straight away, Hattie. I can see you're in emergency gear, I know what it's like,' and Hattie flees.

It is not a fortunate encounter, but not so unfortunate either. Neil has come down on her side. But then, perhaps it was like the rave rejections everyone was now so good at: 'We like your style, looks, demeanour, friendliness and spirit of cooperation: we fully understand your need to be a mother as well as an employee, *but*' – skim the eye down the letter, or the fax, or the email, looking for the *but* – 'just not for us.'

Maternal Panics

Were we born panicky, Serena and I, or did we learn anxiety at Wanda's knee? Wanda, faced with a problem, would lie awake in the early morning worrying, solve it by seven, and have us all out of bed by eight to hear her plan of action. We would have to move house to get away from the neighbours; Susan would leave school because it made her unhappy; Serena would be barred from seeing her friends because she was turning into a lesbian; I would be sent to board in a convent because I was meeting boys on street corners; we would all have to ship out to England because we were developing New Zealand accents. There was no deflecting my mother from her brainwaves, and they were all disastrous.

The worst, I suppose, was when after lying awake all night agonising because my father was with another woman, she decided to have an affair herself and so bring him back to his senses. The 'affair' lasted one night, and she didn't enjoy it a bit. My father found out and divorced her. That was the way things went, in those days. And she loved him.

When Serena got pregnant by David nothing would do for Wanda but she change her name by deed poll and give up her job the better to avoid social disgrace; I was to marry Hammertoes because how else was I to support Lallie and James? – and so on and so on.

If Wanda were alive today she would be in a fine old state about Hattie taking in a long-haired kitten: what about asthma? Isn't it unfair to have solitary pets? Shouldn't they be acquired in twos, so as to keep each other company? Wanda's early-morning solution this time would be to add a puppy to the ménage at once, because dogs and cats got on well if they were reared together and Kitty would be more likely to pat the dog than stroke the cat, thus avoiding asthma.

Wanda's anxieties were always for other people, never for herself. Serena and I are like her in this, though our solutions are, I hope, less doolally. A pain in the heart for us is just a pain in the heart: we may take it to the doctor's, but if it's inconvenient or there's work to be done, we may not. We will wait for it to go away, and it probably will. But for our children, our spouses, our family – that's different. The child with a bleeding nose: *is it a brain tumour?* A pain in its stomach: *quick, to Casualty, it's appendicitis, it will burst!* Late home from school: *waylaid, ravaged!* Late home from the party: *ditto.* The boy's bought a motorbike: *broken and bleeding, he will die. Careful,* as I heard Serena say once, *of that champagne cork: you know four people a year lose an eye through flying champagne corks?* Oh yes, we're anxious enough.

When I think of myself between fifteen and twenty-two, when I disappeared from home for days, nights, denied it even was my home, blamed my mother for 'everything', kept company with druggie artists, got pregnant by a street musician – I am so sorry for my poor mother. How did she survive it? How did she get to ninety-four, enduring the anxiety she did? How will any of us?

Hattie's generation has another worry: take the child with a broken limb to hospital and the first assumption will be that the parent's responsible. If the child-carer takes it along then it's even more likely she did it on purpose. Guilty unless proved innocent. You can go to the school to collect your child and find she isn't there, she's been taken into care, and not even a phone call to tell you what's happening. The child has a black eye. She told the teacher you threw a book at her. So you did; in fun, her homework book, and she failed to catch it. Ever since Hattie failed to go to breast-feeding classes they've been keeping an eye on her. When Agnieszka takes Kitty round to the clinic the child is especially carefully inspected: weighed, measured, given dolls to play with to see if anything suggestive of abuse emerges. She is an abundantly healthy and happy child, but there's a question mark on her notes.

Serena and I both react badly to early-morning phone calls. The harsh tones break into sleep, the hand goes out for the bedside receiver: *What fresh hell is this?* With any luck it's an early call from an airport – the prodigal child on his gap year is unexpectedly home. *Come and fetch me.* Thank God! thank God! But mostly it's a sudden illness, a rush to hospital, death, news that can wait until dawn but not a moment longer. Or it's the police. An accident. No, not fatal, but they'd been drinking.

Or else it's the lawyer from Rotterdam, speaking in stilted English. 'It is my duty under Netherlands law to inform you that your husband is in police custody in Rotterdam. He will be held incommunicado for five days and you must not attempt to communicate with him for this time. No, I am not permitted to give you more information. When the investigating magistrate has concluded his questioning the authorities will contact you.' And the phone goes down. That's all. Rotterdam? I thought Sebastian was in Paris at the Getty exhibition. He wanted to look at the Daumiers. I think it is a dream but it isn't. The bed is cold and empty beside me. I have years to wait until it is warm and filled again.

Bad news comes in the early morning before the birds are singing: good news comes later with the post: a cheque here, a letter from a friend there. Bills, of course, but you know them by heart, and so many are on direct debit you hardly know what you owe to whom any more. Emails are usually good news, unless it's to do with your love life and 'The End' comes up on the screen: *It's time to put some space between us.* Or texts. *We R Fru* came up with a little spurt of announcing sound on the mobile of the girl who now cleans the gallery. We all take turns. She's a student. She'll be okay, but how she cried; I was glad I was not her mother.

As the child gets older anxiety increases, it doesn't diminish. Anxiety serves as a talisman against disaster. Mothers of sons do report, though, that once the boy gets married, the anxiety can be off-loaded onto the wife. Let the wife worry about the gambling, the druggery, the drinking, the fornication that leads to Aids. It's like the curse of the devil – if you can find someone else to pass it onto, you are saved. This works only for formal marriages, not partnerships. I don't worry about Hattie any the less because she's with Martyn. If only she'd marry him formally, she would seem his responsibility: I could relax. But no. Some ceremony was required, and there was none.

Of course Hattie panics when she gets a phone call from Agnieszka. Martyn has told her everything is okay, but she has to know the detail, and she has to know it *now*, see with her own eyes that Kitty is safe and well.

Churchyard Drama

Hattie gets home, breathless, to find the house empty and a note on the table. Before she can read it, Sylvie leaps onto the table and Hattie says automatically 'not on the table, Sylvie, it isn't allowed,' and Sylvie rolls herself up around Hattie's hand into a spitting, scratching ball and draws blood. Hattie shakes her hand, fast and hard, and Sylvie is flicked off onto the floor – for such a mass of fur, and growing every day, she's so light! – where she recovers her balance, arches her back and hisses as at an enemy. Hattie finds this very upsetting.

The cat leaps on top of the dresser and sits there sulking and somehow squashed in on herself so you can hardly see her round orange eyes for her fur – for some reason she has not been combed today – and stares while Hattie reads the note. It's Martyn's handwriting. He's left his mobile at the office, but he's gone down to the church with Kitty and Agnieszka. Hattie could join him there if she wants, but everything's fine. Hattie dabs her deepest scratches with peroxide, which smarts, finds a plaster in Agnieszka's beautifully stocked first-aid box, changes out of her office clothes and goes to find her family among the tombstones.

She finds Martyn on a bench reading the *Guardian* in the early-Spring sun and Kitty wrapped up warm in the stroller, safely wedged between two Victorian tombstones, whose inscriptions are illegible for grey birdshit and greenish lichen. Kitty is gazing at an early daisy. Hattie feels pleased and proud that she is theirs and they are hers, and only a little anxious that she is not at the office warding off attacks from Hilary. She sits down beside Martyn and holds his hand.

'She's gone to see Father Flanahan,' says Martyn. 'She's very upset. I walked down here with her. Two nasty types from Immigration came to see her – some bastard had sent a letter to them saying she was an illegal immigrant. These guys wanted to inspect her passport, but she couldn't find it. They're coming back. We can sort it all out, I'm sure. If the worst comes to the worst, Harold can probably do something through the Home Office: he has friends there.'

'You mustn't try and pull strings,' says Hattie, alarmed. 'It could lead to terrible trouble.'

'We don't want to lose our au pair,' says Martyn.

'No, for sure,' agrees Hattie. 'Only she hasn't lost her passport. It's under her mattress. We have to explain to her that in Britain it's always better to be frank and open with the authorities.'

'You looked under her mattress? You were spying on Agnieszka?' He sounds very shocked, as if the guilt of deception was all on Hattie's side.

'I wasn't spying,' says Hattie. 'I have a duty of care towards Agnieszka. I need to know what's going on.'

'What is going on,' asks Martyn, 'that isn't idle gossip? Anything else I should know?' He's not in a good mood, in spite of looking so happy and handsome on the churchyard bench. He's had to leave work to attend to a domestic emergency. Bosses don't like it, no matter how they mouth their sympathy. Hattie's on the verge of saying he can go back to work, she'll take over, but then she thinks no, why should she? Martyn is a parent too.

'Agnieszka isn't Polish at all,' says Hattie. 'She's from the Ukraine. Just over the border. It's the most horrible example of post-code lottery imaginable. I think she went to school the Polish side of the border but still she's a Ukrainian when it comes to passports.'

Martyn considers this for some time. Hattie absently leans down and picks the daisy and gives it to Kitty, who starts to eat it.

'How long have you known this, without telling me?' asks Martyn. He seems quite hard and hostile. Not like himself at all. 'We could have done something before it got to this stage. Once you're on those arseholes' books, they're like terriers; they don't let go.'

He wrenches the daisy from between Kitty's lips. Kitty's little mouth puckers but she doesn't cry. She is a good brave baby. Martyn is not accusing Hattie of being a bad mother but she knows he thinks it and she also knows he is probably right. What kind of mother lets a baby eat a daisy in a churchyard?

'Martyn,' says Hattie calmly. 'Agnieszka is only the au pair. We lived without her before she came, and we can live without her when she goes.'

'I doubt it,' he says. Then he says he's getting cold, the wind is sharp, and they should go into the church and wait for Agnieszka there.

'Kitty won't like it,' Hattie says. 'Churches are so dark and gloomy.'

'Agnieszka goes to mid-morning Mass once or twice a week,' says Martyn. 'She takes Kitty. Kitty likes it. Didn't you know that?'

'No I didn't,' says Hattie.

'You don't take much interest in your baby's fate,' says Martyn and laughs but it has an odd note in it.

'Incense is carcinogenic,' says Hattie, 'and I don't want Kitty being fed Mother Mary stuff, Virgin, Madonna, whore, all that. She has to grow up to face a new age – thank God!'

'Better to be brought up in any belief system than none at all,' says Martyn. 'Easy to start down the path to unbelief: it's harder the other way round.'

'Oh, put it in an article,' says Hattie. Kitty looks from one parent to the other, sensing discord, and her mouth puckers again. She pushes something out between her lips and it's a single daisy petal. She moves it back inside with her tongue. Neither parent reacts. That surprises her.

'I think we have other things than religion to worry about now,' says Martyn, using his new diplomatic skills. He's been to a course or two on management technique.

'I'm sorry,' she says. 'Sylvie scratched me and it upset me.'

Agnieszka comes out of the church with Father Flanahan. She's wearing Hattie's red dress again and a little false-fur jacket that no longer looks good on Hattie. Hattie knows if she went into Agnieszka's wardrobe she would probably find it full of her own things but that's okay. They either don't fit Hattie any more, or aren't suitable for the office. Martyn says he likes Hattie with a bit more flesh on her, anyway. Not so bony. Their sex life is frequent and lively these days, four or five times a week, though conducted in a silence which Hattie finds oddly exciting.

Father Flanahan waves at them from the church door and goes back inside. Kitty holds out her little arms to Agnieszka to be lifted out. She takes her place in the row along the bench, next to Martyn, with Kitty on her knee. The sun has come out again and everything seems pleasant and permanent.

'I feel bad,' says Agnieszka. 'You have been so good to me, and I've lied to you and now I will be sent home, and my mother is here in Neasden with my sister, and there is no room for me. The pickpocket from the buses stole my boyfriend and now she sends me nasty things on my computer.'

'Oh Agnieszka,' says Hattie, 'why didn't you tell us all this before? You must have been so upset. You know we're always there for you.'

'It was your immigration police told me he was living with her. They find out everything. I had not known, I am so upset. They don't care about feelings, people's lives.'

'Those jobs attract real bastards,' says Martyn. 'But I know they're frightened of the Press.'

'But I thought your mother and sister were in Australia,' says Hattie.

'They came to this country instead,' says Agnieszka. 'Australia is so far and they want to be with me. Now my mother has a little house and my sister has treatment for her cancer.'

'Cancer!' says Hattie. 'Oh, your poor mother – that's terrible!'

'What am I to do? I have to stop my English classes to be with her in the evenings. She is so pale and thin. It is quite safe. It is not catching. I am so sorry to deceive you.'

'Don't worry about that,' says Hattie. Tears are coursing down Agnieszka's cheeks. Kitty tries to kiss them away, manages, likes the taste and looks for more with her tiny pink tongue.

'Salt is bad for her,' says Agnieszka, turning her cheek away. Hattie laughs out of a sheer surfeit of affection for the girl. Martyn looks embarrassed. He is not good at female tears.

'And are your family illegals too?' he says.

Agnieszka nods.

'Only two miles,' she says. 'Two miles to the west and everything would be different for us. They will deport me, I know they will.'

'There's not much about this,' says Martyn, 'that looks brilliant.'

Father Flanahan comes out of the church with a bird held in his cupped hands. He opens them and it flies off.

'Happens all the time,' he calls out to them. 'They get in and then they can't get out again. When God made them, He left the sense out.'

He goes inside again. No one moves.

Hattie breaks the silence: 'Now you have your answer. Why we never got married. Destiny had other plans for us. Both of us are citizens of the European Community, which is our luck: we can share it. Lesbian marriages aren't here yet, so it's going to have to be you, Martyn. You've got to marry Agnieszka. She will be Mrs Arkwright. Agnes

234

Arkwright, if you prefer. I expect she'll make a concession for you.'

Kitty closes her eyes and falls asleep. Agnieszka says nothing, but her cheeks have dried.

'I don't believe this is happening!' says Martyn.
'In name only,' says Hattie. 'I'm only suggesting in name only. Good Lord!' Martyn seems paralysed. He looks at Hattie and away again.
'Nothing changes,' says Hattie. 'I'm still your partner. It is only a piece of paper, a legal document, to bring about a situation from which everyone benefits. After a couple of years you and she will be divorced and everything's back to normal.'
'It is not so easy now to get married,' says Agnieszka. 'The laws have changed.'
'They change so fast no one can keep up,' says Martyn.
'Father Flanahan would marry us,' says Agnieszka. 'I am one of his parishioners. I arrange the flowers. And he knows you too, Mr Martyn: you talked to him about bishops, and he remembers that.'

Kitty sleeps soundly in her stroller. They set off to walk home.
'In the Ukraine a church marriage is not so usual,' says Agnieszka, 'but I have always wanted one.' She says she will make a white dress and one for Kitty too, and they will pick out a beautiful hat for Hattie. 'A hat for Hattie!' she laughs. She seems so happy.
'Say something, Martyn,' says Hattie.
'I suppose it would work,' says Martyn, eventually. 'The

priest would just have to read the banns, three weeks running, that's all. She lives in his parish, so do I. He already has me down as the father. He won't want to make waves. Marry first, argue with the authories later?'

'Three weeks is a long time,' says Agnieszka.

'Not in Immigration-speak,' says Martyn. 'We'll be all right.'

A taxi passes and Martyn takes it: he doesn't want to be away from the office too long. Hattie feels the same but takes the bus. Agnieszka and Kitty walk on home.

Mad Plans

There is a lot of Wanda in Hattie, obviously. Face her with a dilemma and she will come up with a disastrous solution. She doesn't even need an early-morning fit of anxiety before finding the wrong answer. She can do it in broad daylight, in company.

She does not tell me what happened in the churchyard until it is too late. She phones me to tell me that Agnieszka is in some trouble with the immigration authorities, having lost her passport, but Martyn will be able to sort it all out through his contacts at the Home Office, and that she has had to take a morning off work. When she got back Hilary had poached Marina Faircroft by default; Hattie hadn't been around to stop her. She would go to Neil, but she doesn't want to be the one seeming not to get on with the rest of the team. She makes no mention to me of Martyn marrying the au pair to stop her being deported.

Well, I never spoke the whole truth to my mother if I could help it, for fear of her solutions, so why should Hattie speak more than partial truths to me, her grandmother? I am over seventy: what do I know about the modern world? Me, I am just the wife of a jailbird. I could have run off with Patrick the logging tycoon and lived happily ever after but I didn't, which shows what kind of idiot I am.

I have hung Sebastian's two paintings, the bed and the chair, in the gallery window. I won't keep them back for an exhibition; they are out of keeping with his normal work. But they are strong, and I have priced the bed at £1,200 and the chair at £1,000. Unless they are Van Gogh's, beds are easier to sell than chairs. But I can see I don't really want to sell them or I would have priced them at £600 and £500 and thought myself lucky to get that.

Serena says she can see trouble ahead with the authorities. They may argue that Sebastian painting in prison and selling is like a criminal writing a book, and he should not be allowed to profit from his crime. His property can be impounded. I am not sure if she is joking or not. I hope she is. I have had two enquiries already about the chair. It's just a chair, but it's the kind Sebastian would not sit on if he could possibly avoid doing so, any more than he would choose to sleep upon that bed. Perhaps that's what gives the paintings their edge.

Martyn Confesses

'Sorry I was out of the office yesterday morning,' says Martyn to Harold. In his absence an email came through announcing that *Evolution* and *Devolution* were to merge, under the title *(D)Evolution*, or possibly *d/EvOLUTION* – it has not yet been decided. This is the first Martyn has heard of it. He knows what will happen next. The staff will be cut by fifty percent or so, as normally happens after a merger. Those at the top multiply and are not fired: those at the bottom work even harder, such as remain.

Harold is depressed, he seems to have shrunk inside his navy suit. He seems less whiskery than usual, as if the hairs had to fight their way out of his skin, and it had tired them.

'Darwinism is an unproven belief system,' he complains. 'At least devolution is a respectable political theory. They don't mix and match at all, other than that the words rhyme, and it saves printing costs. You'll stay, they like you: you can write jolly articles about the return of Lysenko and the inheritance of learned characteristics, which suits our masters, and three cheers for a vending machine in every school corridor, but what am I going to do? The *Evolution* editor Larry Jugg

239

will get the job. And Debora is pregnant. Think of the school fees, and at my age. Women take what's just talk so seriously, that's the problem. And where were you yesterday morning, as a matter of interest?'

'Domestic emergency,' Martyn explains. 'Our girl had a visit from Immigration and got upset.'

'Not the one you dream about who made the chicken couscous with the marinated vegetables?'

'That one.'

'I don't know how you can keep your hands off her,' says his boss. 'That bum. That mouth.'

Martyn is taken aback. He had thought Agnieszka's qualities too understated to be apparent to anyone but himself. 'She may be deported,' he says. 'Couscous and all. She turns out to be Ukrainian not Polish. Some scumbag reported her!'

'That won't do,' says Harold. 'That's telling tales. It's not as if she was an undesirable, not by any means. Who was it?'

Martyn says he doesn't know and Harold promises to find out for him. He knows people in the Home Office.

Martyn can't help it. He says, actually it's all irrelevant now. He's going to marry the girl and give her citizenship. He's not quite sure himself that he's going to do it. Indeed, he half hopes Harold will tell him not to be a complete tosser but Harold does not. He just laughs and laughs and as he laughs seems to fill out and become hairier.

'You'll go far, lad,' he says, 'I knew you would. You just go in there and get her. I would.'

Strange pains gnaw in Martyn's belly. He's hungry and anxious. What is he taking on? What is Hattie suggesting? Is she so far from loving him that she wants him to marry

240

another, for the sake of getting to work on time? He feels angry with Hattie and that makes him feel he will marry Agnieszka just to pay Hattie out.

'Mind you,' says Harold, 'these days you have to prove you love them, and not just for citizenship's sake. And as, so far as I can see, you're living with another woman and have a child by her there may be a problem at the registry office. But I'd think the au pair would be the best bet. She's certainly the better cook.'
'We're marrying in church,' says Martyn. 'She's a Catholic.' The idea is firming up nicely in his mind. He would like a proper wedding, with a bride in a white dress, and a priest giving a blessing. His mother would want that for him, and it's time he came down on his mother's side and not his father's. She might even come to the wedding. There is more to life than work, politics and principle. Hattie doesn't see it, but at least she has the generosity of spirit to allow him this ceremony.

'Debora started out as a Catholic,' says Harold. 'Now there's the prospect of an abortion it's all coming back to roost. I don't want to pressure her either way, but please just don't invite her to the ceremony.'
'It will be very quiet,' says Martyn. It is going to happen, he knows that now. He would quite like Kitty to stare at a candle and be christened, and that could happen too. The children of Catholics are Catholics. What is he thinking? Kitty is Hattie's child, not Agnieszka's.

An email flashes up on Harold's screen. He has got the job as editor of *d/EvILUTION* (but Harold hopes that's a typo). Larry Jugg is out, Harold Mappin in.

They go for lunch in the pub to celebrate. The barmaid is in the traditional style, with big boobs, big teeth and big hair. Harold admires her. At least, he says, if Debora stays pregnant she'll get bigger boobs, even for a time, though his first wife's shrank long-term.

Martyn wishes Harold wouldn't talk like this. He would rather have a less human boss: it is important to respect the man you work for. But looking at the barmaid, it occurs to him that the pneumatic joys of the female world are not confined to Hattie and Agnieszka, but that there are millions and millions more of them out there, all searching for true love, and somehow his vision had closed in. He has another whisky.

Hattie At The Cattery

'Turns out,' says Hattie to me in a phone call, 'that Agnieszka's mother and sister are living in Neasden.'

'I thought you said they were in Australia.'

'Agnieszka was covering her back, I'm afraid,' says Hattie. 'Fibbing. You can't blame her. Our immigration laws are absurd. They take no notice of family love or human feelings.'

'I am surprised,' I say, 'that you allow your child to be brought up by such an accomplished liar.'

There is silence on the other end then Hattie says I'm sounding very like Wanda.

'Nan! Stop it. The mother's really nice: simple, peasantish and hard-working. She had an allotment and used to grow carrots and sell them but she had to give it up because the sister is really ill. She's dying, Gran. She's seventeen and she's got bone cancer.'

'I'm sorry,' I say, and then because this does sound like a real sob story, and I am beginning to mistrust everything about this Agnieszka of theirs, 'and you have actually been to visit her? She does exist?'

'She exists all right,' says Hattie. 'Her name's Anita and she's thin and transparent but terribly sweet. She sits up in a wheel-chair by the window and grooms the cats. That's all she has the strength to do. But that family is so hard-working they just keep on.'

'Grooms the cats?'

'Agnieszka's mother runs a cattery.'

It sounds so unlikely. I am reminded of the belly-dancing shock. But those classes did exist, they weren't fantasy, they were real enough, Hattie went along and came home with scarves and belts which I don't suppose she ever wore, and gave up after a couple of lessons, as people do. Agnieszka kept going, or said she did. And Hattie has scratches on her hands to prove the kitten is real. So I suppose the cattery in Neasden is true enough.

'The mother has to do something, Gran,' says Hattie. 'She can't claim tax relief because her visa has run out so she breeds Persians in her back garden.'

'That can't be much fun for the neighbours.'

'It's quite a big garden.' How Hattie does want everything to be all right! I fear for her.

'So your kitten didn't just turn up on the doorstep?'

'Well, no. One of the Persians got out one night and the litter didn't breed true. Sylvie's head isn't square enough and its tail's too long so the mother couldn't sell it for more than a tenner. So Agnieszka took it home to save it from being drowned. She would have told me the truth except she'd already said her mother was in Australia. And she knew I'd say yes.'

I was put in mind of Hammertoes' mother, and from Hattie's description they seemed the same kind of person, pleasant and peasanty and tough as old nails, and with long, unplucked hairs coming out of the sides of their chins as if they were in sympathy with the cats. '*She loved her cats more than me.*'

Poor Agnieszka. Perhaps that is what it has been like for her. And I remembered the smell of the cat-filled house, sweet and sour, like Chinese food left out too long in a warm place, mixed up with disinfectant, fumes catching the throat, or perhaps you were breathing in hairs, or the mites were floating down your open mouth. No wonder Agnieszka wanted to get out.

I say I hope Hattie hadn't kept Kitty in the house for long, what with the bone cancer and the litter trays. Hattie says they were there about twenty minutes only: she wasn't too keen to go in the first place, but Agnieszka had wanted her to, been so contrite, had confessed and apologised, and her going to visit the mother had seemed to Agnieszka a token of acceptance, that everything was just fine again, back to normal.

And still Hattie didn't mention the supposed wedding. I had no idea. I think perhaps she too thought somehow it wouldn't happen just because it had been arranged. It wasn't that she wanted Martyn to marry Agnieszka; she was just somehow putting the whole institution of marriage, which had afflicted her family over generations, into its proper place, dishonouring it. As if it really didn't matter. It made no difference to anything.

Hattie says she must stop talking. Martyn and she are to go out to dinner. Agnieszka is babysitting. Kitty now seems to say 'bye-bye and 'love you'. That's nice. It all still appears to be working smoothly, lies, cattery and all, and Kitty continues to be plump, robust and smiling, which is the important thing, so I must stop worrying. I do. As Serena says, parents are just bit-part players in any baby's drama.

Hattie Gets Promotion

'Where were you yesterday?' asks Babs. 'All hell broke loose in here. The computers caught a virus. Marina Faircroft came round with a lawyer who was just to die for and said she was going to sue Hilary for breach of contract. Neil talked to Marina and she calmed down. Then she went to the hairdresser, and the lawyer took Elfie out to lunch. She's the intern who makes a mess of the photocopying. She'll be working at his place next, wait and see. She's very pretty and not very bright. Your Tourette's man came and sat in reception asking for you and refusing to go away unless they changed the title of his book to exclamation marks and asterisks.'

'But we can't do that,' says Hattie. 'He knows that. The publishers have gone to press. He okayed the title.'

'Neil came down and said perhaps we could use the screamers and stars in the next book he wrote, and he went away happy. Neil had to make some compromise, Hattie. You can't have an angry Tourette's man in reception for too long. There are clients coming in.'

'But he hasn't even got Tourette's,' Hattie says. 'He's pretending. Tourette's Syndrome isn't a joke. It's a tragedy for those who have it.'

'If you'd been here you could have said that.'
'I've had a domestic crisis. Visa problem,' says Hattie, shortly. If she told Babs Martyn was going to marry Agnieszka in three weeks' time the whole office would know, if only through the thin partition walls.
'What, the divine Agnieszka? I don't believe it.'

Instead of going out to dinner with Martyn, Hattie baby-sat while he and Agnieszka went for an hour's session with Father Flanahan in preparation for the marriage. Martyn came back banging his forehead, saying, 'How can people believe this stuff?' Father Flanahan was apparently under the impression that the sooner the couple was married the less time they would have to spend living in sin and Martyn had not disabused him. Time was of the essence, before Immigration went into overdrive. Agnieszka wanted a Mass with ceremony, hymns, and everything, which can go on for a long time, but Martyn has said no, the twenty-minute version would do.

Babs has now begun to swell visibly all over; including her ankles, which Hattie is quite happy about. Alastair has booked a Norland Nanny, the very one who looked after him when he was little, which keeps it in the family, as it were, though the nanny is of course quite old. She will be given a young, strong nursery maid to assist her. Babs has lost, or seems to have lost, all interest in poaching Agnieszka.

The true father of Babs's unborn baby, Tavish the TV producer, turns up in the office from time to time. Hattie can see the baby's parentage will soon become the subject of general office gossip, but perhaps Babs would be happy enough if it did. Babs does not like too quiet a life.

All Hattie tells Babs is that someone has snitched on Agnieszka and her passport isn't in order and Immigration is stirring up trouble.

'Well, I wonder who would have done that?' asks Babs.

'I can't believe it's anyone we know,' Hattie says.

'Don't you believe it,' says Babs. 'Could be my sister. Alice was pretty cross after what happened with Jude.'

'What exactly did happen with Jude?' asks Hattie, not sure if she really wants to know.

Babs gives an account of how Alice woke up in the night, and finding Jude not in her bed, went into Agnieszka's room and found him there, half-way into her bed. Jude's excuse was that he'd heard Agnieszka crying so he'd gone in to see what the matter was, and she'd practically pulled him in, like a credit card into the slot at the bank.

'Alice believed him, more fool her,' says Babs, 'and Agnieszka took offence and walked out. So Alice was left with no one to help with the babies, and Jude went into a depression so bad he had to be hospitalised.'

Garble, garble, thinks Hattie, *gossip, gossip*. How did Babs get the job she has? How does she keep it? But Hattie has noticed that Babs never doubts her own decisions. She went to an expensive girls' school and likes to succeed without appearing to. Put any piece of paper under Babs's nose and she will absorb what's written on it in seconds, and within the minute will have responded to it, and put the matter out of her head. Then she has nothing to do but her nails.

That's the way she likes it. No work, no work, no work, and all of a sudden lots of work. Love-life: sex, men, drama, confusion, out of the way, back to the nails.

'But I don't really see Alice having the time or strength to write to the authorities,' says Babs, 'so it was probably Hilary. Hilary the well-known snitch.'

'But why would Hilary do that?' asks Hattie, taken aback. 'She hasn't even met Agnieszka.'

'She's heard about her. And she wants your job as well as her own; without Agnieszka you're sunk. She'd like you to sink in a welter of clinic appointments, visa problems, and time off for domestic emergencies.'

'But people aren't so petty,' protests Hattie. 'Not people like us.'

'People like us!' mocks Babs. 'You sound just like Alastair.' She calls Neil on his extension and Neil actually picks up his own phone. Hattie leaves.

That afternoon Neil calls Hattie up to his office. It's like having an audience with the Prince of Wales. He carries power with him, though it sits uneasily on his shoulders, like an ill-fitting overcoat. Neil sits with his back to the window, and his shadow falls forward across the desk which no one can look at without wondering whether Hilary and old Mr Seltz did or did not. His is the shadow of authority, able to make you or break you at whim. Hattie ought to be nervous but she is not. She knows she is doing her job well enough. True, she was out of the office at a bad time but Neil has children too. What she feels mostly is that her strength is as the strength of ten because her heart is pure. Nothing will go wrong. She is blessed. She has given up something valuable and great for Agnieszka's sake. Agnieszka will become Mrs Agnes Arkwright; her mother, her sister and the cattery will stay in the country. Hattie will stay Hattie Hallsey-Coe. Hattie is a good person and good things happen to good people.

Neil says that Hilary has been transferred to the Frankfurt branch of Dinton & Seltz. Hilary is to manage the new office there: a great opportunity to prove herself. Which means that if Hattie is happy to take on both jobs for the time being – domestic and foreign rights are to be amalgamated – so is he. She will need an assistant, of course – she might consider Elfie, who is very bright and undervalued. There will be more money in it, and the prospect, in time, of a place at the directors' table with share options.

Neil's phone rings. He puts a white leather cushion over it. He says he will put it all in an email and they'll talk more later. Hattie's audience is at an end. But as she goes he says: 'God, that Hilary was a bitch. Babs told me – grassing on your au pair like that. We family folk must stick together.'

Hattie is vindicated. She was right. Good things come to the good. Neil takes the cushion from the phone, hurls it across the room so it strikes the window with a thud, to scare off a pigeon which is crapping on the window ledge. He is lucky it doesn't break the glass. The cost of replacing so large a pane would be phenomenal. But the phone is still ringing so Neil has no option but to pick up the receiver.

And Hattie leaves the newly designer-built brightness which is Neil's penthouse for the older part of the building, down the narrow winding stair towards her office, and feels the breath of countless past employees on her cheek, chilling her, undermining her pleasure. One person's promotion is another's demotion. She has got what she wanted, but she feels she is no longer good.

By the time she gets back to her office the ghosts have gone. Babs does work fast. Did Neil really transfer Hilary because of what she said? Well, that did no harm, and Hilary will hate the new Frankfurt office, where all they do is prepare all year round for the Book Fair. Hilary has no partner or children to offer as an excuse for not going.

Two Weddings And A Funeral

The wedding was lovely. I hear about it later, weeks later. Agnieszka wore a cream dress in which she looked young and delightful and wonderfully happy, and Hattie was a brides-maid in a pink dress also made by Agnieszka, who is so handy with a needle. Actually pink is just not Hattie's colour: it makes her bountiful hair look red rather than golden.

Agnieszka's sister is the other bridesmaid, the one with cancer, now apparently in remission, and out of her wheelchair. The pink suits her pale fragility very well. Martyn wears a new suit and a tie, which makes him look as if he were soon going to make a lot of money, and could be trusted with it. Agnieszka's mother holds Kitty, who settles very well into her bountiful lap, absorbed in trying to take the whiskers out of her minder's chin. Martyn's boss Harold is best man, and his partner Debora, entering the church, can't at first decide whether to sit on the bride's side of the church or the groom's, and settles for the groom's, for which Hattie darts her a grateful look. Debora may not be so bad after all.

Serena hears about the wedding first. I suppose Hattie is more frightened of me than of her great-aunt. I get to hear when Serena calls me and says simply, 'Martyn married Agnieszka three weeks ago', and I go cold, efficient and distant, as I did when the lawyer from Rotterdam rang me up. It is something to do with having been brought up in New Zealand, where everyone, male and female both, knows how to go into emergency mode. It is why New Zealand men – I will not insult them by calling them Kiwis, though they seem to like the term; Kiwis are cautious, frightened little birds, and I cannot think how that bold, fierce land-scape, this noble race, ever spawned them – are found in charge of field hospitals and NGOs, and why New Zealand girls make such excellent au pairs, pausing in your home a little as they gather strength for some amazing leap into future life. If the refugee camp is bombed, the New Zealander does not run away but stays and puts it together again; if the baby falls on its head the New Zealand girl doesn't have hysterics, she just gets it to the hospital.

Serena and I share this ability, though I was born in New Zealand and she was not. Show us a sheep and we shear it: an earthquake, and we know to sit beneath the stairs, a tidal wave and we know when and where to run. It's just when we see men that the knack deserts us: we run into danger, not away from it. I've failed Hattie: my beautiful Hattie, with her upright back and wilful ways; Martyn has left her, left her for the maid.

'I hope to God she's seen a lawyer,' I say, cool and calm.
'It isn't like that,' says Serena. 'They're all still together.'
'What, in one big bed?' I have all the meanness that comes with fury. It is in my voice.
I hear it, and I intend it.

'No wonder she didn't confide in you,' says Serena. 'She knew how you'd react. Of course not in one big bed. It's a marriage of convenience so the girl and her family don't get put on a plane and sent back to the Ukraine. If you didn't want something like this to happen you could always have gone to live with them and helped out. It's perfectly obvious to anyone that Hattie would never settle down and be domestic. She's too bright.'

'What, me give up the gallery? I have to earn a living.'

'Since when?' By which she means: *'think how I have helped you out over the years.'*

Serena and I are having a quarrel. That's what stupid Hattie has done to us. I am so angry. And Serena is upset too, or she wouldn't be referring to what we never refer to: my financial dependence on her.

'Nothing profitable ever happens in that gallery,' she says. 'You hardly ever had it open until Sebastian was out of the picture and you had nothing else to do.'

I find the grace to acknowledge the truth in what she says, and the quarrel is over before it began.

'Okay, okay,' I say, 'you're right. But there wasn't room for me in their dinky little house and they'd have hated having me there watching them and worrying. And then the prison people might have let Sebastian out early, and then we'd be back where we started. As well suggest that you moved in with them.'

'But I have Cranmer,' she says, and we both laugh.

Excuses, excuses. The partner, the spouse, the children as excuse. *'Can't do this because it is my duty to do that.'*

255

Serena found Cranmer quickly enough after she split with George. She knows the importance of a male partner for a woman. Leaving aside matters of love, loyalty and companionship, without a partner for an excuse a woman quickly gets roped in to do baby-sitting, emergency dashes to hospitals, fund-raising, caring for ageing parents (decades out of her life), collecting others from stations. With a partner she has of course another set of problems, all to do with love, loyalty and companionship. But the first, or so Serena demonstrates in her life, is preferable to the second. I'm pretty sure she married the schoolmaster to get away from Wanda. Just as Susan ran off with Piers and I ran off with Charlie. We were all terrified of ending up living with our mother.

Not that there was anything terrible about Wanda: on the contrary, we loved her and admired her, but she did like her own way and she was censorious. And if I were in a room and standing up, Wanda could be guaranteed to come in and say 'why don't you sit down and have a rest?' and if I were sitting down she'd say 'doesn't the window need opening?' or closing, or cleaning, or whatever, so I'd have to get up and do it. She needed to make her mark, change the world as it laid itself out before her, to suit the way she thought it ought to be. Serena complained she couldn't write if Wanda was anywhere near.

Poor Susan, not as adept as her sisters, ended up having to share a roof with Wanda so of course she preferred to die young. Now we are older, we who survive invoke lover-dependents (Cranmer, Sebastian), so as not to have to live with our children.

'You're telling me that Martyn and the au pair had a Catholic nuptial Mass, then they all just went back home, and everything is expected to go on as before?' I have passed from anger to disbelief. I suppose this to be an advance on the road to 'closure', albeit an erratic one.

'I believe Martyn wants Agnieszka to shorten her name to Agnes, so Agnieszka is thinking about it.'

'Does she still keep calling him Mr Martyn?'

'I think so.'

'Stone the crows. But Hattie stays just Hattie?'

'Yes. Thank God. To them it's the marriage certificate which is important; the marriage is beside the point. Agnieszka sends the scrap of paper off to the Home Office, Martyn's boss helps it on its way, and lo! Agnes Arkwright is a citizen.'

'I can't believe they've done this. They're so moral,' I say.

'They're the new young,' Serena says. 'They have a different idea of morality from us.'

I ask for more detail about the wedding. I am calming down. I can see that in Hattie's eyes she has done a good and noble thing. But it's always sad to miss a wedding, and I do think that as her grandmother, and the one who brought her up, I should at least have been invited, if only to refuse.

I didn't tell Wanda when I married Sebastian: we just went off and did it with two witnesses. It was in the middle of Hattie's exams, so she couldn't come. That was more or less how I timed it, to save her embarrassment; who wants to go to their grandmother's wedding? Perhaps Hattie is only doing to me what I had done to her?

Wanda didn't come to Serena's wedding to Cranmer, claiming infirmity of age. The wedding was a couple of weeks after George's funeral, which was perhaps the real reason, the speed of it being scarcely decent. Wanda did not go to the funeral either, saying when you got to her age you were excused family obligations. Before George died she told Serena she should stop moaning about George's desertion because who wanted to look after a man in his old age, and now Serena was free of the obligation and Sandra would have to do it.

George died when he and Serena were in that limbo between decree nisi and decree absolute when nobody is quite sure what anyone's legal situation is. I am not surprised that Hattie has such a low opinion of marriage. But if she had only talked to me, I could have warned her not to bring down so much complexity of practical obligation and legal cost on the unfortunate Martyn's head.

Serena decided it was best not to cancel the wedding to Cranmer, but to get on with it so the children didn't have to go on waiting for her to realise it was madness to marry a man some twenty years younger and an anarcho-conservative to boot. Serena's children, like mine, were all what Cranmer calls lefties, born to go on demos and fight for the rights of the oppressed from the safety of their kindly homes. Serena thought it was worse for her children to wait in false hope than face the fact that this she meant to do: marry again, and not live the left-over life that George had bequeathed her. But she was of course half-mad from grief and resentment at the time, and the more reasonable she thought she was being, the less she was. She could have afforded to wait just a little – any therapist would have told her that.

Some of the children came to the wedding, some did not, and she could not blame them either way. And, come to that, Serena did not go to George's funeral either, to most of her friends' and family's dismay. Widows go to funerals, but do ex-wives? Not if they have any sense. And Serena did not know if she was a wife, an ex-wife or a widow. But she did know that Sandra, in whose arms her husband or ex-husband had died, meant to attend.

I went: I asked her permission and she said I could stand in for her and do her public grieving. I had been very fond of George. He went very peculiar towards the end, and whether that was because of his genes or splashes of oily-blue organophosphate, the Nazi nerve poison, we will never know.

Sandra came to the funeral in an orange dress and a yellow Ascot hat. She was distraught with ostentatious grief. A cortège of friends came with her, all in tears, all in hats, weeping and wailing. I didn't speak to her; few on our side did.

The new-age therapist did not come: she was probably too guilty and frightened: she had wanted his money but not for him to *die*. The day after the death she came round to Grovewood wanting to recover any letters she might have written to George, which his children refused to either look for or supply.

George really has to take some responsibility for his own death: why did he trust such an egregious person in the first place? Poor George. I am lucky with Sebastian. He has managed to get past seventy without going doolally, getting depressed, splashed by nerve poison, changing his nature, trusting demented therapists, chasing after little girls as some men do, forgetting to zip up his flies, dribbling his food, champing false teeth, shuffling in slippers, quarrelling with neighbours, cursing his enemies, shaking his fist Lear-like at the skies: all the things – Wanda is quite right – that men tend to do as they get older.

What he has developed, alas, is a liking for short cuts, which is why he is in the Bijlmer and not with me.

As for Sandra the mistress, she did all right for herself in the end; we don't have to be sorry for her. Six weeks after the funeral she stood pathetically outside a married girl-friend's window looking at the domestic scene within and quietly weeping. They opened the door to her.

'Sandra, why are you crying?'
'Because George is dead, and I envy you so much,' she said. 'I will always be on the outside and never on the inside.' So they invited her in and asked her to stay until she felt better. Six weeks later and she'd run off with the husband: he just happened to be a millionaire. So far as I know, she has lived happily ever after.

Serena tells me more about the wedding. Hattie told her that after the ceremony, when they were all walking home for refreshments – Agnieszka had made profiteroles, little cinnamon cakes and a special bread made with evaporated milk – the bride ran ahead, clip-clop on green kitten heels, to open the front door and get the kettle on. (The heels once belonged to Hattie, but these days she likes to wear higher ones.) And the cattery-mother did a strange thing. She ran after Agnieszka into the house, went into the back garden, took a handful of earth and flung it on the kitchen floor. The others had come in by now. Agnieszka had filled a bucket with hot soapy water and her mother sloshed it all over the floor and Agnieszka took a broom and swept it all out again, earth and all. The sister had mysteriously found the strength to clap her hands, then everything went on as normal.

'Hattie actually said "as normal"?' I ask. 'So what's "normal"?'
'It sounds like some kind of ancient wedding custom,' says Serena. 'And that's not so good. Hattie and Martyn may not think it's a real marriage but Agnieszka and her family probably do.'

Martyn And Agnieszka In Bed

The wedding is three weeks behind them. Hilary has left for Frankfurt, and Hattie now has a nice office with a view over rooftops. Elfie is her likeable if erratic assistant and Marina – who had been suffering from pre-submission nerves when she'd threatened to sue – has finally finished and delivered her manuscript. The book will do well. Agnieszka has found her passport, and written to the Foreign Office forwarding a marriage certificate which no one queries. It seems as if the Ukraine will be part of Europe before long, and so no one is bothering much about from which side of a soon-to-be-irrelevant border someone came. Babs is on maternity leave in Florida, and Debora is not pregnant.

Martyn now works for *d/EvOLUTION*, and his boss is Cyrilla Leighton, a smart young woman of twenty-seven. She is helpful and encouraging – even flattering – about Martyn's work. She can't write but at least she knows it; and if sometimes his articles go under her by-line he is not bothered. Evolution, when it comes to it, is more entertaining than Devolution. The Darwinians and Neo-Darwinians drink more, use shorter words and make more jokes than those steeped in the theory of politics. They may veer to the right, throwing up their hands when presented with human nature, saying what do you expect, rather than earnestly attempting to introduce policies to put things right, but Martyn can cope with that. He knows where his sympathies lie.

When asked about his marital status (and it's amazing how many young women at conferences or parties come straight out with: '*Are you with someone?*'), he replies: 'I'm with a partner in a committed relationship. We have a child.' He does not of course mention the marriage, and is glad that Harold is moving in higher circles, so is seldom in the office to allude to it by suggestive wink or whisper.

Martyn's political prospects advance steadily; he hopes to be adopted by the Party for a marginal seat up North, which he also hopes he will not win. Best to lose this one, then be given a safe seat in a constituency nearer home. He cannot see Hattie agreeing to move far from London.

Agnieszka would follow him wherever he went but he is with Hattie, not Agnieszka.

Agnieszka cares for Kitty as usual, sleeps in her own bed, puts Martyn and Hattie's food upon the table, is sweet and kind – and you would not know anything was wrong, except now she cries in bed, night after night. They can hear the soft, whuffling, gulping sounds just the other side of the wall. What can she want? How can they make her happy?

'Whatever can be the matter with her?' asks Martyn. 'She's keeping me awake, and if I don't sleep I don't write.'

'We can hardly do any more for her than we have,' says Hattie. She would like a little more happy gratitude from Agnieszka than she receives.

Martyn nudges Hattie, laughing quietly – they always speak quietly in bed – and says:

'Well, I suppose we could.'

'You mean take her into our bed,' says Hattie, 'like we used to with Kitty before Mrs Arkwright came into our lives and we learned better? I don't think so, Martyn!' She's joking.

'Don't call her Mrs Arkwight,' says Martyn. 'It sounds hostile.'

'Oh, so she's your wife and you need to protect her,' says Hattie, who now is feeling hostile. 'I'm so glad you have these proper husbandly feelings about her.'

'I don't know what I should do,' says Martyn. 'It was your idea. I can't stand female crying. It's manipulative.'

Hattie has asked Agnieszka what the matter is, but Agnieszka just shook her head and said: 'Nothing.'

Kitty's so bored with the tears she no longer even tries to catch them with her tongue.

A night or two later they make love with a little more noise than usual, they can't help it, and afterwards Martyn says, 'Since we can't live without her, perhaps we'd better do more to live with her.' In the ensuing silence the sobbing from next door gains intensity.

'That does not include her in my bed,' says Hattie, 'if that's what you're thinking.' She should not say such things, she knows it; she is venturing into dangerous territory, but she can't help it.

'For God's sake, Hattie,' says Martyn, 'I'm not thinking anything of the sort. You have no idea what I'm thinking of.' He hates it when she claims to know what's going on in his head. They both take sleeping pills. Hattie sleeps, Martyn doesn't.

Martyn's frightened of his own thoughts. Agnieszka's tears arouse him. He would like to get out of bed naked and bonk her there and then. That would make them stop. He daydreams about it in the office: increasingly. Agnieszka is his wife.

The other day she bent over the ironing board, and she was wearing Hattie's yellow leather skirt and her legs were long and bare: he could see the muscles standing out along the backs of her knees and he had to go and sit in the bathroom to calm down. But he loves Hattie. He does not love Agnieszka. Hattie is his partner, the one for whose sake he does not go off with girls at conferences. Hattie is the mother of his child, Agnieszka is not, though Agnieszka certainly has more to do with Kitty than Hattie does. Kitty has quite a few words now: she pronounces them with Agnieszka's lilt and slight lisp. It melts his heart when he hears her. 'Oh bozzer it!' she will say, in imitation of Agnieszka. She does not emulate Hattie's 'Oh shit'. She knows that sweetness and light are a little girl's best bet, not Hattie's brisk, cross assertiveness.

He loves the tenderness with which Agnieszka smiles at Kitty, the way her upper lip draws away to show her teeth: do other people's mouths do that? He is increasingly angry with Hattie for putting them into this situation, into the way of his temptation. It was her idea. She must put up with the consequences. He falls asleep. It is past five in the morning.

The next night he cannot bear Agnieszka's crying a moment longer. He switches on the light. It is eleven o'clock. They've all been in bed for at least two hours. Hattie, Martyn, Agnieszka, Kitty, and Sylvie too. They all go to bed early, the better to be on their toes during the day.

He gets out of bed, shakes Hattie, and says, 'This is impossible, Hattie. You've got to talk to her.'
Hattie wakes out of a sleeping-pill drowse and says, 'What's happening?'
'You've got to get up,' he says.
'Why can't you just be happy, Martyn?' asks Hattie. 'Everything is going so well.'
'You are a hard-hearted bitch,' he says. 'Can't you hear her crying?'
'Polish girls do cry,' says his partner. 'They're famous for it. It's part of their culture. If she's really so unhappy she can always leave. She's only the au pair.'
'She is my wife,' says Martyn. He speaks loudly. Hattie is really awake now. She knows she has been talking but what has she been saying?

In the next room Kitty starts to cry. Martyn must have woken her up. She can hear Agnieszka getting out of bed, taking Kitty from her cot and going into the kitchen.

What does Agnieszka wear at night, Martyn wonders? He

hasn't let himself think about it before. Does she sleep naked or perhaps in one of Hattie's cast-off nighties, the ones that are now too small for her, that she bought before she was pregnant with Kitty? Perhaps the one in almost transparent silky stuff, two parts, one in pale green, cut low to show the breasts, the darker jackety thing pretending a degree of modesty. Hattie doesn't buy nighties like that now. He only half-liked it when she did. His mother would have been so outraged by the price, his father so scathing about the decency. Usually these days Hattie just pulls on a T-shirt if it's cold, wears nothing if it's not. He likes it when she wears nothing but he's very accustomed to her body by now. It is soft, nice and familiar, and he loves it, and it bore him a child, but it does not bring with it a sense of future shock. He would like to know now what Agnieszka looks like naked. He remembers the time soon after she'd arrived when she demonstrated her belly-dancing skills. Has she gone on with her classes? He has no idea. She is his wife and he knows so little about her.

Hattie pulls on one of Martyn's T-shirts, which reaches down to her knees, goes into the living room and finds Agnieszka there with Kitty. Martyn follows her. Martyn, in the interests of decency, has put on an Indian kurta. The kurta, in white, thin cotton, suits him and reaches to his knees. It is a present Alastair brought back for Babs from India, thinking it was for women to wear, so Babs passed it onto Martyn. It looks good on his broad-shouldered slim-hipped frame. He has been going to the office gym. Cyrilla makes him. Agnieszka always launders the kurta separately, so it has kept its whiteness, and irons crisp and neat.

Agnieszka is in a rather dull-blue velvet Marks & Spencer dressing gown. She is scraping a little bit off a blue tablet and giving it to Kitty on the tip of her finger. Kitty seems to like it and has stopped grizzling.

'What are you giving her?' asks Hattie: her mind is still blurry from sleeping pills.

'A little scrap of vitamin B12,' says Agnieszka. 'Something woke her up and frightened her. In Poland we give it to babies: it is good for her nerves and she is teething. She is not very happy but she will be okay now.'

Agnieszka looks directly at Hattie, and gives her a brilliant, reassuring smile. It is powerful and positive and in charge, but Hattie is glad that at least the tears have stopped. Agnieszka's eyes are not puffy, either. She seems very wide-awake.

'And how about in the Ukraine?' asks Martyn. He thinks the Ukraine is the back of beyond and now they are married is not slow to let Agnieszka know it.

'There too,' says Agnieszka. 'They are not so very far apart.' And she smiles at Martyn, that same brilliant smile.

'Since we are all awake, Agnes,' says Martyn, 'how about making us some cocoa?'

Hattie wonders why Martyn is being so disagreeable to Agnieszka but Agnieszka doesn't seem to mind. She seems to rather enjoy his bad temper. When he calls her Agnes, which she hates, she'll try and get in a 'Mr Martyn', which he hates.

Kitty is smiling now, eyes drooping and closing. Agnieszka puts her back in the cot and goes to the kitchen and makes her famous cocoa, boiling, sieving, frothing, pouring, finding a tray, taking the three mugs into the living room, where Hattie and Martyn sit next to each other at the table, in sleepy conspiracy. And there she drops her bombshell.

'Why are you so unhappy?' asks Hattie, unwisely, but it is the third time of asking. 'Why do you cry all the time?'
'Because I love Mr Martyn,' says Agnieszka, 'and I can't have him and so I have to go away, because it is not fair to you, Hattie, and I love you too.'

Hattie finds her hands are beginning to shake. She has to put down the cocoa. It's very hot and very delicious.
'But you can't leave us,' says Hattie. 'We need you. We depend on you. Kitty loves you. Agnieszka can't leave us, can she, Martyn?'
'It would be against her religion,' says Martyn. 'I am her husband. No she can't.'
'Your poor hands,' says Agnieszka to Hattie. 'Your poor voice! I would do anything not to upset you, but I have. You have been so good to me, Hattie, like an angel.'

Agnieszka goes to the bathroom and comes back with a bottle and shakes out a little blue pill for Hattie.
'What is it?' asks Hattie. Martyn is getting through his cocoa, though it must be too hot for comfort.
'It is a vitamin supplement,' says Agnieszka. 'It is not good when your hands tremble. You have a vitamin B12 deficiency, Hattie. In Poland we give it for the nerves.'
'And in the Ukraine too, I believe,' says Martyn. 'They being not so far apart.'
Hattie takes it. Martyn watches.

'Take two,' he says, and Agnieszka shakes out another pill. Hattie swallows it.

'Let's have a drink to all our futures,' says Martyn, 'whatever they are,' and gets out the bottle of whisky and three glasses and pours out three tots and they all drink.

'I must leave,' says Agnieszka. 'I cannot put you through this. I thank you, Hattie, and I thank you, Mr Martyn. And now I am going to bed and in the morning we will work out the detail of how it is best to be done, for Kitty's sake.'

'Shall we drink to that?' says Martyn, and they all have another tot of whisky, and Hattie's hands have stopped trembling, though how she is to manage without Agnieszka she has no idea. That doesn't seem to matter so much now. She feels quite happy and fond of everyone.

'Bedtime,' says Agnieszka and yawns and stretches and goes to her room.

'Another drink,' says Martyn, and pours one and Hattie drinks it. Now she feels she has to go to bed; that's where she belongs. So Martyn helps her to the bedroom and she rolls over and over luxuriously until she is against the wall. It is a good, wide, expensive bed, bought for them by Serena when they moved in together.

Hattie sleeps. Martyn lies beside her and closes his eyes, and in a minute he is asleep, though this was not what he intended. He wakes to find Agnieszka moving towards the bed as in his familiar dream. A recurring dream, a thing foretold. She is wearing the greeny pieces of froth that once, long ago, Hattie wore. Did he buy it for her?

Agnieszka takes off the top part, so her round small breasts are showing. He is suddenly wide awake. She smiles, and moves another piece of froth aside so her tummy shows and says: 'I have an advanced certificate now. Do you want to see?'

He nods and she moves her stomach muscles in an impressive manner, for all the apparent flatness of her midriff.

'Touch it if you like,' she says. Martyn looks at Hattie but she is asleep.
'It's like a bag of kittens,' he says.
'She'll sleep through quite a lot,' says Agnieszka. 'She is perfectly happy and I am your wife. Kitty will sleep too. We can make as much noise as we like. You two are so quiet. It is very boring.'
'What was the pill?'
'A roofie,' she says. 'Didn't you know that?'
'Rohypnol? But I gave her whisky.'
'All the better,' says Agnieszka.

He stretches out her hand to feel the stomach. The kittens move beneath his hand. He is not sure he likes that.

'And after all, I am your wife and she is only the mistress, and so I am entitled to this bed. I have more right to it than she does. Mine is narrow and small: this is large and wide and room for three. If she does not like it she can go to sleep in my bed but I think if she were awake she would rather it was like this.'

Agnieszka gets into the bed, and lies beside him. The green froth, for all its delicacy, is a little scratchy but he can put up

271

with that. He turns away from her towards Hattie, who smiles in her sleep and reaches for him, and he lets his hand wander. She rolls onto her back and his fingers find her; she sighs with pleasure and murmurs a further invitation. Then he turns to Agnieszka and before he knows it he is on her, forcing her legs apart, pulling up her knees. Her legs are spread wide, and now tangled with Hattie's and both women are his, which was what he wanted since he first set eyes on Agnieszka.

That was Wednesday, the first night.

Two More Nights

'In 1886,' says Hattie to me, three days after the events I have described above, 'Sir Charles Wentworth Dilke, youngest member in the Gladstone Cabinet of the time, was found in bed with both his wife and the maid. The scandal ruined his career.'

'That was then and this is now,' I say, 'and Martyn's career in politics has only just begun.'

'And besides,' she says, 'it was quite clear in those days which one of them was which. Which the wife and which the maid.'

I do not say, as I am tempted to, and whose fault is that? Hattie is in a vulnerable state. She sits at my table, very early on Saturday morning. Her suitcase at her side. It is not yet unpacked. She needs to talk. She has told me about the wedding, about the visit to the cattery, about her promotion at the office and finally she gets around to good-night cocoa, and Agnieszka wearing her green teddy which Hattie now looks ridiculous in, and how Agnieszka was wearing it while in her bed. 'I'm sure I never gave her permission to wear it,' she says. 'The cow.'

I say this to me seems a fairly minor infringement of rights. 'I do remember quite a lot. Rohypnol doesn't blot everything out. It's only a sleeping pill with the pleasure principle added. But I'd had two Temazepam as well, and then two roofies, plus some whisky as well, so it's not all that clear.'

I say she is lucky to be alive.

'When I woke up properly on Thursday morning, Agnieszka was back in her own bed and Martyn sleeping there beside me, only I was on the door side of the bed not the wall side. I suppose she and Martyn thought I would remember nothing about anything, but I did. I might have thought it was a dream but half the bedclothes were on the floor and my green teddy which I never wear any more tangled up in them. The poppers were undone. I left everything as it was and went on down to the kitchen, and there was Agnieszka cutting slivers of apple for Kitty as if nothing had happened. She just seemed rather rosy and somehow smooth.

'Martyn came down for his breakfast and had to get to the office early. He was just as grumpy as ever, and I didn't know what to do, or what to think, but I remembered what my driving instructor said to me once, *'if in doubt, don't'*, so if they weren't going to say anything, neither would I. I would pretend everything was normal while I worked out what to do.

Martyn kissed me good-bye as if he really meant it, with an extra little twitch of my nipples through my office blouse, which is a nice thin material which Agnieszka had laundered and put out for me the day before. It has long sleeves which is just as well because the insides of my arms were really bruised. I didn't know how badly until yesterday when the black-and-blue business started. But the little twitch, the pinch, went straight to my personal parts, you know how these things sometimes do?'

She remembers my age and apologises, and I say I have some vague memories of how these things sometimes do.
'Well, you wanted to know,' she says, and I say that is so.

She tells me that when she got upstairs again after coffee she found the green teddy gone, and the bottom sheet changed and the bed made, and Agnieszka vacuuming away, singing. Hattie was glad she was cheerful. There had been something the previous evening about her leaving but whatever it was it was over. It was going to be a hard day at the office and she certainly felt hung-over – but that was probably just the whisky, not the pills. She remembers the pale gold liquid glimmering in the glass: it had seemed to her so beautiful. Martyn had not been mean with the pouring.

'But I was remembering things, more and more. I remember standing up bending over the bed and Martyn coming at me from behind and she had her tongue . . .' she breaks off. 'Do you think she's a lesbian, Gran, I mean really, or just trying to please Martyn? Because I think she truly loves him. I'm not going into too much detail because it's too rude for you; well, not to mention me actually – you're not a young woman and it might shock you.'

Good Lord, I thought, thinking of the artists and the three-somes and the foursomes, and the tyings up and the pinnings down, and the filmings and what went on in the clip joints, and the buying and selling of this orifice or that, as everyone tried to be at one with one another, even though the another came in twos or threes or more – and the pleasure of pain, and pole-dancing in Las Vegas, when we had to pay our way out of the hotel so Charlie could get to his rodeo – not that he was doing the dancing: he just took the money, lots of it. American girls are better at dirty dancing than the British: they put energy into it and are not ashamed. They see nothing wrong in promising everything, but fulfilling nothing. But I seemed to have a quality few others had: their sins were crude but mine were subtle, and they smiled too much; I was an artist's model not a gangster's moll and it showed. Everyone likes a bit of class, so I made money.

I am sorry about Hattie's bruises, which are stiffening up. I help her unpack in the spare room.

'So Agnieszka has taken the lot,' I say. 'She's got the husband, and the house, and the baby, and Martyn as her meal ticket for life, and status in the world as his wife, and what have you got? Nothing! Can't you even be angry with her?'

She thinks about this a little.

'Okay,' she says, 'Supposing you're right. That was no au pair, that was a shit and a thief and a confidence trickster – and a slut too. She set out to do what she did, every step of the way she knew what she was doing. Even to giving a scraping of roofie to Kitty so she wouldn't wake and be frightened by the noise – so she loves Kitty, then.'

No, I say. That was the worst thing she did.

'I daresay I was very noisy,' she goes on. 'But I don't remember that, and Martyn too, I expect, after all those months of doing it silently because of her in the next room. It was to be expected. Martyn went at it like some guy in a porn film. Perhaps he's missed his vocation.'

I ask her what happened yesterday: she went to work, and it was an ordinary day other than that Babs's Tavish tried to chat her up, because sex, other than normal one-to-one sex, is catching; it hangs round you like an aura and some people pick it up.

'And to tell you the truth,' she confesses, 'I felt so nice, so properly and thoroughly *seen to*, I wanted to get back into a bed and lie in it and wait for something to happen. Actually, anybody's bed would have done. That's the terrible thing. Anybody's. But even I could see Babs's Tavish in the Dorchester for lunch would be a great mistake.

'Around five o'clock I took a taxi home, and Martyn was there before me. Agnieszka was putting Kitty to bed; Martyn and I both helped bath her and still nothing was said. I felt like saying to them both, 'I haven't necessarily forgotten everything: you're both very naïve if you think that.' But I didn't have the energy. So we just all went to bed early in our usual beds. Martyn next to the wall as usual, and I fell asleep at once, and I think Martyn and Agnieszka must have too. And I am sure she did not cry herself to sleep, she just slept.'

That was Thursday, the second night.

It was impossible, I told Serena, not to admire the way Hattie's suitcase was packed. All her best things were laid flat between sheets of tissue paper: ironed knickers were neatly folded, shoes had been put in fabric bags one by one. Every jar of cream, every stick of cosmetic, had been wrapped in cling film and tucked in wherever there was a space to fill. I assumed Agnieszka had done the packing.

'And the next day breakfast was as usual,' Hattie goes on, 'and Martyn kissed me good-bye at the door, and he went one way and I went another, and Agnieszka and Kitty waved from the door. I saw she had a plain gold ring on the fourth finger of her left hand. But I didn't want to be late so I said nothing: Marina Faircroft was coming in to discuss her next novel. She works hard. No sooner is one finished than the next one begun. That is why she can afford to travel with lawyers, even though those lawyers ask the intern to lunch. It may be that Elfie is still seeing him. She comes back after lunch looking so happy.

'But it was a good day and I felt fresh, though I suppose a little numb. And supper was as usual, except the atmosphere was a bit strained. There was the wedding ring, and no one mentioned it. I supposed that Martyn had bought it for Agnieszka, but I didn't like to ask for fear of the answer.

'Bedtime passed, and no one made any attempt to switch off the television, and we gazed as if we were watching it but we weren't. Then Martyn switched it off and poured the three of us some whisky, and the sight of it golden in

the glass made that same kind of quiver run through
me. Then Martyn spoke – he has a nice voice, don't you
think, Gran?'

I say I haven't registered his voice particularly. Actually I
have always thought it had a rather harsh Northern quality
to it, a bit chippy, as if registering a daily protest against
the world. But I daresay his recent successes at work and a
new boss and a new marriage have softened it somewhat.
It might even by now be mellifluous and inviting, as are the
voices of those who are pleased with themselves. Hattie
continues.

'Martyn put his hand on my arm and asked me if I remembered anything about the other night, the night before last,
and Agnieszka put her knuckles up against her mouth and
kind of licked the wedding ring, savouring it.
' "Wednesday night?" I ask. "No, why should I? Except I
remember Agnieszka made us some of her cocoa and I slept
like a log as a result. She makes good cocoa."
'I just wanted to know what would happen, what he would
say.
' "Actually you didn't sleep all the time," he says. "It's only
fair to let you know. Agnieszka was with us in our bed.
Now I don't want you to get upset, but Agnieszka and I are
married, in a church under God's eyes, and you have to
realise that. I have a duty to her. She can't just be left to
cry herself to sleep at night. It isn't ethical."
'I say, "I don't see what someone crying themselves to sleep
at night has to do with ethics. It seems to me to belong
more to the emotional realm."
' "Then you should see," he says. "God, you are so

argumentative, Hattie. But I do still love you, in spite of everything. And Agnieszka loves you too."
'I say nothing.
'Then Agnieszka says: "You have the most beautiful body, Hattie. Nicer than mine. And I wish I had your hair."
'Bet you do, I thought. What do you want now? I could cut it off and make it into a wig and you could wear it. My partner, my child, my baby, my home, my clothes, now my hair? And the thought makes me laugh, the merest giggle. Sylvie the kitten jumps up and pats my cheek with her paw, rather sweetly. We are friends again now. Indeed, I am her favourite person.

' "I'm glad you can take this so lightly, Hattie," said Martyn, losing patience with me. He stands up. ' "So how are we going to work this? Is it to be all three, or one at a time, or you and Agnieszka some of the time, or a rota or what? We need some decisions here."
'And that's when I packed my suitcase but Agnieszka took over and did it properly. Martyn drove me to the station. I made the last train to Bath; and here I am.'

She is brave but trying not to cry. I find her some Nurofen for the pain in her arms – she has bruises on her thighs too – and she swallows them obediently.

'Can I stay here for a while, Gran?' she asks. 'I can commute to the office every day from Bath. I can read manuscripts on the train. People do it all the time. In fact it would be very practical for me.'
'Of course you can,' I say. 'Until Sebastian gets out. Then we'll think again.'

She gets into bed: fresh white sheets, plumped up pillows, red-gold hair all over them.

'I expect he's in bed with her now,' she says. 'Our bed.'

Her mouth puckers as she tries not to cry. Little Kitty does that too. They're both brave. Hattie sleeps.

I call Serena, though it's a bit late.

'Just as well,' she says. 'I never liked him. I'd rather have wicked people who know they are wicked than wicked people who believe they are good. And you have to hand it to Agnieszka. We English are a nation of pushovers.'

We run through lists of au pairs we have known, and how most were so good, and a few were so bad. And how in nature there is one carnivore to eleven herbivores and it's just your bad luck when you run into a carnivore. There you are, happily munching the leaves; there's a squeal in the night and someone's gone in the morning, but the waters of wishful thinking soon wash over memory. Agnieszka is a carnivore. At least Hattie's safely in a family bed, and still has her hair. We agree it was the last straw, Agnieszka wanting the hair, not just Martyn's rota.

We remember a time in the history of Grovewood, when Serena fled to London with the children, George having done something dreadful, she can't remember what. There was a succession of Australian girls: Narelle, Abby Rose, Ebony Jo; so sensible and practical they made her moaning about her fate seem a waste of time, so she stopped sulking and went home to George. Narelle taught Lallie, who must have been staying with Serena, the didgeridoo. Where was

I at the time? I can't remember. I was a terrible mother.

And now what about Kitty?

Serena says she'd better stay with Martyn and Agnieszka, who's a good mother. Better a friendly carnivore than an unwilling herbivore. Hattie can visit. When Kitty's old enough she can make up her own mind. Childhood goes so fast.

We decide we should go to bed. We don't have the energy we did when we were younger, and just as well, or we'd have been round at Pentridge Road tearing the place apart and upsetting everyone. What you lose in strength you gain in wisdom.

Starting on the Monday Hattie commutes daily, taking with her a smart leather briefcase heavy with manuscripts, clear-eyed when she leaves, but red-rimmed by the time she gets home. She allows herself to cry on the way back, never on the journey out. Martyn rings from time to time but Hattie won't speak to him. I ask her about Kitty.
'It's astonishing,' she says, 'how quickly you forget children if they're not under your nose.'
'I've heard men say this, never yet a woman,' I say.
'I read it in a book,' she says. 'Let them just get on with it, if it's what they want, and at least Kitty can have a room of her own.'

At the weekend she helps me in the gallery. Somebody buys Sebastian's chair painting the minute I open. In ten minutes the table has gone too.
'Keep this up,' says Hattie, 'and you'll be as rich as Serena.'

Hattie thinks she'll get a flat in London. She can just about afford it. She says she cried for a week in outrage, loathing, disappointment, shock at her own folly; and because she didn't have Kitty. But it didn't seem to be at all for lost love of Martyn. She'd thought he was one kind of person and he turned out to be another. Martyn won't help support her. Why should he? They were never man and wife.

She's earning, and can look after herself and he has the responsibility of Kitty.

They're sharing the mortgage payments. She has a financial interest in the house, but it has gained equity which she could use as savings, or collateral. Martyn will have his work cut out supporting Agnieszka and Kitty, because Agnieszka will see her future in the home, not out of it. Martyn will have to write articles for *d/EvOLUTION* for ever, selling his soul and charming Cyrilla. Let Agnieszka worry about that. Change one woman, change another.

We walk home from the gallery across Pulteney Bridge and sit for a while in Parade Gardens and watch the River Avon go by. The sun is setting. Swans swim up and down; tourists feed them unhealthy white bread.

'Actually, Gran,' says Hattie. 'I did kind of help this situation on its way. I took Agnieszka along to the christening and pushed Father Flanahan under her nose. I wrote the letter to Immigration. I knew what would happen next. I suggested the marriage. I knew perfectly well what that little blue pill was, and what Martyn had in mind, and even took two. The truth of the matter is, I can't stand domesticity. Any man will do, when you want one, if it comes down to it. I just wanted to get out from under.' I am speechless.

'I did it honourably. Be happy for me that I am happy,' says Hattie. She lifts her white, strong arms – the bruises are fading fast – and stretches her whole body towards the sky, and the sun catches her Pre-Raphaelite hair as it turns to gold. She is a vision, coming from the past into the future, sealed for just this moment like a snapshot of a goddess.

I open my mouth in protest, but I think of Wanda, and myself, of Serena, and Susan and Lallie, her direct antecedents: of Roseanna, Viera, Svea, Raya and Maria, Saturday Sarah and Abby Rose, and all those others, un-named and unaccounted for (for reasons of space as much as my forgetfulness) who had a hand in her creating. And I think of Hattie's baby Kitty and of Agnieszka the minder, next in line – and I close my mouth.

'I am happy that you are happy,' I say, and I am.

P.S.

Ideas,
interviews
& features ...

About the author

2 Cooking the Books: Louise Tucker
   talks to Fay Weldon

8 Life at a Glance

9 Favourite Things

10 A Writing Life

About the book

12 Fiction's Realities by Fay Weldon

Read on

15 Have You Read?

Cooking the Books
Louise Tucker talks to Fay Weldon

What was the inspiration for *She May Not Leave*?
Overhearing a conversation in which two people, a young couple, were wondering about the ethics of hiring an au pair. I thought how lucky they were, and privileged, to be able to worry about the ethics of survival.

Did you ever have an au pair and if so what was your experience like?
All the au pairs in the book are mine, in some way or another. Nowadays, of course, au pairs are more worldly, not like the scared and grateful young women from abroad who used to come and work for us in the days when I had small children. Agnieszka is pretending to be one of this sort, but actually isn't. The lies she tells! But she's sheer invention. None of my acquaintance had designs upon my husband, or perhaps I just didn't know about it. There was one girl, true, who was always tired and we found out she was leaving the house at midnight to work as a croupier. She didn't stay long. She found even better ways of making a living. But whatever they did, you made excuses for them because you didn't want them to leave, especially since the children become attached to them and would be traumatised if they went. That's something that doesn't change.

'Perhaps using child-care is in itself exploitative,' says Martyn. Is it?
Yes, in that our luxuries are often other people's hardships, in the same way that a

designer sports shoe is probably produced in a sweatshop. It's easy to get someone else to do the hard work, rather than doing it yourself, if you can afford it. Obviously you try to be as good an employer as you can be – you pay the au pair, you give her proper holidays – but as Hattie says at the beginning of the book 'people are as moral as they can afford to be'.

Like so many women of her generation, Hattie is caught between conflicting interests. She wants to work, and to stay at home. She wants an au pair, but feels guilty. Do you think feminism has gone backwards, in that now there is so much choice, and that choice is now the burden?

No I don't think it has gone backwards. In the past if a woman wanted to leave home or a husband, she couldn't – there were few jobs that paid well enough to support you and your children. If you left home you had no automatic right to the house. Leave home, and leave the children behind. The employer naturally preferred to employ women without children. (So what's changed?) Now you're free to have children or not, to marry or not, to work or not and there is no longer a stigma about not being married, being divorced or choosing the career above the child. But choice has thrown up all kinds of other problems. One of the most intractable is the one which requires that you either have no children or hand yours over to someone else to bring up. ▶

6 Choice has thrown up all kinds of other problems. One of the most intractable is the one which requires that you either have no children or hand yours over to someone else to bring up. 9

3

Cooking the Books *(continued)*

◄ '"Partnerships" are more fragile than certificated marriages' says Frances and the outcome of the book shows how. Why do you think that is the case?

Because statistics demonstrate that this is the case. Couples in partnerships are twice as likely to split as those in marriages. This may add to the sum of human happiness – but I suspect does not. If your love life is stable and okay, then you can turn your attention to other things. If you – or your partner – are always looking over your shoulder and thinking something better might come along, they might well. It always seemed to me the reason to marry was in case the other one got away, and you needed to invoke all the powers of church and state to hold the other person in place, and if you don't feel like that why be with them anyway? With a partnership there is a sense that the individuals are interchangeable. There's a lack of commitment. Marriage is madness, but it does mean someone wanted you enough to marry you. It's a way of saying, as Frances points out, that this person is my 'final emotional destination'. Even if it doesn't work out, you're saying, with marriage, that at that time you did the committing.

'"Any man will do, when you want one, if it comes down to it."' Hattie's statement seems almost a reversal of what we believe, that relationships are intellectual and unique, not simply an instinct. Is she just more honest?

She seems very typical of today's young women: her relationship with Martyn is

6 It always seemed to me the reason to marry was in case the other one got away, and you needed to invoke all the powers of church and state to hold the other person in place. 9

practical but there's not much passion in it. They live side by side, like many young couples, but it's not really what I'd call love. It's too reasonable.

You've just started teaching at Brunel University. Do you think writing can be taught?
I've only been doing it for a couple of months. Too soon to tell. There are certainly general principles; things which you have found out along the way, which you can usefully pass on. You can, for example, explain the implications of naming your characters. You can point out to a woman that if she calls the men in her novel Michael, David, John or Richard, she's probably writing her men as ciphers. Just all-purpose men. Is this what she wants? (Too often it is.) Names don't come out of nowhere: they shine light onto the social and class aspirations of the parents: all kinds of complexities surface. If all the siblings have names beginning with the same letter, for example, you can be pretty sure the naming parent was a control freak who wanted family cohesiveness at the expense of the individual. But do the naming first; then do the thinking. Hoist yourself with your own petard and then have the fun of working it out. No end to it!

Why do so many people want to be writers?
Everybody wants to express themselves, and why not? There is something inside all of us, an awareness that there is more to ourselves than meets the eye, which does need ▶

> ❝ If a woman calls the men in her novel Michael, David, John or Richard, she's probably writing her men as ciphers. Just all-purpose men. ❞

Cooking the Books *(continued)*

◄ expressing, otherwise the banality of everyday life can get you down. But it's not necessarily writing. It might be better just to go to church.

What's the process of writing a book for you?
It normally takes about six months of active non-writing and three months of writing but writing in quite a concentrated way. The non-writing stage is not so much fun, when you're working out what it is, what you feel, how it fits together. I'm in a perpetual state of guilt and anxiety if I'm not actually writing, but I can't write whatever it is because it's still in the oven. When it's cooked, then you can start.

How do you know when a book is finished?
For me it's when I can't stand it in the house any more. It's a bit like children, it may be too early, it may be too late but you have to let it go.

Unlike the female line in the book, you've had four sons. Did you ever wish for a daughter and if you'd had one, how do you think that relationship would differ from those you have with your sons?
Oh yes. But you get terribly used to boys, and girls are very different. Girls are competitive with the mother whereas boys just bang and crash and need feeding. They compete with each other, with their siblings, and want their fathers to admire them, but they tend to leave their mothers alone: girls try to outsmart them.

❝ There is something inside all of us, an awareness that there is more to ourselves than meets the eye, which does need expressing, otherwise the banality of everyday life can get you down. ❞

What's your next book?
I wrote a piece for *The Times* about what
makes women happy, in which I said
nothing does, at least not for more than ten
minutes. My next book is on that subject,
part non-fiction, part parable. The things
that are meant to make you happy don't;
some people don't even like their children.
What you can't have often stops you from
being happy, as does worrying about what
other people think. For example if your
instinct says 'eat the meringue' but society
says 'what's she doing? no wonder she's so
fat,' then happiness is difficult to achieve. If
you give in to the instinct, eat the forbidden
meringue, sleep with the best friend's
boyfriend, it's hardly surprising. But you do
need to stop yourself doing it more than
once. Just one meringue, not two. If you
persist, then you're in the wrong, and it's
unlikely to make you happy. Just fat.

**After thirty years, do you have a favourite
book, or a favourite period of your writing?**
When the children were small, when I was
just starting out. It was a period of terrific
psychic energy but it was also when I was
doing most damage, filling women's heads
with ideas of leaving their husbands. Yet, at
the same time, I know that men's attitude to
women then, in the seventies, was truly
appalling: we were second-class citizens and
those who did leave their marriages found it
very difficult to get work and survive. So it's
changed for the better in lots of ways but
not in every way. Apparently in Russia, the
cause of the falling birth rate has been ▶

❝ I wrote a piece
for *The Times*
about what
makes women
happy, in which I
said nothing
does, at least not
for more than
ten minutes. ❞

LIFE
at a Glance

BORN

1931, England

EDUCATED

Christchurch Girls' High School, New Zealand; South Hampstead School for Girls, London; and St Andrews University

CAREER

Author of over 30 books, writer of television series such as *Upstairs, Downstairs* and *The Life and Loves of a She-Devil*, radio plays and short stories.

FAMILY

Married to Nick, four sons.

LIVES

Dorset

Cooking the Books *(continued)*

◄ attributed to the 'estrangement' between the sexes. Men and women find it harder than they used to, to get on together. Feminism couldn't anticipate that: you just had to get out of the trouble you were in and it seemed so unlikely that society would change and yet it did, and so fast. ■

Favourite Things

Books
- *Ubik*, Philip K. Dick
- *1984*, George Orwell
- Anything by Hilary Mantel
- Anything by Tama Janowitz
- Anything by Evelyn Waugh
- Anything by H. Rider Haggard
- Anything by Gerald Seymour

That's a lot of books. The best writers usually write a lot. They can't think of anything else to do with their lives.

Food
- Scrambled eggs, but not done in a non-stick pan which leaves the lumps too big
- Irish stew
- Caviar, though I'm happy with the Avruga kind, with blinis, sour cream, chopped egg yolk and chopped onions

That's more than enough. My cholesterol count is rising horrifically.

If I had lots and lots of money I'd have a . . .
- Chauffeur
- Housekeeper
- Gardener

I love . . .
- Landscape

A Writing Life

When do you write?
All the time unless I can't, unless there's something else I have to do. In my head I write non-stop, in real life days go by and I write nothing!

Where do you write?
Before I had a computer I could write anywhere, on the stairs and in bed, but now I write in my office. A pity.

Pen or computer?
Computer. I used to do a first draft with a pen and then type; now I type and then do a second draft with pen on the printout, then somebody else types that.

Silence or music?
Silence.

Why do you write?
Because I want to persuade everybody to agree with me about everything, for their own good.

Do you have any writing rituals or superstitions?
It used to be A40 pads and Pentels, lined, wide-spaced paper and a soft-tipped pen, but the modern Pentels are too soft and I have yet to find the right pen after ten years of looking. And I like writing out of sleep, as I get up. Now I go straight to the computer but I used to wake up and start writing in bed which was very annoying to anyone else who happened to be in the bed.

Which living writer do you most admire, if any?
Hilary Mantel, she's quite amazing. She seems to have extra antennae planted in her as to what goes on in the world.

What's your guilty reading pleasure or favourite trashy read?
Thrillers, though I'm not sure I'd call them trashy. I've just read a Gerald Seymour and he is very far from trashy: I bought another title for the train and then discovered I had already read it. I all but cried. He holds you, he really does. A good thriller is hard to find but once you've found one they're extremely satisfactory. There is no need to read anything guiltily. Though I admit back in the sixties I used to tear the lurid covers off *Amazing Science Fiction* before reading them in public. ■

Fiction's Realities
by Fay Weldon

Having lately for my sins become a Professor of Creative Writing at Brunel University, I ask my students what the novel they propose writing is *about*. They start to tell me the plot, and I say that is not what I mean, so they start to tell me about the characters or the setting, and I stop them short. Plot and character is not enough, I say unkindly, unless you are writing a genre novel, which from the sound of it you are not – readers of the 'literary novel' require something more from you. You are asking them to give up hours of their life reading your book: give them something in return: at least offer them food for thought. They want bread: do not give them stones. Grown-up novels are no different other than in sophistication from the book the child likes to have read to it at bedtime: a story with a beginning, a middle and an end, which makes sense of the chaos of real-life experience, and in which the good are rewarded and the bad punished.

Asking myself that same question about *She May Not Leave*, I am grateful to be able to give the kind of answer I require from my hapless students. '*It's to do with what Hattie says at the beginning, about morality being what you can afford.*' As well as telling the story – which is an old one, though a good one, I hope, being about the wicked au pair who uses her wiles to run off with the master of the house – it charts Martyn and Hattie's slow descent into moral chaos. Martyn deceives himself about the morality of his job: he sells his integrity to please his political bosses; he is motivated by lust, while pretending he is acting out of kindness when he first marries, then takes Agnieszka into the marriage bed. Hattie persuades herself that it is okay to let another woman bring up her child, so great is her desire to be free of motherhood and domesticity. Both, in fact, in spite of their initial good intentions, are guided by 'want', rather than 'ought'. And that's not good.

The other answer I could give is *'Oh, it's about the changing face of motherhood through the decades.'* I've tried to give this aspect of the book less prominence: it being my own preoccupation, not necessarily the reader's. But what I find fascinating is not how much, but how little it has changed. Mothers still fear being swamped by the needs of a baby who demands her time, her strength and her attention. If she works she is torn between the conflicting demands of child and employer. If she doesn't work she feels she is drowning in a sea of domesticity and boredom. Nature has not made it easy for her. With motherhood, most women revert to a pre-liberation state.

And then there's Frances. What is she doing in this book? Well, she narrates, thus saving the author from doing it. Frances is not me, but my sister. I invented her years back when some journalists came knocking at the door when I did not want to speak to the press. I opened it inadvertently. ▶

> ❝ Frances is not me, but my sister. I invented her years back when some journalists came knocking at the door when I did not want to speak to the press. ❞

Fiction's Realities *(continued)*

◀ 'Hello, Fay,' they said.

'I'm not her,' I said, brazening it out. 'I'm her sister Frances.'

'You look like her,' they said, suspiciously.

'I would, wouldn't I,' I said. 'If I'm her sister.'

They believed me and went away and wrote Frances up in their columns. I have always wanted to make her true, give her a real life and a history of her own: someone brought up as I was but with a different temperament and body. She has many of my views but not all. I would hate to have a little art shop in Bath which seldom opens and I daresay I would have run off with the bear-like man from Canada. I am probably more like Serena, taken to country living.

So this is the third book of mine with what I could describe as autobiographical leanings. *Auto da Fay* was straight autobiography and ended when I started writing in 1967. *Mantrapped* was half-novel, half-autobiography, as I tried to work out if the two forms can indeed be separated out as many writers (including me, until I tried) claim. *She May Not Leave* is mostly pure novel but with a strand of autobiography which takes me up to the present – and I can now leave autobiography altogether, which I rather thankfully do. ■

❛ I would hate to have a little art shop in Bath which seldom opens and I daresay I would have run off with the bear-like man from Canada. ❜

Have You Read?

Fay Weldon's other books include:

Auto da Fay
In this, the first volume of Fay Weldon's autobiography, the author takes us from New Zealand to London, from being an unmarried mother to a CBE. Young and poor in London, unmarried mother, wife, lover, playwright, novelist, feminist, anti-feminist – there are few battles Fay Weldon hasn't fought. An icon to many, a thorn in the flesh to others, she has never failed to excite, madden or interest.

The Bulgari Connection
Take one wealthy businessman on his second marriage to an avid, successful young woman; one ex-wife who happens to be a saint; one artist, and a portrait for sale; two women wearing Bulgari necklaces: add a touch of the supernatural, a big dose of envy, stir, and see what happens.

Puffball
Richard and Liffey, a young married couple, follow their dream of moving out of London to a country cottage in the middle of Somerset. Richard continues to live and work in London, coming to stay with Liffey at weekends. But Liffey's pregnancy, the odd neighbours and Bella, Richard's lover in London, all threaten the rural idyll she has imagined for so long. ▶

Have You Read? *(continued)*

◄ *Remember Me*

Madeleine, ex-wife of Jarvis, wants revenge.
Hilary, their daughter and witness to the
wrongs her mother suffered, grows fatter
every day under Madeleine's triumphant
care. Jarvis, happily remarried, fends off his
ex as best he can but she is determined to be
remembered . . .

Mantrapped

The second volume of Weldon's
autobiography moves beyond the non-
fiction of *Auto da Fay*. Juxtaposing her
fictional characters with real ones, she plots a
course through both worlds that questions
who we are, and who we become.